DE... THAN A DODO

BY GENE HUSTON

outskirts
press

MAPPING THE MISSION

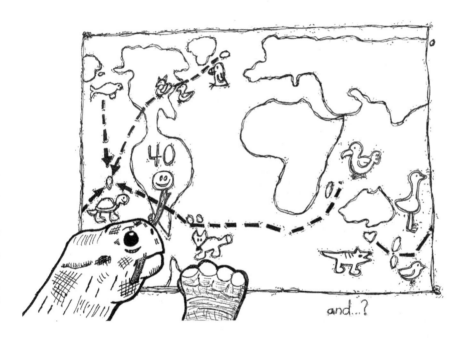

and...?

Outskirts Press, Inc.
http://www.outskirtspress.com

Paperback ISBN: 978-1-9772-4702-5

Outskirts Press and the "OP" logo are trademarks belonging to Outskirts Press, Inc.

PRINTED IN THE UNITED STATES OF AMERICA

CONTENTS

Chapter 1:

FAMOUS SINCE 1971

"Why do I hate you? Let me count the ways. I hate your yappy little dog. I hate the fact that you are staring at me with that high and almighty grin again. I hate the fact that you have no control over your child. I mean seriously lady, are you even paying attention to what your kid just did or do I have to come over there and say something?"

"*Excuse* me! Who are *you* to tell me how to raise my sweet darling? It is good for him to have the freedom to express himself and..." she replied.

"Express himself? Your kid just threw a rock at me and laughed. You think allowing your little monster to hurl rocks at me is funny and a freedom of expression!? Why don't you come over here and let *me* express *myself*! I'll just add your lack of parenting skills to the reasons I despise you!" I retorted.

"But you don't even know me. How can you say you hate me? Who do you think you are?"

"I know your type. I don't have to know *you,* to know you. You people are all the same in the end. I don't even know why I bother talking to you people. You're lucky I don't have thumbs, or I'd come over there and grab hold of you and..."

That was how the conversation would play out in my mind with those people who stared at me every day. But when I screamed at them at the top of my lungs, all that came out was, "Hssss! Hssss!

Hss! Hss!" The people thought that was *so cute*, which only made me angrier.

Who am I? 'Lonesome George' they called me. The "most endangered animal" and "rarest reptile" as deemed by the people from the Guinness Book of World Records for the past 40 years. They said I was "effectively extinct while still alive". That title pretty much explained my plight. One is the loneliest number might seem cliché to say, but knowing I was all alone, totally alone, made my daily life depressing.

Sure, if I was a tourist basking on the deck of some cruise ship sailing the Pacific, I might love my life here in the Galapagos, but I was simply a tortoise, a slow-moving behemoth. Until 1971, people would stop by Pinta Island, like the rest of the Galapagos Islands, to see the tame creatures like us tortoises. "Pinties" they used to call us. Being a tortoise, I couldn't tell anyone that all the Pinties were disappearing. I also couldn't explain how angry I got when I would see a tuft of grass, start moving toward it, only to have some hippity hoppity goat beat me there first. I never understood why people put those goats on our island in the first place. There was nothing I could do but wallow in self-pity (and my mudhole) waiting for some person to turn me into soup, like the rest of my family and friends.

People were supposed to be *so smart*, but I had yet to see evidence of that. I mean seriously, it took a little girl stopping by Pinta Island to point out to her tour guide that I seemed lonely. Well, of course, I was lonely! I had not seen another Pintie in years! Soon after that, some scientists showed up, talking about how excited they were to find me. At first, the feeling was mutual. Finally, someone could get rid of all of these goats and leave me alone. That dream was short-lived though, as they gathered around my shell and took measurements while flashing their toothy smiles.

Those scientists finished measuring me, and before I knew what was happening, they hoisted up my left side, slid some kind of rope under me and tied me up. They were making *me* leave, not the goats! I knew I was supposed to be a tame, pleasant-tempered Galapagos tortoise, but that day I was hissing mad. I didn't know what was happening at first, but I was lifted off of the ground by some sort of log with ropes and carried off by a bunch of people. I must admit that that experience itself was a bit exhilarating, until they dropped me in some crate, slammed the lid shut, and left me peering through six small holes as we ventured out to sea. In that one day, I had flown like a frigate bird and sailed through the water like a marine iguana, but that would be the last exciting thing I'd ever do.

I was taken to a concrete enclosure at the Charles Darwin Research Station. I was there to be studied, measured, tested and talked about. They really made a big deal out of me. I had overheard them talking about a 150-year-old female Galapagos tortoise somewhere in Australia. At first, I was still optimistic that one of my relatives had survived being made into tortoise soup. I wondered what it'd be like dating a tortoise that old, but she turned out to be a different subspecies. If nothing more I could wait at the research station in peace and quiet, away from those obnoxious goats until I met my end.

The scientists of the CDRS scoured the earth; all of the world's zoos and private animal collections for a female Pinta Island tortoise, but their efforts were fruitless. Realizing I was actually the last of my species was a real low point for me. I would never have an awkward first date, have tortoislings of my own, or even get to talk to another Pintie again in my life. I regretted not dating when I was in my forties or fifties. I thought I had a good hundred years to meet someone. I figured I was too young to settle down back then, but now I knew for sure I'd never get a chance. The people at the CDRS even posted a $10,000 reward for anyone who could find another Pinta Island Tortoise. They could have offered ten million dollars, but it would not have helped.

It would bother me so much when some kid would stand there with his family and say, "Mom, I don't understand why he's called Lonesome George when he's in there with two other Galapagos tortoises. They look the same to me."

Even though I knew he couldn't understand me, I would hiss,

"They look the same to me? They look the same to me! We are completely different subspecies! How'd you like me saying, yeah that little boy and that monkey look the same with their big eyes, weird smiles, and opposable thumbs. Why don't they form one big happy family?"

The conversation wasn't any better *in* the enclosure with those two tortoises from Isabela Island.

"I don't know what your problem is Georgie," Isa said. "You have a great life here with us. We get fresh grass and vegetables every day. We have beautiful weather and for whatever reason people line up every day to see *you*."

My body tensed up every time Isa called me Georgie. That was a name reserved only for family and close friends, which she was not.

"And don't forget our watering hole. It always has water in it, and you don't have to walk over hot volcanic rubble to find it as you did back on your island," Bella added.

"All you do is hiss, hiss, hiss. You hiss at us, and you hiss at them. We're probably going to be in this enclosure together for the next fifty years, so can't we make the best of it Georgie?" Isa reasoned.

Truth be told, I had stopped talking to Isa and Bella a few months after meeting them. Even the scientists thought if you put two subspecies of Galapagos tortoises together, you'll get more tortoises. Obviously, that's not what happened at all. I couldn't stand their thick Isabela Island accent or their cheery demeanor. They didn't understand how *Georgie* was feeling because there were still 2,000 of their kind left. I tried explaining it to them once, but they are kind of slow, even by tortoise standards.

I needed to find some space by myself, so I walked over to a corner of my enclosure, my backside pointing toward the two tortoises and the people. They always sighed disappointedly when I did this, but their disapproval gave me a momentary joy before I turned in for my midday nap.

Sleep was never restful because with sleep came the nightmares. It was always one of two dreams; the Starving Time after the goats arrived, but the worst ones were always about the Last Raid. It always started out the same way, walking up to the lookout, with my bale to watch the sunset. I could feel the air beginning to cool, and we looked out over the ocean from our favorite cliff.

"Georgie, it's going to be a great sunset today," my mom said joyfully.

"Mom, of course, it's going to be a beautiful sunset. It's pretty much always the same here. We are on an *island* you know," I replied.

"Haha. I guess you're right, but I just love a good sunset. I don't know where you get your restless spirit, Georgie. It must be from your father," Mom joked.

I sarcastically replied, "How do I know you really are my mom? I mean you just laid me in a pile of sand in the rubble and walked away. Maybe I'm the son of someone else in our bale, like Aunt Brenda? Have you ever thought of that?"

"Well as you love to point out all the time, we live on an island. We're *all* related here. But Aunt Brenda is just that, *Aunt* Brenda. I know your smell. You smell like your father," she said.

"You mean like a tortoise? Yeah, we all have the leafy, ashy smell," I replied.

"Oh Georgie, you're so stubborn sometimes. I know you by your smell. Some day when you are older you will understand," she explained. "You should rest up Georgie. It's going to be another exciting day of eating prickly pear in the valley."

"Good night, Mom. I'm going to go for a little walk. See you in the morning."

"Just be careful," she said in that loving yet annoying way.

"Mom, we're on an island, a *Galapagos* island. I think I'm a little too old to be scooped up by a frigate bird," I joked.

"I love you, Georgie," she said.

"Yeah. Yeah. See you, tomorrow Mom," I said.

Then the dream would always jump from that last sunset when all the Pinties turned in for the night (meaning they simply fell asleep where they were) to the following morning. Since I had been off by myself, I was late getting to the prickly pear cacti. That's when it happened.

I was heading down to the valley when I heard shouts of terror coming from my bale. That's when I saw them, the only real danger for us. It definitely wasn't a flock of frigate birds. From my vantage point on the hill, it looked like a group of whalers. These men came every year during whaling season to stock up on food supplies, namely us tortoises. They had, of course, stopped before and taken a few tortoises, but this time they seemed to be rounding up our entire bale. I was terrified.

I watched as the whalers herded my family and friends together. I heard them talking as they wrapped harnesses around my friends. I noticed the first older whaler smile a toothless grin.

He exclaimed, "Those other whalers were right! These dumb tortoises are easy pickings. We can just take them on board our ship and eat them later. I heard these things can live for over a year with no food or water."

The man holding the other end of the hoisting pole replied, "We might as well take as many as we can. These things easily weigh 150 - 200 pounds. That's a LOT of good soup."

The first man responded, "Let's clear them out. I hear they'll be putting goats on this barren island next year anyway."

"I make a mighty tasty goat stew. That's something to look forward to next whaling season. But for now, these pathetic tortoises will have to do. Let's round them up and fill our cargo hold. It's gonna be a long whaling season this year," the second man replied.

That's when the nightmare always went from bad to worse. I knew that as a tortoise there was nothing I could do, but that's when I saw her fleeing toward the rougher terrain. I heard my mom screaming to Aunt Brenda and the others to run for it. I saw she had a chance. I willed her to crouch down behind a large rock, but she didn't.

"Go!" she screamed toward the others. "I will divert them."

"No! Run, Mom! Run!" I pleaded from up on the hill.

She glanced up the hill at me and then back to the others before throwing herself between two rocks, blocking the path of the whalers. I watched in horror as she flipped upside down, which I knew could be fatal in and of itself for a tortoise. I saw the two whalers spot her flailing to right herself.

"Look. This old girl has herself wedged," said the first man scanning the surrounding land. "Come help me with this one. We'll come back for the rest later."

They took quite a while unwedging her from the rocks, but when they did I heard the second whaler say, "She's a biggie. We might as well take her straight to the fire. Cook her right in her shell."

"Easy pickings and easy cooking. Tortoise soup even comes with its own decorative bowl," the first whaler joked while running his hand along my mom's shell.

I snapped awake with a jerk and looked around me. The two whalers were replaced by a crowd of smiling people outside of my enclosure. I always woke up from those nightmares feeling great sorrow and extreme rage, but the people just ogled at me for being awake. I hated going to sleep, but I hated waking up and seeing those people staring at me even more. I hadn't had a peaceful night's sleep since the Last Raid, and that was just before the goats arrived in 1958 on our "barren" island. Pinta Island was far from barren. It was statements like those that spawned my hatred of goats and the people who brought them.

I knew I was a bitter old tortoise, but how could I forgive the people for not even trying to help me until I was alone? Even after the Last Raid, people could have protected the remaining few Pinties from the Starving Time brought on by the goats. I saw no reason to be joyful or to wake up being grateful for anything. I had seen a lot in the past century. But even at 106, I was only middle-aged for a Galapagos tortoise or so the sign outside my enclosure said. I still had a long time to go until my extinction came, but as far as I was concerned it couldn't come soon enough.

To be fair, there were a few people at the CDRS who had tried (in vain) to make my last days as positive as possible. As Isa and Bella so often pointed out, the people did pamper us by adding lush greenery from Pinta Island as well as one of my favorite sunning rocks, which on the side they had engraved 'Lonesome George'. At night I would slowly pile rocks to block out the 'Lonesome' part. Seeing that addition to my name was a constant reminder to me of my fate.

Fausto was one of the keepers who tried his best to make me happy. He was the one who pushed to have some other types of giant tortoises in my enclosure. Although those two female tortoises talked too much and annoyed me to no end, I knew Fausto meant well.

There were only two times when I was even remotely happy; one was when I dreamt about my youth when I was with my family back on Pinta Island watching the sunset over our favorite cliff before the Last Raid. The other was late at night when Fausto returned to the research station to check on me, read me stories, or play songs for me on his guitar.

Fausto walked over to the fence with some plants in his hand, patted my shell and whispered, "Are you ready for another song that I wrote just for you my friend? You seemed extra unhappy all day today, and I just wanted to cheer you up a little bit. I also brought you some fruit from my home that isn't on your approved diet list inside the station." This made me smile a little bit (on the inside at least, since I didn't have lips).

"I can only imagine what you must be feeling," he continued. "Even though you are one of the most famous animals on earth, loneliness is not a very pleasant thing to be famous for is it? When I look at that rock over there with your name engraved on it, it makes me a little sad, my friend. 'Lonesome George' is just a dreary name." I could only think about how much I agreed with everything that he was saying.

"George, my friend," Fausto said, laying his warm hand on my head. "From now on you are just George to me. How does that sound?" I raised my head off the ground and looked at Fausto. "Well George, I will take that as your nod of approval."

Fausto read some stories to me and played a few songs on his guitar until I pretended to be asleep. Then he snuck off to his home and family on the other side of the island. Once he was out of sight, I lifted my head from the dusty ground one last time to take in all that was to be my life for the next 100 years or so, before drifting off to sleep and another nightmare.

Chapter 2:

MY WAKE UP CALL

"George, you need to wake up," an unfamiliar male voice said.

"We don't think he's going to wake up. Do you really think this is a good idea? We just don't think he's going to go for it anyway. Have you read his scroll? He's really not the most agreeable animal we have ever met, you know," declared a fast-talking female voice.

"George, we would like to talk with you for a moment," said the first voice in a calm tone.

I felt uneasy that these voices were talking directly to me. Fausto was the only one who talked to me like I was an individual and not an animal on display. I pretended to be asleep as I tried to figure out what I should do, not that I had a lot of options. I only heard two voices, so I figured I might be safe. I weighed close to two hundred pounds, so I knew I was not easy to move, especially if I wiggled around a little. I knew this because a few years ago some angry Ecuadorian fisherman had tried to kidnap me and hold me hostage because they were angry they couldn't fish in the ocean near the Galapagos Islands. The fisherman knew I was important to many people around the world, and they wanted to get the attention of Ecuador's government, since Ecuador owned the islands. I just didn't want to be tortoise-napped for a political statement, so I started waving my feet back and forth and hissing. This seemed to slow them down. Fausto appeared around the corner to stop them. He had come back to visit me that night and was just in time to call the authorities. I was grateful that he was there to save me that night.

"George, we know you're awake and can hear us. We need to ask you a very important question that will affect the rest of your life," stated the first voice again.

I slowly opened my eyes and noticed a few things. The first was that my enclosure was not my enclosure. I was in some type of jungle that was full of lush green plants with a crystal clear stream that ran through the center of it. The smell of fresh fruit lingered in the air from somewhere in the distance. The golden sun beat down onto my shell, and I noticed that there wasn't a cloud in the sky. For some reason, which didn't make sense to me, I felt warm and tingly. Not because of the sun, but because I seemed to be content and happy for the first time in a long time. It was a strange sensation, which made me wonder, *Did someone tranquilize me while I was sleeping and move me into the jungle?*

"No. No one drugged you, and you are not exactly in a jungle," assured the male voice.

"You're not in a jungle. It's more of a garden. We just wanted to ask you if you want to join us on a mission. It might be dangerous, but it could be a lot of fun at the same time. Do you want to join us? Do you? Do you?" inquired the rapid talker again from somewhere in a tree above me.

"Martha, I think you need to slow down a bit and give George here a chance to ...to get his bearings," the male voice stated.

As I listened to these two talk about some kind of mission, I realized something. Somehow the first speaker had heard my thoughts and answered my question before I spoke. How was that possible? Now a fresh wave of panic swept away my warm tingly sense of contentment.

"I don't understand what's going on. How did you . . . I mean . . . Can you understand what I'm thinking?" I asked, trying to pinpoint the speaker.

"We can all understand. Here we all can communicate clearly. There are not any language barriers here," he affirmed.

"Who are you? Where am I? And what do you want with me?" I blurted out a little more panicked than I meant to.

I frantically looked around me to identify who the speakers were and to understand what was happening, but I couldn't locate either of them. So I raised my head to get a better look, and slowly I rotated my neck to get a look behind my shell. As I did, I came face to face with the owner of the first voice, who I discovered had been sitting on my shell the whole time!

"Hello, George. I'm Eldey," he said.

There, just a few inches from my nose, sat a strange bird standing a little taller than my neck. At first, I thought I was looking at a large Galapagos penguin, but the beak didn't look quite right. It was also about twice as tall as most penguins that I had seen back at the research station. Its beak was a grayish hue with black stripes. The strange bird's wings weren't penguinish either. They didn't have that firm, flipper look. His wings looked like those of a Galapagos cormorant, except stumpier and tucked back to his sides.

I must have been staring because Eldey continued, "I know this must all seem very strange to you, so let's just take things one step at a time. My name is Eldey, or at least that's the name I've chosen for myself here. I was known as the great auk. I don't want to bore or overwhelm you with a bunch of facts about myself. I want to answer some of *your* questions."

My questions! Yeah, I had quite a few questions for this three-foot talking bird who could read my mind. "Where am I exactly, and how did I get here?"

"Nothing like starting with the difficult questions. It is kind of hard to explain exactly," Eldey said, adjusting his dark webbed feet on my shell. "You are in the Garden at the moment, but you are not totally here."

"Not totally here?" I retorted. "What does that mean?"

"As I said, it is not that easy to explain since you are not totally here yet. We want to propose an idea to you; a sort of mission that we need your help completing. We brought you here to explain the plan to you and then give you time to decide whether you would want to join us or not. To simplify things, at this moment you are sleeping next to your watering hole at the Charles Darwin Research Station..." Eldey said matter-of-factly.

"So, this is a dream then?" I asked.

"Not exactly. It is a little more than that," he said, almost laughing. "You are also partially in the Garden too, so this is not a dream. You are kind of between two places; the one there and the one here."

"You are going extinct, and we all went extinct, and we came here, and we want to go back, and we want to have you help us do that because we want to make sure that we help out the people because they need our help, you know?" said the female voice somewhere up in the tree, which I assumed was Martha whom Eldey had addressed earlier.

"So there are two of you? And you are asking me to join some type of special animal trio for a mission to save the people? Save them from what? Killer bees? Yappy dogs? Their own stupidity?" I chuckled. Another tortoise stereotype was that we were very patient because we are slow. That had never been my experience. We were slow by nature, but not by choice. Conversing with these two was almost as frustrating as talking to Isa and Bella back at the CDRS.

"There are many of us here in the Garden but only a few who are interested in going back and helping the people. Many don't have the same compassion for the people as we do," replied Eldey crouching down and leaping from my shell.

"You said that you are a great auk? How is that possible? Aren't you supposed to be *extinct*?" I asked.

"Yes, actually I am surprised that you know that," replied the great auk ruffling his black and white feathers.

"Well, I have seen a lot of information posted around the CDRS and heard people talking about other animals that have gone extinct. Being the last of my kind, that's a normal topic of conversation around my enclosure. It was always disheartening to hear about the sad end to so many creatures."

Eldey continued, "I *am* extinct and have been so for some time, but in the Garden, we are given some 'options' if we choose not to be extinct anymore," Eldey said air quoting with his minuscule wings next to his head like I had seen people do while talking before.

"How can you be given the option to be extinct? I don't understand. I mean I'd personally love to go extinct and just end it. It's so lonely in my enclosure, and I miss my family so much. This is the first conversation I've wanted to be a part of in over 40 years," I said trying to avoid tearing up.

"I know your time at the CDRS has been a difficult one and that you have so much time until your extinction will come, but that is also why we wanted to talk to you about some 'options' you have given your unique circumstances," Eldey stated.

"Yeah, you have lots of options, you know? You can stay here in the Garden, or you can go back for another 23 years, 6 months, 3 days and 46, 45, 44 seconds; if you want. That choice is yours, but if you go back you wouldn't be able to help out the people or have an adventure with us. Personally, we wouldn't like being stuck in a small enclosure by ourselves for that long; especially not when you can hang out with all of us doing awesomely helpful things," Martha yammered.

"Before you help me understand everything that you're trying to tell me, can you let me know who you are exactly?" I replied, straining to locate Martha in the trees above.

Just then, a brown, mossy green dove descended in a circling pattern from a tree at the edge of the woods. She landed right in front of me and began pacing with her coral red feet, head bobbing back and forth at the same rapid rate at which she spoke. I looked into her bright red eyes as she prepared to ramble on.

"Our chosen name is Martha, but then again you figured that one out already. You're really, really smart, you know? We're not actually a dove-like you were thinking. We were...or are, passenger pigeons. You probably heard of our kind in all of your extinction conversations at the research station too. Right? Did you know that we were once the most populous bird in the whole wide world? A flock of us could take days to pass by one place, blocking out the sun for hours. We were pretty amazing actually. After we flew by, there was sometimes an inch or two of poop, like snow covering the ground. We know that's gross, but it's also pretty amazing. Don't you think so?" Martha asked dreamily, staring off into space.

I was grateful when Eldey interrupted Martha's rambling, "Martha talks in plurals as you may have already picked up on. Being the most abundant bird in the world at one time, she is used to big crowds. Martha has trouble focusing on one thought at a time, even here. You will get used to it after a while."

Eldey seemed to sense my uneasiness. "I can see that you are a little overwhelmed by everything that has taken place. Why don't you and I head over to the brook and talk? I will send Martha to get the others for our meeting later."

"Martha, please go round up some of the other animals who have expressed interest in pursuing the mission with us," Eldey said looking at the frantic little bird, "and see if you can try to avoid Inca."

"We will see what we can do. See you at the meeting grounds in a little bit," Martha said as she flew out of sight.

"Inca? Who is that?" I asked.

"He is a Carolina Parakeet. Maybe I should not try to exclude him from this mission, because he has a wealth of knowledge, *but* he just makes so much noise and has a shorter attention span than Martha, if you can believe that," Eldey joked, trying to lighten the mood. "I honestly think he would be detrimental to what we are planning. He likes to be the center of attention, and he is overly friendly. Those are admirable traits in many circumstances but not when we are trying to stay off the radar."

I felt so dumbfounded by all that was taking place that I just wanted to lay down. Still, there was an unexplainable excitement in me that I hadn't felt in a long time. Eldey put his stumpy little wing around me and waddled over to the crystal clear brook that was flowing out of a large rock near the tree line.

"I know how overwhelming all of this must seem, especially since you are still in between both places. I don't know why, but once you are totally here, things seem to make more sense. Why don't you take a nice refreshing drink from the brook, get something to eat, and then hopefully I can explain what we have in mind a little more clearly."

Chapter 3:

THE GARDEN

N ever in all of my days on Pinta Island or at the CDRS have I ever had such sweet, tender grass. The flavor was like all of the ripest fruits and leaves I've ever eaten blended together at the same time. The water tasted even sweeter. "I feel so refreshed and energetic. That's a pretty big deal coming from a tortoise you know," I said, cracking a smile.

"It is nice to see you smile, George. Hopefully, now that you are relaxed and 'energetic'," Eldey said air quoting with his stumpy wings, "things might make a little more sense."

"You mean you can see me smile here?" I asked, astonished realizing the corners of my beak were actually curving upward.

"Yes, George. As you have noticed, things in the Garden are a little different." He stated pausing slightly. He shook his head and slapped it with his stumpy wing. "I need to remember my manners. I never even asked you if you like the name George. You see, we animals in the Garden get to choose our names. Many of us have chosen a name that has to do with our last days back there on earth before our extinctions. Being mainly a food source for sailors and a stuffing for European pillows, I did not have a given name from the people. I guess I could have gone for Delicious or Pillow, but they didn't seem appropriate, so I chose the last place where great auks once roamed and consequently where the last three of us were taken."

I noticed a sadness appear in Eldey's eyes, and he turned away as he recalled his past, especially at the mention of the last three great auks. I wanted to ask him more about the last three and what happened, but I figured I had more than enough questions for him. I'd be sure to ask him more about his past at a later time. It sounded like we'd be spending a lot of time together on this mission.

"The name Eldey sounded a lot better than our other last homeland which was referred to as Funk Island. Imagine being called Funk or Funky after the terrible smell emanating from our nesting colonies," he said laughing to himself. "It's funny how smells, even terrible ones, so clearly bring back memories, isn't it? Anyway, enough about me. Let us start with what you would like to be called."

That was a hard question to answer. I thought about hearing Fausto call me simply George back at the research station, and how it made me feel good. I told Eldey that I'd stick with the name George while I was here.

"Fausto!" This thought of him made me wonder what was going on with him back at the CDRS. "You said I am here and there somehow. What is going on at the research station now if I am here? Won't Fausto realize that I am missing? I don't want to worry him," I said while realizing my disappearance could cause Fausto distress.

"I am glad that you are worried about what the people will think when you are not there George. That is progress from your initial attitude, even since you arrived here," Eldey said with nodding approval.

I felt anger well up in me at the mention of the people and my apparent concern about them. I think that came out in my response to Eldey, "I don't care about the people, but Fausto has always been kind to me. I'd hate to hurt his feelings. I know he would miss me terribly if I weren't to come back."

"Well caring about one person is a start," Eldey said with a smile. It was something about his eyes that made me feel peaceful. "So George, as Martha had interjected earlier, we are trying to organize a rescue mission to help save other animals from the fate of most of us here. We are also trying to help save the people from themselves. I know you do not care about the people in general, but I want you to think about Fausto back at the CDRS. Keep him in mind as you decide whether or not to join us."

I wasn't sure if I really wanted to know what this mission to save mankind was going to entail. Here in this garden, I was content for the first time since before the Last Raid. I was tempted to let Eldey know that I wanted to be left alone for a little while to enjoy this place. His eyes drew my gaze, and I could tell it wasn't quite that easy. I tried to look down at the ground, so I could say no, but he cleared his throat causing me to look up again before I could utter another word.

"I think I am being too hasty, asking you to join us when you do not even understand where you really are. I do not think that I can explain the Garden to you as well as Astuto. Maybe we should take a short walk over to the tree," said Eldey pointing his wing.

I tried thinking back to all of the famous names of extinct animals I had ever heard of back at the CDRS, but *Astuto* didn't ring a bell. We began walking toward the tree, and I noticed that I was able to walk almost gracefully along the brook. I had the feeling of flying, the way I did that day I was hoisted into the air on Pinta Island before being jammed into the crate that would take me to the CDRS. I also noticed that Eldey seemed to almost fly with his tiny wings that I had assumed were useless.

We came to a tree that towered into the sky above us. It had golden leaves like I had never seen before, and there on the lowest branch of this golden tree, I noticed the unmistakable pillar of extinction, the dodo. He appeared to be reading some sort of scroll as we approached. He had a round gray body as I had seen in so many pictures, tiny white wings, and three rounded poofy feathers sticking out of his rump. But the thing that stood out to me was his face. His beak looked like a yellow squash with a brown spot on the end. And his face, well it wasn't exactly pleasant to look at. It had the appearance of a person's foot after being in the ocean too long. He was ugly.

"Astuto, we have brought George here for the mission. I have not told him what we would like his part to be. As we expected he is a little confused by what is going on, so I thought it might be helpful for you to explain the Garden to him *before* we discuss the mission itself," Eldey said, catching the dodo up to speed.

Astuto looked at Eldey and simply nodded. Then he looked carefully at me with a stern look. He seemed to be able to see into my very core, and it made me shiver. His eyes stared at me from within his fleshy face. He frowned slightly and shook his head.

"You know Tortoise, you aren't much different from the people you love to hate," the dodo said bluntly, placing down the scroll he had been reading.

This statement hit me like a slap in the face. I didn't know what to say, and I found myself getting angry that he would accuse me of such a thing. I mean, I never killed anything, unless you counted some clumps of grass at the research station.

"But you...you don't even..." I stammered.

Astuto cut me off and continued, "I can hear your thoughts here in the Garden. I can hear your judgments of my appearance and it stings, like how did you put it....like a slap in the face."

I was speechless. Who was this creature? Was he reading my thoughts right now? That dodo had no right to be in my brain making judgments about me. He didn't even know me or what I had been through.

"You are right. I shouldn't be listening in on your thoughts. You are still of that world, and not yet of this one. It is not your fault that you feel animosity toward me and the people. All this hatred was not how it was meant to be, you know? It's important to know where you are before you choose where you will be. Don't you think Tortoise?" Astuto said, forcing a small unconvincing smile.

I simply nodded my head in agreement. He adjusted his stout feet on the golden branch and hopped to the ground beside me. The dodo beckoned me to have a seat on a rock at the base of the golden tree.

"First let me introduce myself. As you have deduced, I am in fact the dodo bird. Whereas you are the poster boy of endangered-ness, I am the international symbol of extinction. Did you ever hear the quote by William Cuppy about my kind at the CDRS? He once stated that 'The Dodo never had a chance. He seems to have been invented for the sole purpose of becoming extinct and that was all he was good for.' Tell me that isn't a cruel statement. I didn't plot out my extinction or plan for my ill-gotten fame. We all have our baggage, Tortoise. Whereas you hate the goats that made your family starve and the sailors who 'soupified' your family, I could say I hate the rats, cats, pigs, and sailors who ate dodo eggs and killed all of us from the island of Mauritius, but where would that get me? Hatred doesn't accomplish anything except to breed greater hatred," Astuto said, peering straight into my eyes; straight into my soul, letting his final statement sink in.

I couldn't help feeling sorry for Astuto, but how could he say I shouldn't be angry? That's all I'd known for over 40 years and probably for the next 40 as well.

"I do understand the temptation to be angry with me for saying that Tortoise. I can't make you let go of the anger you have, but I do hope that sometime in the future you will find peace," Astuto replied.

"We can agree to disagree on how I should be feeling," I told him. "Let's get back to why I'm here and why Eldey brought me to see you."

"Eldey is helping me and some others organize a rescue expedition of sorts. He brought you here to talk with me because I've been here in the Garden longer than he has. I understand its 'dynamics' a little better than he does. Let's start with simple things first and get to the more complex ones later. My chosen name is Astuto, which is the Portuguese word for 'intelligent' since the name *dodo* comes from a Portuguese word for...," he paused searching for words, "well let's just say it's a Portuguese word for the opposite of intelligent. Dodo was one of the nicer, more respectable terms that the people had for my kind."

"So can you explain to me where I am exactly?" I asked.

"Well, you are *there* in the present outside of the Garden at a place you call the Charles Darwin Research Station. You are also *here* for the time being with us in the Garden until you make your choice about whether to join our mission. Either way, you will end up here eventually," Astuto said, cocking his head to see how I'd respond.

"I thought I was having some kind of strange dream. So am I dead then?" I asked.

"Not exactly. There is a time for that if that's the option you choose, but that time is appointed for a later date," Astuto explained.

"Yeah, in 23 years and 6 months or something..." I said under my breath.

"Oh, I see you have been talking to Martha. Well, that would be one choice. To continue on at the CDRS until your 'official' extinction date or you can choose to leave there voluntarily now and come here to help us with our mission," Astuto said, air quoting *official*, then scratching the underneath of his beak with his claw.

"So you mean I can choose to live there with Fausto for the next 23 years or come here?" I probed.

"Indeed. Except I can't guarantee Fausto will be with you the whole time," he said.

I could tell he must have some insight into Fausto's personal extinction date too, but I didn't want to know. Instead, I chose to redirect the conversation back to this place. I had to admit, I enjoyed the peaceful, almost joyful feeling this place had to offer as well as the food, but I didn't know if I was ready to be officially extinct just yet.

"So where exactly is *here*? You keep referring to it as *here*," I asked hoping for more of a clear, concise explanation.

"You are there and here," Astuto said much to my dismay. "The Garden is known by many names, but it is best known as the Garden east of Eden."

"Wait! Do you mean to tell me this is *the* Garden of Eden? Like from the Adam and Eve story?" I asked sarcastically.

"I am surprised that you have heard of it, but yes, Tortoise. That is exactly what I'm saying," Astuto stated.

"Fausto used to read many stories to me when he'd sneak back to visit me at night. That was one of the stories that intrigued me because people and animals seemed to live at peace with one another, which was so different from what you and I have experienced back there in real life. But I always thought that was something of a fantasy story; a nice thought, but nothing more," I clarified.

"Well I can see you don't believe it, but there *is* truth to that story, Tortoise. You see, we were created for mankind to have dominion over us. That was the original plan at least. We tried our best in the olden days to help the man out, but we weren't designed for that position. The dog got the closest and was deemed 'man's best friend', but even the dog couldn't fulfill the role of helper, which the man required. The man named all of us, and we lived happily alongside him in the Garden eating all the fruit we wanted. It was a good design," Astuto recalled with a sigh.

"So you're saying we were all here in the Garden living happily until Adam and Eve ate the fruit from this golden tree, and then we all got kicked out of the Garden because of the serpent or something like that?" I mocked, rolling my eyes.

At the mention of the serpent, Astuto and Eldey shuddered, but Astuto continued, "Yes, that's the short and simple version. The serpent had told Adam and Eve to eat of the tree of knowledge. That is not this tree. This golden tree is the tree of eternal life, which Adam and Eve never partook of before getting exiled."

"Is that why you can live here in the Garden for so long?" I asked a little more humbly.

"In a way, George. The Garden is a refuge of sorts for all of creation. There, on earth where misery exists, we can go extinct, but here there will always be a representative of our kinds. That is why in the Garden there is only one of each of us. We represent our entire species from beginning to end; the good times and the bad," Eldey explained. "If you remember the Garden story and some of the finer details, only the man, the woman, and the serpent were *directly* cursed..."

"And the ground," Astuto interjected. He seemed to want to make sure that Eldey remembered *all* of the finer details.

"Yes, and the ground," Eldey said, correcting himself. "That is why the man and woman had to start growing their own food. It is also why the food there does not compare with that which you will find in the Garden. But I know you have already discovered that."

"Oh," was all I could say trying to make sense of everything I had just been told. The Garden of Eden was a real place. Extinction was real, but it wasn't. Here I could live happily ever after, but back there at the research station I would face another 23 years of pictures, people feeling sorry for me, and personal sadness possibly without Fausto.

Astuto's next question caught me completely off guard, "So Tortoise, are you ready to save the world?

Chapter 4:

THE DECISION OF MY LIFETIME

"Excuse me?" I knew the look of shock must have been written all over my face.

Seeing that Astuto had finished the explanation of the Garden and here and there to me, Eldey walked over to me, again placing his wing around my shell, "George, the reason we have brought you here from there is to ask you if you would willingly join us in our endeavor. You see, as extinct creatures, we have options," Eldey said, "but our options are very limited compared to yours."

"Yes. Yes. You see, you are not quite extinct there, and have such a long span of time until you go extinct, that you can choose how and when you want to go extinct before your scheduled time. It's an anomaly really, a 'loophole' in the realm of extinction that hasn't happened in a long time. Most creatures go quickly or surprisingly. The people don't usually even notice or care until it's much too late. You, on the other hand, have 23 years left there if you choose, or you can decide to leave there now to join us here, to go back there," Astuto stated without further explanation.

"I was with you until the last part. Why would I leave the CDRS there, to come to the Garden here, and then head back there again? That seems like that would be against the rules or something," I interjected.

"The *rules* as you put them are simple. If an individual here wants to go back there, they can, as long as they choose to go back to the same location where they were originally placed," Astuto explained.

Eldey could see that I wasn't understanding, so he altered his approach to fill in some gaps in Astuto's explanation, "So if *I* went back there, I would have to start off on Eldey, an island near Iceland in the North Atlantic, and Astuto would have to go back to *his* home island of Mauritius in the Indian Ocean. We cannot simply go back together to the same location, which is one of the complications with this mission."

I guess those rules made sense in a strange sort of way. I wondered how I'd be able to help them since the Galapagos Islands are in the Pacific Ocean far away from the islands of Eldey or Mauritius.

"Some species have chosen to do this successfully in the past. The takahe is a good example," Eldey explained.

"Tacky? What is that a good example of? Glue?" I joked.

"The *takahe*," Eldey enunciated, "is a flightless blue, green bird of New Zealand, who chose to go back there with great success but returning from the Garden can be difficult to do. Many of our homeland environments have been devastated since our extinction dates. The people there may also choose to simply eat us back into extinction. Any bad experiences back there would be felt by us when we return back to the Garden. It is the biggest downside to trying to be a 'Lazarus species'," Eldey clarified.

"Wait a minute," I said trying to keep my facts straight, "A Lazarus species?"

"Yes, that is simply a term that the people use to describe a species that they think went extinct which they miraculously find again. It usually is not because those animals were not extinct. Some animals here, like the takahe, simply wanted to go back and try to give the people a second chance there. It is a personal decision which most animals here would never consider. You can see that there are a lot of perks to being in the Garden and not a whole lot of motivation to go back there. Our fate involving the people is always a very uncertain thing," Eldey said trailing off.

He excused himself to get a drink from the brook which flowed through the Garden. It seemed that something was bothering him, but I didn't want to ask and offend him; especially after he had expressed such genuine care for me during my time here.

Astuto came over beside me, watching the great auk walk slowly over to the brook and cleared his throat. "I don't know how much you know about the extinction of Eldey's kind, the great auk, but all of this talk of going back to help the people has mixed emotions for him. You see Tortoise when one of us here in the Garden decides to go back there, there are *rules* as you put it; a certain rhyme and reason as it were."

"What kind of rules are you talking about? You mean more than just the rule that you have to start out where you ended...I mean went extinct?" I asked.

"Let me try to explain this by asking you a seemingly trivial question, Tortoise," Astuto said softly. "Which came first; the chicken or the egg?"

I said, half laughing, "Are you going to ask me why the chicken crossed the road next?"

"Huh?" Astuto said, with a blank look on his face.

Seeing that the dodo was serious about the chicken or the egg question I responded, "It's a trick question. If I say the chicken, you will ask where the chicken came from? If I say the egg, you will ask who laid the egg? It's just one of those riddles that have no right answer."

"That's where you are wrong Tortoise. That question has an answer. You see, when an animal leaves the Garden, it still has the directive to "be fruitful and multiply". When an animal leaves here to return there, one becomes three."

I felt my face scrunch up in confusion, and it was obvious to Astuto who continued with a sigh, "What I mean is, if I were to become a Lazarus species and return there, I would start off as three of my kind; a male, female, and an infant, or being a bird, an egg. You see Tortoise, the question has a direct and sensible answer," Astuto clarified by puffing up his feathers to show the absurdness of my thinking.

Under my breath, I retorted, "Well you were the one who didn't know that the chicken and the egg crossed the road to get to the other side."

"You are a strange one, Tortoise," was his only reply.

"Thank you for clarifying one of life's mysteries to me Astuto, but why does discussing the Lazarus species bother Eldey so much? Shouldn't he be content and happy to stay here in the Garden? I mean, what's not to like here?" I asked, sweeping my front leg toward the breathtaking scenery surrounding us.

"You see; many of us here have struggled, like you, with resentment about being forced here because of the disregard of the people for our well-being. I honestly wasn't always in agreement with helping people like Eldey. Sure I've made my peace with my extinction, but Eldey has always wanted to *do more*," Astuto explained, "You see Tortoise, he *did* go back."

"You mean to say that Eldey went extinct twice?" I asked.

"Yes, that's exactly what I am saying. When Eldey went extinct and came to the Garden he was adamant about going back to help people once he found out that he had that choice. Having been here for a century and a half at that point, I tried to tell Eldey it was a bad idea, but he insisted. Eldey said that he saw people who were trying to save the great auks. He saw a renewed compassion on the part of the people that hadn't been there before. He said many of the remaining great auks died off due to a volcanic eruption during a nesting season, *not* because of the people." Astuto explained.

"So, what happened when he returned back there, to the Atlantic Ocean I mean?" I prodded.

"Eldey formulated a plan to go back to Eldey Island, which was once a great auk breeding colony. He returned hopeful and was in the midst of hatching the egg amidst a group of smaller seabirds when a group of sailors sent by a collector pulled up on a nearby shore. Eldey started toward the men, hopeful that this would be his chance to save his kind and show the people that conservation could work. Unfortunately, this hope was short-lived.

As Eldey got closer to the men, he saw they had a bag and

several clubs. He still held onto the hope that if he didn't run, they would simply take him back to England or Iceland to be observed and cared for. Eldey's mate, on the other hand, panicked and headed toward the sea to escape the men, but she slipped over some rocks. One of the men drew back his club and..." Astuto sighed, seemingly deciding whether to finish his sentence or not.

Even though I couldn't hear Astuto's thoughts as he could mine, I knew the answer before I asked, "So she didn't make it? What about Eldey himself and the egg? Did they survive and make it to the collector?"

"Sadly, no. One of the other men accidentally stepped on the egg in the nest. At the sight of this, Eldey fled toward the ocean still holding onto the hope that he, himself, could somehow find someone who would be more compassionate. He never made it to the ocean and a big part of him died on the cold, rocky beach that day. There's a pain in suffering and in facing your demise, but to do so *twice* is more than most can bear."

"What did you say to him when he came back to the Garden? This place must have helped him deal with his loss, right?" I inquired.

"For a long time, he never spoke to me or anyone else. But after a time, more and more animals were going extinct at a faster and faster rate. This seemed to motivate Eldey, and he again expressed a strong desire to help the people. He knew simply starting again on Eldey Island would be in vain, so he brainstormed many ideas that could possibly work. He was figuring out other options and learning what choices we have here. I told him that it was too much for one animal to take on alone. That's when we realized there was an option we'd never considered," said the dodo, cocking his head and looking straight into my eyes.

"So what you're saying is my 'situation'," I said air quoting as Eldey had done so many times since my arrival, "... is the option you hadn't considered before?"

"Yes, that is where you come in, George," said Eldey from behind me. I wasn't sure how long he had been there, but the sadness in his eyes again flickered with passionate optimism. "If you are willing to join us on our mission, you would be able to start off anywhere in your species' range, which for you is simply Pinta Island. But *you* would have the ability to communicate with each of us who undertake this mission. You would be an integral part of this mission. In fact, you would be the most important part of our mission. I do understand if you choose not to join us. It is a lot to ask of you. It is ultimately your choice to make, but we are asking you to consider it."

"How would *I* be able to communicate with all of you? Would I have to take a cell phone from the CDRS or something?" I asked.

"That is not exactly clear, but we know you *will* be able to do so... at least for a time," Eldey explained.

"May I ask what the downsides are to saying yes to joining you on whatever mission you all are planning? I feel you've been a little vague on some of the specifics," I said.

Eldey and Astuto exchanged a brief look of concern.

"For each of us in the Garden, going back means adding potential hardships to add to our memories, which is a reason so many don't choose that option. Double extinction is a fate few have ventured toward. Added sadness from those memories is something that *we* need to worry about here. Even though we are at peace here in the Garden now, we can all recall each and every act of cruelty we experienced back there," Astuto said sadly.

"Well I don't know how adding one more bad memory for me would be that terrible. Plus all I'd be adding is the memory of my own demise right?" I asked.

There was another long awkward pause and Eldey slowly continued, "Well George, for each of us here *in* the Garden that is the case, but for *you* it is different. You see, since you have not officially gone extinct back there yet, and you are not yet here, eating off the tree of eternal life like us, you are in an 'interesting' position," Eldey air quoted, mocking me, mocking him, trying to cut the tension of the situation. "If you would be killed during this mission, you would be extinct, for real, with no hope of ever coming back here to the Garden."

Wow, that didn't seem fair. This seemed like another heavy burden to bear, which I wasn't expecting. For them, it was a matter of discomfort, but for me and my kind, it meant real extinction? For 40 years I had been hoping not to see another day of loneliness back at the CDRS. Every day I woke up was the beginning of the worst day of my life. There was no hope, and I had begged for my own demise. But knowing that it could be a fate *worse* than death, seemed like an even more difficult pill to swallow. I found myself in a place more difficult than I had been facing back at the Charles Darwin Research Station. What was I supposed to say? Should I wait to go extinct or go *really* extinct? I would be deader than a dodo.

"What happens if we can complete our venture without me being exterminated? Is there any chance that I can make it back to the Garden or are we talking about a no-win situation for me?" I grumbled.

"There have been a few others that have been in your position in the past. Most have chosen to simply go extinct in their planned time, but a few creatures have volunteered. Once you leave there, come here, and go back there, you are stuck there unless you can complete the mission you have started...or are killed," Astuto said matter-of-factly.

"Have you ever heard of the Gigantopithecus or the Plesiosaur?" Eldey asked.

"Yeah, you know; Bigfoot, Sasquatch, Yeti, Skunk Ape or Nessie, the Loch Ness Monster? We don't know how much you know about these creatures, but they are some of the ones who tried to do what we're trying to have you help us do," the unmistakable voice of Martha burst in. "What did we miss? Did he decide to help us? Everyone is on their way to the gathering place to hear his verdict when he is ready, but there's no rush...unless you already know your answer," said the passenger pigeon bobbing her head up and down while frantically pacing back and forth.

This was a strange turn in the conversation, and I had no idea of how Bigfoot could possibly fit into the Garden of Eden and saving mankind. Like a lot of things since I arrived here, it just didn't make sense.

Turning from the hyperactive, little pigeon back to the two, larger birds, "You mean Bigfoot and the Loch Ness Monster? How in the world do mythical creatures fit into the Garden of Eden and a 200-pound tortoise saving the earth?"

"Well, they aren't exactly ... *mythical.* They both tried the same mission that you are attempting and to this point, they have been unable to get back to the Garden," Astuto explained.

"They are real then? Why hasn't any person ever caught them then? I mean those are two *large* well-known creatures you're talking about. It's not like Martha hiding amidst a flock of pigeons in a crowded city." I responded.

"They *are* large, and *that* has been part of their problem. You see, they are in the same position that you will be in if you come here and go back there, except they are feared by the people. Fear makes people do horrible things. Nessie the plesiosaur was stuck alone in the depths of the North Atlantic awaiting her ultimate extinction for quite some time before we approached her with the same proposal we are giving to you," Eldey explained.

"I tried to warn her that people might fear her, but she wouldn't listen. She thought she knew better than an old fuddy-duddy dodo bird. As a 'boomerang species', Nessie got to choose where she would return within her species range," Astuto added, seeing if I was following his logic.

I must say for a dodo bird, he was quite...well quite astute.

"The ability to choose your return location is what separates you and them from one of us, already extinct animals," Eldey added.

"Well, that and the fact that I can really go extinct and die forever and you can't," I scoffed.

"Well yes; that too. As I was saying, Nessie decided to come to the Garden ahead of schedule and her return location was in Scotland where sailors had known about her kind because of their breeding grounds in Loch Ness for some time. She had hoped that, by starting in a smaller location than the Atlantic Ocean, she could befriend and eventually approach the Scots. Her attempt at returning was a total failure. Her enormous girth and ferocious appearance made approaching the people of Scotland a ruefully, unwise choice. She approached a small girl washing her toy off in the loch. The girl seemed genuinely intrigued by Nessie and beckoned the plesiosaur closer," Astuto explained.

"You see George, younger people seem to be the most accepting of things hard to understand. The girl actually reached out to pet Nessie's snout, but as she reached her hand out, her mom screamed, "Help! It's a monster! It's the Loch Ness monster, and it's trying to eat my baby!" The people quickly rushed to the shore screaming and shaking sticks at Nessie. Of course, Nessie retreated under the waters of the loch and was unable to attempt further communication with that little girl." Eldey explained.

"Now Nessie is stuck fleeing the people she wanted to return to help. Even though Scottish law protects Nessie from hunting, people are seeking her for the wrong reasons that won't help our cause. Now she can either be captured and put on display in some zoo or be killed by one of the people seeking personal fame," Astuto explained, shaking his head regretfully.

"I had hoped Pat would have better luck on her mission," Eldey continued.

"Pat? Who's Pat?", I asked.

"Pat is the chosen name of the Gigantopithecus, better known as Bigfoot or Yeti. She named herself after Roger *Patterson* who was the first person she tried to communicate with," Eldey explained.

"We thought about using you Tortoise even back then in 1967," Astuto explained, "We knew the last Pinta Island Tortoise died in an Australia zoo earlier that year, but the people didn't even know who you were at that point, so we chose Pat. We thought since Pat looked more like a person and was less intimidating than a thirty-foot dinosaur swimming around in the murky water of Loch Ness, she would have better luck."

"Well, is an eight-foot-tall hairy ape-man that much less scary than a dinosaur?" I mocked, "I mean I've seen people run away from tiny lizards back at the CDRS."

"Yes, I have to agree. People's reactions are very difficult to predict. I did not think the people would respond to her as dramatically as they did. I thought given the fact that she looked *similar* to the people, they might accept her more willingly. I also had hoped that she would be able to communicate with them using sign language which she had mastered before her 'boomerang mission' began. Having opposable thumbs and individual fingers would give her a greater communication advantage with the people over creatures like us," Eldey said, showing off his tiny wings.

"Unfortunately for Pat, on the day she tried to approach the man, Roger Patterson, in the woods of northern California, she startled his horse causing him to fall to the ground. Pat panicked and ran away for the entire world to see. She has good reason to be fearful of the people. She is constantly being hunted by people seeking fame and fortune. Pat has been trying to find a place to hide, but no matter where she tries to hide, in the thick remote forests or the highest mountains in the world, people are always looking for her," Eldey explained.

"That is why we chose you now. People can easily make judgments and overlook an entire group, but give them one individual, like yourself, to get to know and their hearts are much more compassionate. Plus, tortoises are about the least intimidating creature in the world. Very few people suffer from chelonaphobia, the fear of turtles, and I'm pretty sure Fausto isn't one of those people. You are the least scary creature who has ever been in your 'unique' circumstances and many people already have compassion for you. If you were to die, people around the world would take note. The trick will be for us to arrange your death at the Charles Darwin Research Station, since you are in a zoo, bring you back here, and then boomerang you back to Pinta Island," Astuto continued.

"I still don't understand what you're asking me to willingly sacrifice my life for?" I asked.

"Our mission is to go back and rescue Pat and Nessie *and* to help people understand what they are doing to creatures like us. People aren't aware of how they are affecting some of us. Even zoos, as well-intentioned, as they might be, aren't able to reach the people like we might be able to. We can't give you all of the specifics, because we have never tried anything on this scale before, but we want to help those who we were meant to live in peace with," Astuto continued.

"You mean the people? You want to restore things to how they were...I mean how they are here in the Garden?" I asked, trying to tie everything together.

"I know this is a lot to ask," Eldey added, sensing my uneasiness.

"Yeah, it is. How long do I have to make a decision?" I asked.

"You have until you go to sleep again to give us an answer. After that we won't be able to hear your response until it's too late, about 23 years from now," Astuto clarified.

"Take your time and think it over," Eldey said, placing his little wing on my shell. "We have all made sacrifices to get to this point, and I am sure there will be many more sacrifices to make. Although you may not care about *most* people, I know that some people like Fausto have sacrificed much because they *do* care about you. Think about *him* as you weigh your decision, George."

With that, there was a flash of light.

Chapter 5:

THE SUN BEGINS TO SET ON MY ANGER

Slowly my eyelids opened, and I immediately noticed the weight of my shell and the familiar smell of my enclosure back at the research station. It did *not* smell like fresh fruit. Even though I had the decision of a lifetime to make before sunset, I woke up with a certain sense of peace about being back here at CDRS.

Hindered by the returned weight of my shell and the yapping of those two female tortoises, my only thought was that by the time I found some space to myself in my confounded enclosure, the day would be half over. My thoughts battled in my head. Why should I sacrifice myself for the very people who caused me to be the rarest animal in the world? I didn't ask to be a part of this special mission to save mankind. The people should have to figure this out on their own. But I knew there were animals out there facing the same fate as my species to consider as well. This was not an easy decision at all.

"Good morning George, my friend. If you hurry up, you can have an apple that I brought you from home. The missus won't miss it," Fausto laughed.

I wondered if he could *see* my eyes roll at his terrible puns. I tried to muster a smile but realized that it was fruitless here. I was in a bad mood, wrestling with my thoughts and as much as I appreciated Fausto's generosity, all I managed to get out was a slight hiss.

"Oh really? I guess you're a little temperamental this morning. Do you want to come over for this apple or should I just leave it here for you?" Fausto said, placing it inside the enclosure.

My mind was at war with itself; a perfectly chaotic blend of appreciation for the one person who really cared about me and the bitterness about my past, my family's demise, and my current abysmal situation. I wasn't the one who caused these problems. Good for them. I wasn't the one who listened to some serpent and got kicked out of the Garden, which I guess, really happened. I still had a rightful place back in the Garden when my time did come. I wasn't the one who was so self-focused, that I didn't see entire species vanishing before my eyes. Astuto's first words to me resounded in the back of my mind, "You aren't much different from the people you hate."

I decided that the apple did look good and that I should at least show Fausto my gratitude for his kind gesture. As I bit into the apple in Fausto's hand, the thought occurred to me that I *was*, in fact, being just as self-focused as the people I had grown to hate. I had spent years wishing for my own demise, and not caring about the people or any other animals.

Over the years at the CDRS, I had in fact grown increasingly jealous of 'cuter' more people-friendly animals like the giant panda; the poster child for endangered animals and conservation. I was tired of being compared to them. One day, two years ago a family visited my enclosure and the conversation went like this.

"Daddy, why did we come to see a dumb, old tortoise?" a little girl asked.

"Well, he's the last one of his kind dear. This is the only Pinta Island tortoise in the whole world. Didn't you read the sign?" the dad asked.

The girl continued, "Why would I read the sign about a smelly, old tortoise. It's not even cuddly or anything. Pandas are much cuter, and they can smile. I like the way the pandas in the zoo back home eat bamboo. This tortoise is a slob. Look at all that grass just hanging from his wrinkly, old face."

That's because I don't have any paws. I'd like to see you try not getting messy eating without your hands kid!

"He *is* a little freaky looking. He's just staring at us," the mom added. "That tortoise has only moved two feet in the past ten minutes. Is there anything else to see in this place, or can we head down to the beach now?"

Why was the fluffy, cuddly, bamboo eating panda, with paws, and 'clean' eating habits deemed worthy of saving, but an old tortoise was only seen as a smelly old freak? As much as I hated comments like those, I realized my resentment was truly toward the people, not the pandas.

Again engrossed in these thoughts, I heard Fausto saying, "George, you are crying."

I could taste the salt of tears roll down into my mouth. Fausto hopped over the railing and bent down right next to me even though the sign forbade it during visiting hours. He patted my shell and looked me straight in the eyes and tenderly said, "George. If there was some way that I could see you happy, even for just one day, I'd do it for you. It breaks my heart to know there is nothing I can really do for you, my friend. I hate knowing that my grandkids will never see a Pintie like you, other than in some book or on the internet."

Something in my heart melted as Fausto kissed my beak, and a solitary tear rolled down his cheek landing on the top of my head. I felt a terrible sense of guilt overtake me. It was as if the dam that had been holding back five decades worth of anger was cracking. I looked into Fausto's eyes, and I could tell he really would have done anything for me. In that moment I knew what I had to do for Fausto, for pandas, and perhaps even for the people. The day rolled on, and I cherished each moment with Fausto mulling over his emotional reaction to my situation.

That night as I closed my eyes, Fausto read me the story of Noah's Ark. I thought about how this story, like the Garden of Eden story, had always given me a wishful feeling inside. To be at a point in time when animals and people were able to live in peace and harmony seemed like a dream that was out of my grasp. As Fausto played songs for me on his guitar that night while the sunset glowed behind the Charles Darwin Research Station, I thought as loud as I could, *I'm in!*

Chapter 6:

EXTINCTION COMETH

"He's here! He's here! He's 23 years, 6 months, and 2 days early, but he's here! George, we're so glad that you've come back to join us in our adventure to save the world. Not everyone thought you'd come back, but we knew you wouldn't let us down. We just knew it!" Martha exclaimed.

"It's nice to see you too Martha. So now that I've made my decision to join you, where is this meeting place you told me about last night?" I asked.

Overhead Martha was circling, beckoning me to follow her up the hill, past the golden tree of life, and across the crystal clear brook, I drank from the night before. I again snuck a cool, refreshing drink on my way across the brook. I squeezed my shell between some trees, enjoying how much more nimble I was here. As I cleared the row of trees I came out to a clearing near a white sandy beach. There I saw an amazing menagerie of animals.

All eyes were on me as I ventured toward the semi-circle of creatures. Many animals looked familiar from books about extinction that I had seen at the research station. At the thought of the CDRS, I felt a sense of great loss, knowing that I could never go back; never again hear Fausto sing to me at night. At the same time, I was flooded with a great sense of pride that all of these animals were awaiting *my* arrival, George, the Pinta Island tortoise, to save the world.

"George, I am so glad you have decided to return and help us with our rescue mission," Eldey said, coming around an enormous barnacle-covered log protruding into the sea. "I think the best way to go about this is to introduce you to everyone."

"I'm really excited to meet some of the animals that I've heard and read so much about at the research station," I said eagerly, "I can't wait to hear from all of you, and I am honored to be amongst you all. You have no idea how at home I feel amidst all of you who can relate in so many ways to what I've been feeling for so long."

I realized two things while introducing myself to the group. One; I was rambling like a passenger pigeon hyped up on too much coffee, and secondly, I felt more at peace and confident in taking on this mission to save the world. For the first time in a long time, I didn't feel alone.

"Tortoise, we are really limited to how much time we have. We should start the mission immediately," Astuto said, raining on my parade.

"Okay, but I'd love to... to meet everyone first," I stammered, still amazed by these creatures; my personal heroes, I was about to meet.

Eldey tried to appease both Astuto's desire to get started and my desire to meet the members of this world-saving group. "Let us go around quickly and say our species, our chosen name, where we are from, since that *is* important to our mission, one interesting thing about you, and wrap things up by stating your extinction date. Does that work for everyone?" Eldey asked, looking over at the dodo who was obviously annoyed.

"I guess it makes sense to do introductions now so that the plan might make more sense to everyone," Astuto grumbled under his breath. "We've waited this long, what's a few more minutes."

"Okay. I am glad to have your support Astuto. We are going to need to work *together* if we want to have any chance of pulling this off," Eldey emphasized for Astuto and the rest of the group to hear.

"Let us start in order of our extinction dates. That might help this run a little smoother. We will start with Moana over there, and we will end with you George over here," Eldey said, directing every-one to regroup around him.

There was a lot of moving around as we all sought our extinc-tional order. I had never been a fan of cheesy ice breakers. I had seen enough absurd introductory activities with volunteers at the CDRS, but in this case, I was excited to hear from everyone in this group. Just looking around gave me goosebumps. There before me were some of the greatest most iconic examples of extinction that I recognized right away like the Tasmanian tiger and giant moa. Many others looked vaguely familiar. There were a few animals missing which I had hoped to see, like the quagga, the brownish half horse, half zebra looking creature. I didn't think now was the time to ask whether the quagga might be joining us. I also didn't want anyone to feel disrespected. I quickly reeled in my thoughts, knowing that animals here, well at least Astuto, could hear my thoughts.

Now that we were in order, all of us turned our attention to Moana, a giant bird that towered above everyone. She looked like a twelve-foot tall ostrich/kiwi mix with no visible wings. Her feath-ers resembled shaggy brown hair and her head was proportionally smaller than the rest of her gargantuan body. There was a deep blue color lining the bottom portion of her head that ran partway down her throat. Moana turned toward Eldey who encouraged her to share. I wondered why such a large creature would be so reserved.

I didn't think she was going to speak, but then she cleared her throat and began in a voice that was oddly tiny in comparison to her great size. "Giant Moa. Moana. New Zealand. Pacific. Don't like holes. June 6, 1492." Her voice trailed off, and I waited for more from this giant bird, but it was obvious she wouldn't be speaking anymore.

But a tiny voice near Moana from somewhere above me began speaking, "Moana is a giant moa from New Zealand in the Pacific Ocean southeast of Australia."

I wondered if Moana talked in the third person or had multiple personalities or something, similar to how Martha spoke in plurals, but I didn't want to interrupt while she was speaking to ask her. I also thought it awkward that Moana, a girl, had such a manly voice representing a possibly different personality, but I kept that thought to myself too. I even thought to apologize for that thought in case she heard my internal conversation.

The lofty tiny male voice continued, "Her chosen name in Moana because she feels it represents her species, the giant moa well. Honestly, she also isn't known for her creativity. Moana is very loyal and honest and went extinct on June 6, 1492, when her kind was finally eliminated by the Maori people who had arrived in New Zealand years before. Even though she is huge, she is relatively shy and scared of enclosed places. Moana is *very* claustrophobic due to the fact that the Maori people would herd giant moas into large pits to capture them, sometimes leaving them in those deep pits for days at a time."

Moana bowed her head and took a step back into line.

"Thank you, Stephen, for helping Moana with that. You can stay right there until it is your turn to share," Eldey said appreciatively.

I strained to see this Stephen character, but I couldn't locate him. Maybe he was some extinct insect or something. Either way, I'd be hearing from him again soon.

Eldey motioned to the dodo. Astuto still looked annoyed by these proceedings, especially since he had already told me about some of his extinction stories, but to appease Eldey and the group he informed us, "I am the dodo bird. My chosen name is Astuto because I think it better represents me than my species' given name. I'm from Mauritius, a small island in the Indian Ocean east of Africa. Dodos are curious and of course, we couldn't fly, so when sailors came to Mauritius life became difficult. Those of us who weren't eaten outright lost our battle for survival to rats and dare I say... snakes that stowed away on the ships the people sailed to my homeland. I'm not a big fan of rats, and I know none of us are fans of serpents. The dodo's extinction date was February 3, 1681." He bowed and returned to his spot, giving the floor to the next in line, which appeared to be Eldey who had joined the ranks of our little squadron next to that barnacle-covered log oddly protruding into our semi-circle.

As much as Eldey was encouraging us to share, he remained silent, staring at the log. About that time, the log began to twist around, and I could see that it wasn't a log at all. It was a large whale-like creature with the face of a manatee. I had seen plenty of manatees in books about endangered animals around CDRS, but this creature was different and much, *much* larger.

The behemoth creature cleared her throat and began speaking in a deep, earthy voice, "I am the Steller's sea cow, and the name I have chosen to take for myself is, Stella. Like Moana, I am not very creative at all, but it is a name that represents how the world came to know about me, all 27 years of my *known* existence at least. Georg Steller was a naturalist who studied wildlife on a Russian exploration in the Bering Sea region. He and the rest of Captain Bering's crew were stranded on the Commander Islands and had to partake of some of my kind in order to survive. They even said we were yummy, better than beef, which I personally consider a compliment."

I thought it was wrong to be flattered by what people thought of your flavor. Being tasty is not a good thing. I never considered people eating a nice bowl of me an honor.

Stella continued her story, "Even though this was not a pleasant time for my kind, it was understandable given their circumstances…"

Understandable? How can being eaten be something that is okay with you?

"Stella, remember we are trying to keep our introductions concise," Eldey said motioning toward Astuto who was pacing now obviously growing even more impatient.

"Oh yes. I do apologize Eldey. So my chosen name is Stella after Georg *Steller* who sketched and described my kind in his journals. Unfortunately, his journals led other Russian explorers to our island and ultimately to our demise. My extinction date was July 15, 1768. I'm not really fearful of much other than maybe a pod of killer whales, but I'm really good at being 'stealthy'," she laughed, emphasizing the 'stell' part of the word.

She was also air quoting with proportionally tiny flippers. I really wondered why everyone here did that. It was so out of place, but that was one of my least pressing questions in that moment.

Next, it was Eldey who gave his concise introduction, "As you all know, I am the great auk, a flightless bird found on islands in the northern Atlantic Ocean. My chosen name is Eldey after the island where I last went extinct."

I felt pain for him as he recalled the story of Eldey's tragic return that Astuto had told me earlier.

"The great auks were used as a food source for sailors and our feathers were used to stuff pillows. People passed laws to end great auk hunts, but the volcanic eruption of 1830 that sank our nesting island of Geirfulasker did not help my kind's cause. My kind went extinct on July 13, 1840, in Scotland when a group of people captured a great auk and kept it in a cage. I had hoped that these men would help to save my kind, but that night there was a horrible storm. The people thought the great auk was a witch, so killed it. As many of you know, I have been trying to find a way to help the people and decided to go back and try a second time. But sadly, my plan failed, leaving the great auks to become re-extinct on June 3, 1844. I am honored that so many of you turned out tonight eager to help too," Eldey added before nodding toward the next in line.

I turned to the next in line and saw some sort of small wolf. His fur was very shaggy and had a brownish, gray hue. The tip of his long tail was white as snow. The thing that stuck out most to me about this creature was his deep yellow-orange eyes. I had been trying to guess each species before they shared their names and backgrounds, but I could only recall one wolf species that had gone extinct, the English wolf, but that was supposed to be a very *large* canine.

Wolves had been bred to work with the people and now dogs were everywhere. I had always envied dogs because they had such a close relationship with the people and were known as being 'man's best friend'. Tortoises had never really had that luxury. Although animals like the red wolf and Ethiopian wolf were endangered, I couldn't recall any canine species which no longer existed. Maybe this was an English wolf, but I honestly was guessing.

While I was pondering this, the wolf began to share, "I am known by many names, the Falkland Island Dog, Wolf or Fox, or as the Antarctic Wolf. Like the dodo, we were also called by a degrading name which I don't like; the *warrah* which translates as "foolish dog of the south.""

I noticed Astuto listening a little more intently to this portion of the wolf's sharing, shaking his head. He mumbled, "People can be so unkind with their labels."

The wolf looked at Astuto and nodded his head in agreement. He continued, "My chosen name is Strong. It's not because I'm proud and have a lot of strength like you might be thinking. It is to honor Captain John Strong, the English explorer who first discovered the Falkland Islands, where my kind once roamed. Captain Strong took one of us on board his ship as a pet. We bonded very quickly, and it is one of my favorite memories with the people. I was known as being kind to people, but I've always been a little skittish, especially around loud noises," Strong admitted looking around at the others.

"One day while sailing with Captain Strong, his crew spotted a French ship and fired their cannon. Having never heard a noise louder than a flock of penguins, it terrified me so much that I jumped overboard and drown. Sadly that was one of the last good encounters with the people as they continued to visit and eventually settle on the Falkland Islands. I suppose, like any predator, the people began to see us as a threat, and soon we were hunted for our soft fur. We were also poisoned into extinction by sheep and cattle farmers who settled on my islands. We were not foolish at all, but being a trusting species became our downfall. We went extinct on Christmas Eve, December 24, 1876," Strong explained.

"And where are you from geographically speaking?" Astuto prodded knowing that that information was the most crucial to our mission.

"Oh yes, The Falkland Islands are located in the southern Atlantic Ocean near the tip of what the people refer to as South America," the Antarctic wolf added. He too bowed and took a step back into line.

The tiny voice, referred to earlier as Stephen spoke, not from his extinctional position after the wolf, but from somewhere above the giant moa spoke, "I am the Stephens Island Wren and as Eldey stated earlier my chosen name is Stephen. The Stephens Island wrens once flourished around the island known as Stephens island for a long time before the people came. Like many others here, our downfall was not being able to fly and living on a small island. The people built a lighthouse to keep their boats from running ashore. We were excited at first and very curious about the lighthouse which opened on January 29, 1894. David Lyall was the lighthouse keeper on the island and seemed nice enough, but he was lonely. He brought a cat which he called Tibbles to keep him company. Tibbles ran amuck, killing my kind indiscriminately. That is why I have a slight case of ailurophobia, which is a fancy word meaning I have a fear of cats. I mean no offense, but I agreed to join this mission as long as no cat species would be joining our quest." Stephen explained.

A few of the animals looked further down the line at the Tasmanian tiger, but she simply smirked.

Before he could finish sharing I blurted out, "But why are you above Moana during our meeting tonight? I can't even see you up there."

Many in the group scowled at my rude outburst. I swallowed hard, realizing I may have inadvertently offended a member of this extinction group. I saw a flash of movement up on Moana's back and a scurrying brownish, yellow figure moving along the moa's back. Moments later Stephen emerged from behind Moana's massive leg and stood upon the giant moa's toe. The wren was brown in color with golden splotches from head to stumpy tail.

"The Tasmanian 'tiger'," Stephen said air quoting, "is more of a dog mixed with a kangaroo, so I don't count her as a cat. I'm not scared of tiger lillies either in case you're wondering..." Stephen joked, ignoring my rudeness.

His wings blended in with his speckled body and could only be seen only when Stephen fluffed his feathers before continuing, "Being from the New Zealand area myself, I have a regional friendship with Moana. Plus I feel more comfortable having a big friend to keep me safe from any felines I might come across. I'm definitely still fearful, but Moana gives me the confidence to try to help out with this mission. It's kind of a symbiotic relationship if you will. I help her communicate more clearly, and she ensures my safety. Although I trust Strong," Stephen said looking over to the previously introduced Falkland Island wolf, "and Benjamin who you'll meet soon, I still have trouble trusting predators, especially when we return to our homelands. Here in the Garden, we're all vegetarians you know, but back there it's *not* that way. Better safe than sorry when you're so small. Don't you think so?" Stephen said, smiling at me.

"Now if you don't mind, I'll climb back up there," the little bird stated, pointing his tiny beak up to the massive bird's back, "Oh I almost forgot. My kind went extinct February 5, 1895, just one year after Tibbles arrived on Stephens Island."

Stephen disappeared and nestled into the thick fur-like feathers around Moana's neck. Next in line was Martha, who I had met several times in the short time I had been here in the Garden.

Her olive colored neck let out a slight cooing noise as Martha cleared her throat to speak. I braced myself for a flurry of details from this fidgety little bird. Martha ruffled her feathers and began pacing back and forth bobbing her head as she began to speak, her rosy eyes peering around at those gathered, "We are the passenger pigeon and our chosen name is Martha, a name we chose because that was our last name while back there. We were alone for some time ourselves George," she said looking at me. "We were kept in a small enclosure at the Cincinnati Zoo, and we saw firsthand that the people really did care about us. The people realized they had only themselves to blame for our demise. The people at the Cincinnati

Zoo did their best to help the last few of us survive, but it was fruitless once our numbers were so small. Being the most numerous bird species to ever roam the earth, we were used to lots of noise and chaos. The isolation of the zoo enclosure, as nice as it was with the little trees and birdbath, and that little cup that held our food, was just too lonely even with several of us in there."

"Similar to our little friend Stephen, we also have a great fear; monophobia, the fear of being alone. Sure it wasn't for nearly as long as you had to be alone George, but when you're used to being around others, silence can be soul-crushing. Our species once roamed all over the eastern coast of North America and were a food source for many poor people. We know that the people needed us for food, but the ways that they chose to kill us were very cruel indeed, but that is one thing we don't want to talk about."

The pigeon trailed off looking around and bobbing a little less enthusiastically, and I wanted to ask about the cruelty endured by the passenger pigeons at the hands of the people, but I thought better of it after my last outburst. Sensing this thought, Martha looked at me with a sadness I've never seen in her red eyes and turned away to finish her debriefing. "The passenger pigeon went extinct at 1 pm on September 1, 1914, at the Cincinnati Zoo," Martha stated, strutting slowly back into line.

There were now only two more creatures in line until my turn to share, and I had trouble focusing on what was being said. Another bird began to share. He looked like a small chicken of some kind, like the kind I have sometimes seen around the research station, but he had reddish-brown bands running around his plump little body. This chicken-like bird had a very stumpy, rounded tail and a set of two longer triangular feathers jutting down from his throat.

"I am the heath hen, and my chosen name was originally Ben, but given the fact that her name is Benjamin," the heath hen said motioning to the last creature in line, "I've decided to take on one of my nicknames from when I was among the people, Boomer. True they called me "Booming Ben" because of my elaborate dance moves, but I think Boomer has a little more pizzazz," Boomer said enthusiastically.

Then he put his head down dragging his wings along the ground and inflating some sort of small orangish balloons on the side of his throat similar to the frigate birds which flew around the CDRS back on the Galapagos Islands. He definitely could dance in ways that I could never dream of, but I realized my head, like many of those in line, began involuntarily bopping to Boomer's rhythmic beat.

As he stood up again, recovering from his spontaneous dancing, Boomer continued, "Heath hens were never known for being shy. We really liked to be the center of attention and were even at the first Thanksgiving in the New World. Like the passenger pigeon over there, we once roamed the eastern portion of the area known as the United States. Heath hens were once very plentiful and served as a food source for the servant people. Like many of us here, I have faith in the people to change which is why I have joined this mission. They tried many times to help my kind. As early as 1791, some people in the United States passed a law protecting heath hens, but many people misinterpreted this law as protecting "heathens", which is what they called the native people they were fighting against at the time. Needless to say, the law didn't help my kind. In 1870 the people did notice that heath hens were rapidly disappearing, so they rounded up the remaining 300 or so of us, and put us on Martha's Vineyard, no relation to the chatty passenger pigeon over there. The people said we'd be safe there, except the wild cats on the island took their toll on us. By 1908 people came from all over to see us do our dances and our population was 'booming'," he said air quoting and smirking at me.

"The people were confident we'd recover until the untimely fire of 1916. This decimated our population, and we never really recovered. The last two females died in 1927. By December of the next year, I was the only one. I danced my heart out for the people," Boomer said proudly. "I knew they did their best to try to save my kind, but after my grandest dancing ever, I bowed out March 11, 1932." Boomer strutted back into his spot.

My eyes turned to the thylacine, the Tasmanian tiger. Besides the dodo and perhaps the great auk, the thylacine was probably the most well known extinct animal I had ever heard the people speak of. I gave my full attention, trying to be attentive, but not ogle at him. He looked like a midsized dog of sorts with the unmistakable thirteen black stripes running down his back. His feet *were* sort of kangarooish, and I wondered if he could hop as well as run. While these questions were bouncing around in my head, the thylacine began his speech.

To my surprise, *he* turned out to be a *she*. The thylacine began sharing her sad story, "I am the thylacine, better known as the Tasmanian tiger. Although semi inappropriate, I have chosen to take the last name given to my kind by the people whom Boomer had alluded to earlier, *Benjamin*. I also waited for my extinction at a zoo. The zookeepers at the Hobart Zoo in Tasmania thought I was a male, hence the masculine name. Still, I know they had tried to save my kind after our unfortunate termination," Benjamin said, shaking her head.

She continued, "Like any predator, the people feared me. As the people began settling in Tasmania and raising sheep and chickens, we had our run-ins. Someone took a picture of a thylacine running out of a hen house with a chicken in its jaws. The people circulated that picture, igniting a hatred for my kind. The Tasmanian government even paid money to any person who brought in a thylacine dead; male, female, or pup. By the time some people began to care about our declining population, the damage was done. Some people captured us and put us in zoos, but others still tried to eradicate us. This is when I saw the people's capability to have compassion for us. The last of my kind, Benjamin, died of malnourishment and exposure the night of September 7, 1936." The tiger dropped back into her place.

I felt pity for Benjamin and the rest of the creatures assembled, but I could feel my face begin to flush as it was my turn to speak. I wanted to impress this group that I was supposed to lead. *Okay species, chosen name, location, an interesting fact, extinction date.* I reassured myself that I could do that.

"George, you share as much as you want to. Most of us here know something about you anyway, and you are the one who this mission centers around. No pressure," Eldey said, smiling at me.

"Oh... I'm a...I'm a Pinta Tortoise Island. I mean a Pinta Island Tortoise. I chose the name George after the name I have been given by the people since they found me alone on my island in 1971. The people used us tortoises for food while they explored the Pacific Ocean or while hunting pods of whales for oil. Pinta Island is part of the Galapagos Island chain near the country of Ecuador, South America in the Pacific Ocean. I really hate... I mean I really dislike goats. The people put them on my island, and we tortoises couldn't compete with them. I have spent the past 40 years, alone at the Charles Darwin Research Station known as the rarest and loneliest animal on earth."

I saw looks of sympathy and compassion from the group. I paused, thinking I had said my piece but then remembered to add my final requested piece of information, "Even though I apparently had many years left back there, I have chosen to go extinct ... today... June 24, 2012." I exhaled a deep breath, bowed like the others before me, and stepped back into line.

Chapter 7:

THE MISSION

"Now that we have gotten our exciting ice breaker out of the way, I'd like to get things moving," Astuto said, annoyed. I wondered why Astuto seemed to be so time-sensitive. I thought it was nice to get to know everyone on the team since my life was the only one truly on the line during this mission,

"As you know we have assembled to try to set things right between us animals and the people, the way it was intended to be. I will let Eldey go over the specifics of the mission with you in a minute," Astuto looked at Eldey. "I know many of you see me as an old fuddy-duddy, but time is of the essence during this mission. We will have only 40 days to succeed or fail our mission."

Eldey interjected, "That is why Astuto has been trying to move things along. Our mission is already on the clock. It officially began the moment George entered the Garden tonight. It is also important for us to know one another's strengths and weaknesses. Teamwork will be of utmost importance."

After so many years being 'Lonesome George', I was happy to be surrounded by friends. There it was; a new thought, a happy thought, *Lonesome George was no longer all alone awaiting extinction. I was now 'extinct' surrounded by peers who understood me.* I mentally added air quotes to this thought to mock that apparent custom here in case anyone was listening to my thoughts.

"As most of you know, when we choose to go back there, we

get to go back in sets of three; a male, a female, and a young one," Eldey said, turning his attention to me to make sure I was following these apparent rules. "I was one of the few species who went extinct and chose to go back and become extinct a second time. It was by no means an easy experience, but it will be worth it if there is a chance to set things right between us and the people."

Many nods of agreement were exchanged. We all looked around to wonder what male and female animals would be paired up, as well as how young ones might fit into this picture. I could see this bothered Stephen, the smallest of all the animals gathered and he piped up, "By young one, do you mean each of us will return there with a mate and a baby? Won't that make things more complicated? I mean rather than just ten of us, we'd be talking about thirty animals, ten of those being babies or eggs? Is that what you're saying?"

"This return will not be like any that have ever been attempted in the past. When we originally left the Garden, we left with three of our own kind. When we left the boat after the Great Flood, we left with three of our own kind, but when we return this time we will return not as mates and young ones but as three groups of three; or as I like to think about them, 'triads'," Eldey clarified.

Wait, did he just say *left the boat*? Like the Ark boat I had heard about or some other boat I didn't know about? I was feeling overwhelmed again. At first, I didn't catch the mathematical quandary about Eldey's last statement, but then it hit me. *Three groups of three were only nine animals. What about the tenth one of us? Was I going to be left alone on this mission since I had chosen to become extinct early?*

"Yes. Yes. The rule of *three*," Astuto interjected in annoyance. "We all know that certain numbers carry significance here in the Garden and back there. That is why we must return in groups of three, but this time our return is different. It's not to be fruitful and multiply like both previous returns there. It is to help."

"Numbers are in no way trivial. The number three is unifying, a number which tends to link to power. The number forty has always held significance as well. It is a number that has always been connected to washing or cleansing. For instance, during the Great Flood, the rain washed over the earth there for *forty* days. This was to clean the world from all of the corruption and evil that had built up over time. Once George arrived here in the Garden on his own free will, the time to complete this mission to help cleanse the earth again had begun," Eldey explained.

Martha had been extremely quiet, but this last tidbit seemed to get her brain spinning. "Eldey, are you saying that our mission will be to go back and flood the earth with water and then clean it up with little brushes? We don't see how that will help the people or help 'reset' things back to a less corrupt state."

"Martha, we are going to try to help clean up some of the corruption back there, but we can't do that with water. That was prohibited long ago, after the Great Flood. Our missions in these groups of three over forty days will get at least seven of us back together in the same place. This should give us the power to help temporarily 'reset' the earth. Similarly, the Great Flood did not eliminate evil from the earth, but it helped usher in a small time of peace. We are hopeful that during this 'reset period' we will be able to work with the people to set up a new age where people and animals can again live together in relative peace and harmony," Eldey clarified.

There he went with his tiny winged air quotes again. Seriously, amidst the seriousness of this conversation, I still had to smirk seeing him do that. So in two days or two nights, I wasn't quite sure how much time had actually passed, I had learned that the Garden of Eden was a real place, not just a fable. I had just learned that Noah's Ark seemed to have been real too. All of the animals of earth had actually crammed into a little boat with old Noah and his family two-by-two. It really got me wondering what else may or may not be true. I could probably spend the whole forty days asking Eldey and Astuto questions about these two events alone, but I knew there wasn't time for that in that moment.

"So Eldey and Astuto, can I ask why you think that forty days might not be enough time to complete this mission to 'reset earth'.

I know that I am probably the slowest creature amongst us, well other than maybe George," Stella turned her proportionately small head over to me and smiled sweetly, "No offense George, but I don't understand what our mission is and why we can't do it in forty days."

Astuto and Eldey exchanged glances almost silently asking who should answer that question. Astuto had begun tapping his foot while waiting, so Eldey stepped toward the enormous sea cow and explained, "Stella, as you know there have always been some *rules* of sorts; here and there that we animals must adhere to. When we go back there from the Garden, we must go back to groups of three. Until this mission, that group of three has always been composed solely of members of *one* species. That is how we returned after the Great Flood, and how I tried to go back on my own to save the people. We were told to go forth and multiply, and we did. Along those same lines, when we return we have to return to a proper location back there. For instance, as a Steller's sea cow, you have to return to the cold arctic waters where your kind once roamed, so in the northern Pacific Ocean. You can't simply show up back there in the warm waters of Hawaii. Does that make sense?"

Astuto, trying to speed things up again and preempt follow up questions, added on to Eldey's carefully delivered statement, "You see our mission is to be able to willingly come together at a certain location back there from our *starting points*. This has only ever happened once in history, and that was in the time before the Great Flood. We were summoned to come and fill the giant Ark before the floods came. Now of course not all of us animals were blessed with the abilities to make that great journey. The dodos, for instance, had no feasible way to walk to the desert region of the Middle East. We have always been a flightless bird on the island of Mauritius, so we had no way to make it to the Ark like many other animals. After the floods subsided, we were given the option to go back there with the people or stay in the Garden where many species who didn't make it to the Ark had retreated to during the Great Flood."

Upon hearing that I felt many more questions welling up and just before I was able to express some of my questions, I heard Astuto's voice inside my head say, *Just hold off on this question Tortoise, and I'll explain more to you personally in a little while. I know I said that I'd stay out of your head, but we need to get the rest of the animals here started on their part in this mission.* I turned toward Astuto and simply nodded slightly to let him know I had heard him and understood his directive.

Eldey continued addressing the group, but kept his eyes on Stella, "You see Stella when you go back, you must begin your part of the mission in the region where your kind once lived. To put it simply we will be in groups of three starting in our geographic starting points, attempting to all come together at the same point on earth. There is a certain power that we have when we band together. That is why when many animals came into the Ark from all over the earth; there was the power to reset the earth."

"Wait a second," Martha interjected, "if that were the case; shouldn't zoos like the one where we went extinct be super powerful? We mean, we were in a cage next to a lot of other birds from all over the world. There was this one guy from..."

"Sorry to cut you off Martha, but the simple answer to your question is that although zoos have animals from all around the earth, those creatures did not go to those zoos *willingly*. Animals must make the journey voluntarily," Eldey explained. "Now to clarify your original question Stella, we will have 40 days to locate every animal from our group of returning triads, and then to make it to Pinta Island, George's homeland, in the Pacific Ocean."

What? Why were all of these animals trying to go to Pinta Island? There was nothing there but a bunch of goats and grass. Again, Astuto's voice cut into my thoughts, *Tortoise, you need to be patient, and Eldey and I will explain things to you in greater detail once we start our mission.*

"For instance Stella; as you've stated, back there you are *not* a speedy animal. In fact, you can only swim about ten miles an hour. Isn't that right?" Astuto said a little too bluntly. Stella bashfully nodded her head. "Simple math says if Pinta Island is 4,600 miles away from where you will be starting. At ten miles an hour it would take you twenty days of straight Open Ocean traveling to make it to Pinta Island," Astuto calculated.

"But Astuto and Eldey, I can't swim in the Open Ocean. I'm not built for that, and I know it might sound odd coming from a massive sea creature like myself, but I have a fear of drowning," Stella stated.

"I know Stella. This mission is in no way going to be easy for any of us. We will all have to get over our fears to complete our part. You will need to decide what you can and cannot do once we return, but if seven of us do not make it to Pinta Island forty days from tonight, our mission will fail and our hope to reset things between us and the people will fail," Eldey explained first to Stella and then making eye contact with each member of the group.

"But why only seven of us? What about the other three?" I asked, concerned about the losses we could apparently be facing.

"As I explained earlier, there are certain numbers of significance here and there; forty, three, and seven. Six of us must make it to Pinta Island and join the tortoise within the forty days, or we will fail. Seven is the third number of significance," Astuto said. To drive this point home he slowly and bluntly announced, "We have forty days, working in teams of three, to get seven of us on Pinta Island."

Eldey now seemed a little more concerned about the time this meeting was taking, and he called us all over to an open area of sand. He asked us to make a circle around him, and he bent down and drew a quick sketch of the world as we knew it in the sand with his black and gray striped beak. Eldey drew the outlines of the continents and added our homelands to the sketch. Then he put our names in the locations where we'd be starting out and placed numbers next to each name. To this sketch in the sand, he added dotted lines, outlining the journey as he saw it.

He then explained the teams and the mission in greater, yet concise detail. The first team of three, or 'triad' as he quoted them, was deemed the Southern Triad. This included Moana, Benjamin, and Stephen. Benjamin would have to travel from Tasmania to New Zealand, meet the two birds, and then get to Pinta Island.

The second triad which Eldey deemed the Northern Triad would include himself, Martha, and Boomer. They would team up and travel across the North American continent on foot. They would then travel the rest of the way south via the Pacific Ocean.

The third group, the Scattered Triad, would have the most complicated journey because their return was so... well, so scattered. The Scattered Triad would include Astuto who would travel the long distance from Mauritius in the Indian Ocean, across the Atlantic Ocean to the Falkland Islands where he would join Strong. They would then travel north to Pinta Island where they would meet up with Stella who would be traveling twenty-some days straight south to meet them. In theory, they should be the first triad to join me on Pinta Island.

This plan seemed simple enough, but Astuto and Eldey explained that we would not only have to worry about making it to Pinta Island in forty days, but we would have to face our fears and travel in ways that we'd never thought possible. They explained that I would be in charge of directing the triads because going extinct before my appointed time gave me the ability to communicate with each animal in a similar way to how they seemed to communicate while in the Garden.

The complication for the other animals was that they couldn't communicate with any of the other creatures until they were *with* them. If we didn't all reach Pinta Island in forty days, I would apparently lose my ability to direct them, and they'd be totally on their own. It seemed that the longer an animal was away from the Garden, the less clearly they would be able to communicate. I had no idea how Astuto and Eldey knew this, but I knew I had to trust them because my life was in their hands...or wings.

One part of this explanation really scared many of us, and Astuto didn't sugar coat it. "Some of us might not make it, but it is critical that at least six of us can make it to join the tortoise within the forty-day window," Astuto said with sternness in his voice.

Eldey quickly added to soften Astuto's direct tone, "That is not to say that all of us cannot make it back to Pinta Island within the forty-day window. Since we must return in triads, our options were either to send two groups of three or add a third triad to make sure we had a better chance at resetting things. We want to make sure that if anyone did not make it, the mission could still succeed."

"Then there's the serpent to worry about," Astuto added, dashing any positive spin Eldey had attempted to establish.

Again as the serpent was mentioned there was a simultaneous shudder that seemed to go through the group. I could only assume that this serpent was somehow connected to the original serpent in the Garden, but I had no idea how right that thought would turn out to be. I also wondered why Astuto couldn't sometimes just add a little more compassion into the facts he delivered so bluntly, the way Eldey always managed to do. Didn't Astuto realize that if he painted things a little more positively, we might find it easier to listen to him?

"Yes. We all know that Lusadé, the serpent, is still a very real danger to this mission. Indeed, he can only be in one place at a time, but still, he must have some idea that we are planning something. He is very aware of many things, and I have no doubt his suspicions are up now that George went extinct much earlier than was originally planned. Lusadé will do anything and everything in his power to try to thwart each of you. He is a crafty creature who has no desire to see the people reset things *again*. This is why it is so important that you find the fellow members of your triads before he finds you. Alone we are vulnerable, but together we will be able to withstand his attacks," Eldey added.

"That is yet another reason we have asked so many of you to be a part of the mission. When others like the tortoise have voluntarily gone extinct early to join our cause, Lusadé was able to get to them, play on their fears, before they could reset things back there," Astuto explained.

"Many of you know that is what happened to Nessie and Pat when they returned to try to reset things between us and the people. We are hoping as a side effect of this mission, that they too will be able to get back to the Garden," Eldey said. "They have been gone for such a long time that we have no way to contact them, but hopefully this mission will allow them to safely return with us to the Garden where they belong. They are brave animals who have been trying in vain to help out the people. I hate knowing that they are out there in part because I sent them without fully understanding the ramifications."

"So now to begin; let's get in our triads," Astuto barked.

The animals quickly fell into ranks. I looked around as the animals scattered, flew, and waddled to their respective groups. I tried to take it all in and admire these famous natural 'failures' who were returning to try to help the very people who had erased them from the earth in the first place. I felt a little clearer about what we were doing, so I intensely studied Eldey's map in the ground, trying to memorize it the best that I could. I knew it would be crucial knowledge for me to have as the apparent leader of this mission.

The Southern Triad gathered together next to the crystal clear stream that I had taken a drink from before. They all took a long drink from the stream themselves, ate some orange fruit from beneath the tree, and then circled together. Moana, the giant moa, stood silently unmoving, seemingly taking it all in. Stephen, the little flightless wren, darted this way and that along the ground before scurrying over to the towering bird who lowered her proportionately tiny head to the ground. Stephen then burrowed himself deep in the fur-like feathers of Moana before peeking back out.

The thylacine, Benjamin, took another long drink from the stream, before heading toward the two birds of the Southern Triad. Her short tawny fur glimmered in the light of the day, and her striped back danced side to side as she walked. Benjamin placed her front paws in front of her and stretched out her back. The muscles of her back rippled beneath her short fur as she let out a massive yawn. I'd seen this in pictures of the Tasmanian tiger, but to see it in person was really a sight to behold. I wished I felt as confident as Benjamin appeared to be.

Benjamin was the only creature who I never mentioned a fear. I wanted to ask her about it but before I could speak, Eldey gave them final instructions, "Remember that timing is of the utmost importance. Once you enter through the light, you will find yourselves in your homeland. Remember to try to reach New Zealand and rendezvous as soon as possible. You will have to be creative; finding ways to travel while avoiding the people. If any of you is captured by the people, try to save your captured teammate only if a rescue seems possible. But if it seems too hazardous you may have to leave someone behind. I know this will not be an easy thing to do, and I sincerely hope that none of us have to make that decision. We do not want to lose anyone, but losing an entire triad would be devastating to the mission. Remember that until you reach one another, George will be your *only* line of communication."

It seemed that my part of the mission was to spend at least twenty of the forty days alone on Pinta Island with the goats. I wasn't too thrilled that my last post extinction days would be spent with the animals I hated the most. I wanted to ask about that, but I remembered Astuto's voice that had asked me to be patient. I decided that patience should prevail for now.

While I was still thinking these thoughts to myself I watched the three animals of the Southern Triad bow and disappear in a flash of light. With that, only two triads and I remained. The instructions to the Northern Triad were similar, but most of their journey would be across the North American continent. They would have to avoid the people which might be easy for Martha who was a pigeon and an excellent flyer, but Boomer, being a heath hen, was too heavy to fly very far at all. And Eldey, well he was a swimmer, not a long-distance walker. I couldn't imagine how they would be able to cross such a vast distance in so little time.

They also went and got a drink from the crystal stream and ate some food before congregating in the same area as the previous group. Before they were taken away by the flash of light, Eldey came over next to me. His deep brown eyes sparkled with excitement, but the compassion was there as well. I bent my head down to him and he whispered in my ear, "George, I know you can do this. I know there is still anger at the people and possibly even some anger toward me because of your part in this mission, but I am proud of you for the sacrifice you made for Fausto. You are more crucial than you know, and without you, even if seven of us arrive on Pinta Island in time, we cannot complete the reset mission. You are the one who matters the most, and I will do everything in my power to help you. But rest assured that when Lusadé finds out you are back, you will be his main target. You must be strong George. Remember that even when you are *alone* on the island, you will not be without your friends. They need you and *I* need you, George."

With that, the great auk took his place with the passenger pigeon and the heath hen, disappearing into the flash of light. With the Northern and Southern Triads gone, the Scattered Triad fell in line. Stella, the massive Steller's sea cow, dunked her head under the water where she had moved and came up chewing some brownish-green seaweed, humming a tune to herself. Astuto waddled over to the stream bending down to get a drink, flinging his shriveled beak back to swallow. He picked up an orange fruit and swallowed it whole. Strong, the Falkland Island Wolf, splashed in the water and came out twisting his body; throwing mist into the air around him. He too took a long drink and partook of some of the orange fruit before walking over to the lagoon where Stella was waiting. He made a jovial yip and leaped onto Stella's back. He stood there waiting for Astuto.

Astuto came over to me, cocking his head to the left and then to the right. His yellow-orange eyes seemed to peer deep into my being and he said, "Good luck Tortoise. I know that you still have more questions than answers now, but over the next forty days, Eldey and I can take turns explaining what we can to you. Even though I've been here in the Garden for a long time and know many things, there are still many things I don't understand myself. Once you have gone extinct, there are many things that you simply understand without explanation. There are many other things which wouldn't make sense even if they were explained. Tortoise, do your best to worry about the things you can understand and be content with not knowing the things you can't."

With that, the final triad flashed out of the Garden, and I was left alone. I let out a deep sigh, knowing that I might have just sealed my doom, eternal extinction. I walked over to where the others had stood, took a drink, ate some orange fruit, and hoped for wisdom and strength to do my part, even though my real mission wasn't totally clear to me. The last thing I remembered was a blinding flash of light before total darkness.

Chapter 8:

ALL ANSWERS LEAD TO MORE QUESTIONS

"Maaa! Maaa!" a little goat screamed at me. It jumped up on my shell bleating incessantly. It seemed to be mocking me, jumping all around me. I could feel my blood begin to boil (which is a lot for a cold-blooded reptile). Just as it leaped to the ground, ready to frolic some more, I reached out my neck and snapped my mouth right on his little waggly tail. As the kid bleated in pain I let go and laughed like I hadn't laughed in a long time. Then I saw Eldey looking at me with a solemn, disappointed look. He said nothing, but I instantly felt a wave of guilt.

I opened my eyes and squinted through the blinding afternoon sunlight. I looked around and at once realized *exactly* where I was. I was home on Pinta Island under my favorite prickly pear cactus that I hadn't seen since the afternoon I was taken from Pinta Island to the Charles Darwin Research Station. The trunk of the cactus was brown and round and there were a plethora of spiky cactus pads and some prickly pears scattered throughout the spreading branches. I took a long deep breath, taking in the sights, sounds, and smells of home.

Something was missing; the goats. I guess I had been dreaming about the little goat because Pinta Island appeared to be goatless. I remembered them talking at the research station about eradicating all of the goats from Pinta Island in the early 1990s, but I never knew if that came to fruition.

Even though the attack on the small goat had only been a dream, I still felt guilty about what I had wanted to do to that kid. Then my mind caught up with my present circumstances. I had almost forgotten I was part of a mission. Although I knew that I could somehow contact the rest of the group, I wasn't sure how to do it. My leadership role didn't come with an instruction manual.

I knew that in the Garden, animals could, if they wanted, listen to the thoughts of other animals. I wondered if they could hear my thoughts and might be laughing at my angry outbursts toward the goats in my dream.

I waited a few seconds to try to see if I could *hear* anyone, but all I heard was the crash of waves against the rocky shore down at the end of the valley below and a few distant sea birds screaming at one another. I wondered how I was supposed to call the others. I figured it'd be easy, and that it would just happen since I hadn't been instructed differently.

"Hello? Can anyone hear me?" I yelled to the sky.

All at once I heard a cacophony of voices simultaneously asking questions, talking about their locations, and saying they could, in fact, hear me. I couldn't make out anyone's voice in particular, but I assumed the voice that kept talking at such a rapid rate was probably Martha.

I decided to try again and make it more specific, "Eldey can you hear me?"

The chaotic voices were replaced by utter silence. The silence seemed to linger forever, but was broken by Eldey's lone voice, "Yes, George. I can hear you."

"Why did everyone start talking at the same time? I'm not sure what I'm supposed to do as the communication center. You never really explained it to me," I said honestly.

"Yes, I am sorry about that George. Astuto and I thought it would be best if we got everyone started on their portion of the mission, and we would fill you in on things as we went. I guess we should have at least told you how to contact us. Sorry for the miscommunication about communication," Eldey joked.

"Can you explain it to me now then?" I asked, wanting to clarify what I was supposed to do around Pinta Island for the next forty days.

"Just a second George," Eldey panted.

"Eldey are you okay?" I asked, wondering if he was already in trouble. I felt a wave of guilt that the others might be in serious peril, while I was here waiting in my favorite place in the world under my old cactus.

"George. I am here now and can talk. I have been swimming the past day trying to reach Martha and Boomer. I know that the most dangerous part of our journey will be crossing a whole continent overland without rousing the people's suspicions," Eldey said, still trying to catch his breath. "I figure that I should be able to catch up with the other two in another day or so. I was only about 900 miles to the north, so reaching them in New York should not take too much longer. I calculated 3 days for my solo part of this trip since I am swimming against the current to go south."

"So Eldey, can the other animals hear me talking to you right now?" I asked.

"No. Not at this moment since you only called to me. But the first time you spoke, we all heard you at the same time. I am sure that is why you did not respond to our combined answers. I'm sure it's a little overwhelming," Eldey said, trying to reassure me.

"Is there a way to talk to two of you at the same time? I mean, can I speak with you *and* Astuto, or should I try to talk to one creature at a time?" I asked.

"George, I know that things may seem overwhelming to you right now, and I think you are doing a great job. To answer your question; yes you can speak to two of us, a whole triad, or all of us at the same time as long as you call us by name. Only those you call will be able to respond," Eldey explained calmly. "Who to contact and when is something that you must discern on your own. One of the hardest parts about leading is the fact that sometimes keeping some of the details from those you lead is the best thing for them. They might not always understand what you are trying to accomplish, but that is part of the burden of leading."

"Like how you and Astuto had to lead me during my first night you called me to the Garden?" I inquired.

"Yes. You see George; you needed to make the choice to risk your very existence on your own free will. We could not make that choice for you, but we could not lie to you about what we knew. We gave you the details we thought were pertinent to your decision, but we did not want to overwhelm you with all the details," Eldey explained.

"Would now be a good time to have you and Astuto answer some of my questions or would it benefit you to travel a little more first?" I asked, not wanting to hold up Eldey's long swim through the Atlantic.

Eldey told me to wait a few minutes until he reached a secluded piece of rock to rest and chat. He said it was too difficult to swim and talk at the same time. Eldey explained that we were communicating by talking, so it was more than just me reading his thoughts. To properly give my questions the attention they deserved, he would spend the next day answering all of the questions I had been waiting to ask.

Eldey told me to contact Astuto while he headed to a place of rest. He directed me to call him again in an hour. Astuto wasn't quite as enthusiastic about stopping his part of the journey to talk so soon, because he also had a long difficult journey. I wondered how an iconic fifty-pound flightless bird would be able to cross over 6,000 miles of Open Ocean to reach the Falkland Islands without being spotted.

Astuto told me he planned to try to stow away on a plane to cut his travel time down a bit. He also added in an almost giddy, well giddy for him, fashion that it would be nice to cross 'flying' off of his bucket list.

Astuto also told me that I needed to be careful when doing an all-call like I did the first time I tried to contact the team because other animals not on the team might be able to hear those communications. Even Astuto wasn't sure about this, but he warned me to be selective because we didn't want to give Lusadé any idea about what we were planning.

Eldey said that he had found a place to rest where he was out of sight of any people. He was on a remote rocky ledge some-where along the Canadian coast. Astuto said that he too had found a secluded place to hide in the dense shrubbery around the base of a Tambalacoque tree, also known as the 'dodo tree' ironically enough. Astuto had ventured away from the coastline where most of the towns were located. He also said he was surprised by how much his homeland had changed since he was last there. I remind-ed him he'd been extinct for over three hundred years, but I prob-ably should have bit my tongue.

"So George we can give you a little time to ask your questions and get some clarification from us on as much as we know. But then we really must join the rest of our triads and head toward you on Pinta Island. Time really is of the essence. It may not seem like it, but we have already used up 2 of our days, simply in getting our bearings and beginning our journeys," Eldey explained.

The multitude of questions that had been swimming around in my head back in the Garden struggled to align in a way that made sense. It was times like this that I wished I had an opposable thumb and a pencil-like the people so that I could craft what Fausto used to refer to back at the Charles Darwin Research Station as a "to-do list." I figured I would start asking my questions, and hopefully get to everything I had wanted to before the triads reformed. Once the groups were together it might be overwhelming to have simultane-ous conversations.

So I figured that I'd begin with what I thought were the most important questions first, and then move onto some of the more trivial ones if I had time.

"Back in the Garden before we dispersed, you were talking about the Ark and what happened. Were you saying not all ani-mals made it into the Ark two-by-two as the story says?" I asked. "So many of us here would have already gone extinct in the past, especially us island-dwelling animals? I'm assuming no Pinta Island

Tortoises were able to swim across the Pacific Ocean to make it into the Ark in the Middle East either."

With a great sigh the old dodo explained, "You see Tortoise, there have been times when the people have been punished because of their disobedience in the Garden, but other than the serpent and the ground, none of the rest of us were ever *directly* cursed. Were we affected by people's bad choices? Definitely. We wouldn't have gone extinct if everything was perfect for us. Many creatures didn't want to go back there after making it to the Garden during the Great Flood."

For the first time, Astuto seemed almost as nurturing and considerate as Eldey. I had not expected to hear such compassion or patience from the old dodo, so I listened intently as he continued, "You see when we left the Garden, we were charged to be fruitful and multiply and fill the earth. The people were directed to do the same, but it was added that they should, *"fill the earth and subdue it and have dominion over the birds of the heavens and over every living thing that moves on the earth."* In other words, people were always given leadership over us."

"Well, that is not fair at all. I mean the people were responsible for cursing the earth and passing along the negative consequences of their actions onto us. Why should they be given dominion over us or over anything for that matter? I honestly think you or Eldey would do a much better job," I blurted.

"Haha. Tortoise, it isn't for us to decide what's 'fair' or not. You haven't been in the Garden long enough to understand that this command was a good one for us and the people. You see they were called to have dominion over us, but before the Great Flood, there was always a sense of peace and harmony between us and the people. The people were the ones having problems amongst themselves which is why the earth needed 'cleansed' in the first place," Astuto said seemingly air quoting. "You see we were there, but it wasn't until *after* the Great Flood that the people's disobedience truly hurt us, creatures."

"Really, because I think getting kicked out of the Garden was a pretty big negative effect," I retorted.

"Leaving the Garden was a terrible thing, but we interacted peacefully overall with the people. It wasn't until *after* the Great Flood that a new command was given to the people, which would change our existence with them on earth forever. Noah and his surviving family members were told *to be fruitful and multiply and fill the earth*. This mirrored the first command but with a caveat; "*the fear of you and dread of you shall be upon every beast of the earth and upon every bird of the heavens, and all the fish of the sea. Into your hand, they are delivered. Every moving thing that lives shall be food for you.*" This additional directive changed our relationship with the people. Now we needed to fear them, and those who didn't take this seriously were some of the first creatures to go extinct at the hands of the people," Astuto explained.

"You see George, before the Great Flood the animals had no real reason to fear the people because the people only ate the plants they grew. After the flood animals had a choice; go back and live with the people in fear or stay forever in the Garden," Eldey clarified.

"I'm sorry. I'm still not following. Are you saying that the animals on the Ark had a choice about whether to go back with the people or not? Why wouldn't everyone simply stay in the Garden?" I asked.

"Those are two difficult questions to explain. Let me start with the first question. Put simply; the animals on the Ark did *not* have a choice about whether to come back to fill the earth with the people. They were commanded to be fruitful and multiply. So the animals like the great auk that made the trip and stayed *on* the Ark were destined to fear the people and couldn't stay *in* the Garden because they never returned *to* the Garden," Astuto clarified.

"I can answer the second question. You see George, the animals that did not or could not make it to the Ark because of distance or being trapped on various islands like the dodos or the Pinties, were wiped off the face of the earth in the Great Flood. In a way, those animals went extinct but were given a choice to return to the earth if they wanted to. Remember George that we, animals, still were not the ones who were cursed. But we were affected by the curses on the people. The animals in the Garden were aware of the new command given to Noah and his family. Many animals chose to stay in the Garden instead of living in fear with the people," Eldey explained.

This was a curious idea to consider; animals going extinct and then going back after the flood. I guess it wasn't as simple as entering the Ark two-by-two, waiting 40 days, sending out a dove, and multiplying. There were other things I needed to understand, but I wanted to ask one more question about the Great Flood.

"What about the dinosaurs, Eldey? I mean as a nearly extinct animal myself, I heard all the time about the extinction of the dinosaurs. If you are saying that all animals after the flood had the option of coming back, why wouldn't the dinosaurs come back? I mean two flightless birds and a slow 200-pound tortoise have something to fear, but an eighty-foot dinosaur, why didn't they return?" I asked, waiting for a clear answer.

"I know you asked Eldey to explain, but let me," the dodo interjected, "The people tend to fear larger animals, especially carnivores. Larger animals that people fear tend to be hunted. That's the main reason animals like Strong and Benjamin were hunted to extinction. So although being a terrifying thirty foot T-rex would seem to be an advantage, it was not. The people hunted the few dinosaur species who decided to return after the flood back to extinction very quickly."

"Some species did better than others. The people referred to these returning dinosaurs by many names including *sea serpents* or *dragons*. Of course, the remaining dinosaur species went into hiding very soon after returning, but the harder they tried to avoid the people, the harder the people pursued them. Legends of dragon hunts show up in people groups all around the world. The land-based 'dragons' soon regretted choosing to stay with the people and were the first species to find extinction at the hands of the people. Being creatures of deep water, plesiosaurs were one of the species who fared the best, which is why Nessie lasted so long before I called upon her to try to reset things by herself," Eldey said with a twinge of emotion in his voice.

"Okay, well that explains why the people and animals can't live in peace anymore. I'm sorry I have so many questions," I said.

"That is okay George," Eldey said, "Of course you are going to have questions. You have only been in the Garden for a night and a day. Plus since you went extinct early, you did not get the knowledge that we seemed to have acquired once we entered the Garden after our own extinctions. You see, you think we know a lot, but we always feel as if we only know a small portion of things. We are just like you George. There is a certain design to everything and certain rules which we have come to understand. There is a 'rhyme and reason' to the world around us, which we only ever have a small glimpse of. We have time for one more question before I must get some sleep. I have a long swim tomorrow and hope to join up with Martha and Boomer in a few days."

"I agree Tortoise. We want to explain more things to you, but we are finite creatures who need sleep and food and water. Like you said, or thought, it will be hard for an iconic fifty-pound bird to travel 6,000 miles undetected. I will need to plot out my journey. Mauritius is a world away from Pinta Island," Astuto stated in an almost joking way.

Rather than asking some deep philosophical questions, I decided to ask a more personal, extinctional question.

"The quagga?" I asked. "Where was the quagga in the Garden?"

"Really? That's the last thing you need to know tonight? You want to know why the *quagga* wasn't in the Garden?" Astuto said, returning to his usual gruff self. "I was starting to expect better of you Tortoise"

"What do you mean George? I would love to understand your question, but the quagga is not extinct," Eldey said in a perplexed tone.

"The quagga isn't extinct? I'm sorry Eldey, but you must be mistaken. Maybe you just never saw one in the Garden. I mean there must be an unfathomable number of animals there. Next to the dodo, the thylacine, and the great auk; the quagga is one of the most iconic extinct animals I know. I've seen them in many of the extinction books that Fausto read to me back at the research station," I explained with certainty.

"I am sorry George, but there was no quagga in the Garden. Yes, there are an unfathomable number of species in the Garden, but there is also an unfathomable amount of time to meet them. What is a quagga exactly?" Eldey inquired, trying to appease me.

"A quagga looked similar to a zebra, except that it was brownish and white rather than having the bold black and white striping pattern of a zebra," I explained.

"I think I might have an idea of where the confusion is on this question. You see, the quagga isn't a *real* animal species," Astuto said before I cut him off.

"What do you mean it's not a real animal? I'm not talking about a unicorn or a griffin here. I've seen the pictures and heard about them for the past 40 years at the research station," I objected.

"George, I think you should give Astuto a chance to fully explain his thoughts before jumping to judgments about his intentions," Eldey said calmly but firmly.

Eldey's statement sent a quick powerful wave of conviction through me over my lack of self-control. I didn't think that I'd ever been able to truly relate to others with joy or patience the way the other Garden animals seem to be able to do.

"I'm sorry, Astuto. I do want to hear your thoughts on the matter," I said like a scorned dog.

"I know my tone can seem harsh or overly direct, but this time I was simply trying to explain a simple fact to you which you may not have considered. I know you wanted to end tonight's conversation with an 'easy' topic. And yes I did just air quote that," Astuto said laughing to himself. "You see Tortoise; many easy questions have very complex answers. I believe the quagga was a variation of the common plains zebra. You see, just because an animal looks a little different from others of its species, does *not* mean it *is* its own species," Astuto explained.

"Variations?" I asked.

"You see George, after the Great Flood, to survive the new parameters of the post-flood command, we animals were given the ability to adapt to our surroundings in new ways. Things you might think of as camouflage or mimicry were the results. I believe this quagga of yours is, in fact, a ghost of sorts. The quagga is simply a brownish variation of the plains zebras; not its own species. They no longer need that particular variation to survive. Species and adaptations can get quite confusing. You see it is not an easy question to answer," Eldey clarified.

"I guess that makes sense. It's just a little disappointing," I said sadly.

"It's disappointing to you, but not to the plains zebras which number close to a million. You see what's good for one creature isn't always good for another," Astuto said frankly.

"To clarify this for you, George, think about dogs. There are many variations or breeds of dogs, but they all came from the same species of wolf. People bred dogs to emphasize certain traits or variations they found most helpful. The quagga was a simple variation of the common plains zebra. Variations can be a tricky topic. For instance Boomer, the heath hen, looks similar to the lesser and greater prairie chickens which still range around the prairies of North America, but he went extinct, so he was, in fact, his own distinct species. As much as they do know, the people do not always get these connections right themselves," Eldey stated.

"I mean they've been trying to find you a mate from a different species back at the CDRS for how long? Tortoise, you know firsthand that a species can't simply be determined by similar traits, but you can't determine a species because things look different either," Astuto explained, "Honestly we only know which animals are their own species for sure when they show up in the Garden."

Chapter 9:

BRINGING EVERYONE TOGETHER

Eldey bid me goodnight, and Astuto said he needed to figure out how he would begin his part of the mission. According to Astuto his leg of the mission was over 6,000 miles. By boat, it would take about fifteen days. Assuming everything went perfectly, he would arrive to meet up with Strong around day 18. It'd take another ten days or so by boat to meet me at Pinta Island. It still seemed so easy. I mean sure that would put Astuto and Strong with me and the others on Pinta Island on day 38, but that was still a two-day buffer.

Before going, Astuto told me a little more about my role on Pinta Island. He told me that it wasn't as easy as sitting under my favorite prickly pear cactus waiting for 40 days. As he explained things I had two main roles; one was to get in contact with Fausto, and only Fausto. I told him I was confused because I thought I left Fausto to come on this mission. I didn't understand why I had gone extinct to get back to Pinta Island to go back to Fausto at the CDRS. I could have simply contacted Fausto while I was living in my enclosure *at* the Charles Darwin Research Station.

Like most aspects of this mission, things were never straight forward. My biggest challenge would be getting in touch with Fausto who was on Santa Cruz Island. Now it might not sound like much but as I understood from the maps of the Galapagos Islands that hung around the research station, my trip between islands would be 75 miles. Giant Tortoises aren't known for their great swimming abilities, which is why most tortoise species never had a chance to mix in the past. It might take me the remaining 37 days just to reach Santa Cruz assuming I didn't drown first.

If that would be my easier role, I didn't want to know what my other job would be. Astuto explained that I'd need to discern how and when to talk to various members of the group. It would be critical that I speak to each animal of a team individually over the next several days to encourage them to link up with the others in their triad. Once the members of the team were together they should be safe and wouldn't be as susceptible to any onslaughts by Lusadé. This led to Astuto's most stern warning; beware of doing 'all calls' within the group. Astuto seemed to believe, though not sure, that when I did all calls like I had originally done when yelling to the sky when I first arrived on Pinta Island, other animals might be able to listen in to the group's conversations. If that were in fact the case, all calls could put members of the group and the whole mission in serious jeopardy.

"Tortoise, you need to remember what each creature shared in the Garden and coach them through their fears. That is why I allowed us to spend some time in the Garden doing those terrible ice breakers. *You* are the most important link to this mission; not Eldey and not me. You, Tortoise, have the power to help others, and your ability to communicate will be the key. Remember that it's not always what you say, but sometimes what you don't say that can move things forward. Use discernment and compassion when speaking with others. I know this is not always an easy thing to do for you," he paused before continuing, "or for me. If you don't know what to say or what to do; think about what you think Eldey would do. I know you can do it Tortoise and remember even though you are alone on that island, you are never truly alone. Good night," Astuto said in a softer, compassionate tone.

I was stunned by this short conversation with the old dodo bird. For a creature known as dumb, he appeared rather wise. He had a softer side to him, but it did bother me that he still referred to me as *Tortoise*. Maybe I should just call him *Dodo* then.

Before letting bitterness about names overtake my thoughts, I decided to check in with members of the Southern Triad first. From the sketch in the sand back in the Garden, it seemed like Stephen was going to meet up with Moana somewhere around the northern tip of southern New Zealand. At least that's what I remembered from Eldey's sand sketch. I also decided to draw Eldey's sketch in the dirt at the base of my cactus to the best of my memory. That way I'd be able to semi-track the teams' movements as they approached Pinta Island. I was still getting used to having this one-way communication system, but in some ways, it made learning how to talk with others a little easier.

"Stephen? Stephen, can you hear me? I just wanted to see how things were going for you on Stephens Island," I said waiting for a reply.

"George, it's nice to hear from you. It's a little ironic to say to you, but I was feeling a little lonely myself out here. I heard you call us all earlier in the day, but I hadn't heard from you after that. How are the others doing?" the little bird asked.

I told him briefly about my conversation with Eldey and Astuto, which he was delighted to hear. I told him I wasn't too excited about trying to island-hop across the ocean. He said he could relate.

"George, Stephens Island is a very tiny grass-covered rock about two miles from a much larger island called D'Urville Island. I have to find my way across a small channel to the mainland of southern New Zealand. Hopefully, Moana will be there to meet me near the city of Nelson," Stephen explained.

"I will try to contact Moana now," I said, getting ready to invite her into this conversation.

But the little wren stopped me before I could. "George, before you contact Moana, could you give me some ideas about how you are planning to cross the ocean to reach the research station? I've been standing here on this beach for the past day and a half trying to figure out how I should go about doing the same thing. Thankfully there are no cats to be seen on Stephens Island anymore. It's still a loud, bustling nesting colony for seabirds. Anyway, do you have any thoughts, George?"

"I know you can't fly and you're probably a poor swimmer like me, so...," I said thinking, "Can you speak to a seagull, and hitch a ride?"

"I actually can't seem to communicate with any other creatures, except with you. Plus seagulls can be very careless creatures. The thought of falling to my death is worse than learning to swim," he said.

"If I remember right, there used to be a lighthouse on your island. Is it still there?" I asked.

"Yeah, it's just a short hike up to the lighthouse from this beach. Why? What are you thinking?" Stephen asked curiously.

"Well, the people at the CDRS always leave garbage around, so maybe you can find a bottle or a small container in the trashcan to use to float across the channel to D'Urville Island. Maybe you can also find a spoon for a paddle or something?" I said trying to sound helpful and encouraging.

"I had walked near the lighthouse cautiously, not knowing if there were still cats and I didn't see any people around. I think the people have set things up so that the lighthouse runs by itself now. It's not a very big island at all, so it's pretty easy to see who is here and who's not. Just another reason my kind couldn't hide from Tibbles the cat," he said. "I will head back up to the lighthouse to see what I can find and let you know. Are you planning to sail 50 miles in a giant bottle too George?" he mocked.

I enjoyed hearing from that little wren. He hid his obvious fears well for such a small fellow, plus he had a fun side about him that Eldey and Astuto lacked. I told him I'd try to contact Moana while he climbed back to the top of the hill.

"Moana, can you hear me?" I asked. It seemed weird to be talking so clearly with animals that were not actually with me. There was no response, so I called her again. Still no response.

"I'm here," Moana's faint voice finally replied. I remembered that even in the Garden she was a very soft-spoken, straight to the point talker.

"Are you getting closer to a rendezvous point with Stephen?" I asked.

Again, a long wait with no response, so I continued, "Stephen is going to try to find something to use to float across two miles of ocean to get to D'Urville Island. Then he is planning on meeting you in the town of Nelson in northern Southern New Zealand. Does that make sense to you? Are you anywhere near there right now or are you further south than that?

After another long, awkward pause, Moana simply replied, "Yes."

"Yes you are near Nelson or yes you are further south?" I said trying to clarify things for myself and for Stephen who I could hear panting in the background running up the rocky ridges back to the lighthouse.

"Yes," the giant moa replied again.

"Let...me...try...George," Stephen chimed in. "Moana, are you closer to Nelson, Christchurch, or Dunedin?"

"Dunedin," she replied.

"Stephen, how far does that make Moana from your rendez-vous point?" I asked, directing the conversation toward the more outspoken wren. I tried to appear like I knew what I was talking about, but I had never heard of any of these three places. Even asking about northern Southern New Zealand sounded more like a riddle than a place, but I left it up to their regional expertise.

"I think that's about 350 miles or so from here. So that means Moana could be here in ten hours or so," Stephen said matter-of-factly.

"Wait. I thought you said Moana is 350 miles away," I said thinking like a tortoise. "How can Moana possibly get there in half a day?"

"Well George, that's simple. She's huge! I mean an ostrich can sprint up to fifty miles an hour over short distances, but a giant moa is much, much larger and much, much faster. Watch what I mean," the wren said happily. "Moana, how long do you think it'll take you to reach me?"

Almost confidently Moana replied, "Eleven hours."

"Well Moana, that's a little disappointing. You're slowing down in your old age," the little bird mocked. "I'm just kidding Moana. You know I love you and that I can't wait to sit up on your shoulders and feel the cool breeze as we 'fly' across the ground."

"Moana fly," the colossal bird laughed heartily, getting the little wren's joke.

I checked in with the third member of the Southern Triad and as expected Benjamin was full of nothing but confidence. She told me and the other two birds that she was already on a large shipping vessel sailing toward Nelson. She should be there in another 3 days. I asked her how she had snuck onto a ship with so many people on board, and she said it wasn't that difficult.

She had said there was only one tense moment for her when she got near the city of Hobart in Tasmania. A tourist had spotted her running across an open field to reach a pocket of trees. Benjamin said she thought the tourist might have caught her on film. Her concern was realized while she was hiding behind some dumpsters. She heard many people talking about some amazing video that was all over the news. Since Benjamin had gone extinct in 1936, she was familiar with the people's video technology. In fact, I had seen some of the video clips of thylacines myself back at the CDRS.

"I should have gone around the clearing, but I wanted to make my portion of this trip as short and easy as possible," the Tasmanian tiger said, disappointed in her carelessness. "I shouldn't have rushed things, and now the people are looking for me around Hobart right now. They may have it on film, but the people won't be looking for me on a ship heading south to New Zealand. Every person knows that wild animals don't willingly get on boats," Benjamin said, regaining her confidence.

"So you're saying the people know about you being back in Tasmania? Isn't that a bad thing for our mission?" I said, a little annoyed by her apparent arrogance.

"George, the people have been saying I never went extinct for a long time. They report seeing thylacines all the time; mixing us up with feral dogs or dingoes. People will see what they want to see and will believe what they want to believe. Plus, there still are no thylacines *in Tasmania*; at least not as of 2 days ago when I boarded this ship and hid down in the cargo hold. The way I figure it, I should be in Nelson, New Zealand in about 3 days. Hopefully, I can meet up with Stephen and Moana when I arrive, and we can find another ship headed toward the Galapagos Islands. By my calculations it should be a 19-day boat ride getting us to Pinta Island by day 25; in plenty of time to save the day! Now if the three of you don't mind, I'm going to go get ready for a good night's sleep and think about how to hide a twelve-foot tall bird on the next boat," Benjamin said sarcastically.

By now the sun was starting to set on Pinta Island. I figured that I would check in with Stella before getting a good night's sleep myself. I figured Martha and Boomer would be asleep like Eldey, so I'd contact them first thing in the morning. Plus, I wasn't sure I could handle a Martha conversation right now. Talking to so many creatures all day in my head was exhausting for an introvert like me. After my morning conversations the next day, I would try to concoct some kind of plan to swim across 50 miles of Open Ocean to the closest island.

"Stella, how are things going for you?" I said.

"Great!" she replied almost instantly which surprised me. Most of the other animals had to reach a stopping point, or take a moment to gather their thoughts or formulate short one-word answers.

"Great? Well, that's... great," I said before I could formulate my thoughts. That sounded so dumb, but I couldn't take it back. "So are you doing okay then?"

"As I said, I'm doing great George," she said again, overly excited. There was something in her extremely happy tone that seemed *off*, but I didn't want to question her.

"Well, that's nice to hear Stella. If I remember right, you can cruise at about ten miles per hour, and they had said in the Garden that your leg of the mission should take 20 days as the Steller's sea cow swims? I think you'll be the first one to reach Pinta Island. It will be nice to see someone from the group again," I confessed.

I thought I must have offended her with something I said because there was such a long pause, that I thought I was talking to Moana again.

"George. I know the team is depending on me, and that my trip is supposed to be the *easy one*, but I'm not sure... ," Stella stammered. "I'm not sure that I can do this."

Now it was my turn to pause for a moment and consider how to respond. I didn't want to offend or discourage Stella. I thought back to the advice Astuto gave me earlier and tried to think about how Eldey would approach a situation like this.

"Stella, I know that you can do this. I have complete and total faith in you," I said hoping she didn't sense any worry in my voice. "What is keeping you from leaving the Commander Islands and swimming south to me? How can I help you along the way?"

"Well George, as I said back in the Garden; I fear the deep open water of the ocean. Steller's sea cows weren't known for our epic migration routes like whales or other large sea creatures. Like everything else we do, we vanished *slowly* from coastal regions around the northern Pacific. Even at our last stronghold in the Commander Islands, we didn't move away from the hunters when they approached us. It's not that we couldn't leave, it's that our fear of the Open Ocean kept us close to the shores of the islands," she admitted rather despondently.

"Just because you couldn't do it as a species long ago, doesn't mean it's impossible for you *now*. I know that you can do this Stella. I will make sure that I'm in contact with you every day to help," I assured her.

"I want to make the long swim, George. Maybe I could swim along the coast south to you on Pinta Island. No, then the people might see me. Plus it would take me so long that I might not make it by day 40," Stella said spiraling deeper into despair.

Thinking on my feet of how to support her, I blurted out the first thing that came to mind. "I have to swim almost 200 miles myself," I said, exaggerating the truth. "I'm like a 200-pound rock, and I *really* can't swim, but I have to find a way. If a nearly 200 pound, sinking tortoise can make it almost 200 miles, then a big seafaring creature like yourself can do it."

"What?! *You* have to swim. I thought tortoises can't swim," she said, pondering my previous statement.

"I can't swim at all. That's what's funny about it. But I have to and so do you, Stella," I said, forcing a laugh.

"So Stella we both have a big, impossible adventure ahead of us. We can do this *together.* I promise to help you out as much as I can every day. I don't think either of us has any desire to swim across open water in the dark, so why don't we do this. Let's get a good night's sleep, rest up, eat a good breakfast, and get started tomorrow. Let's hear some more of that positive talking that you started out with tonight. Okay? Things are going to be great Stella, and I know that you'll do a *stellar* job," I said trying to reassure her.

"Good night George and thanks," the sea cow said with a hint of confidence in her voice.

"Good night Stella," I said, yawning.

Chapter 10:

MY MISSION BEGINS

As the sun rose in the distance, I tried mustering some positive thoughts to fight this intense terror that had kept me awake throughout the night. How exactly does a 200-pound tortoise swim? It's a scientific fact that we can't. Pinta Island isn't exactly a tourist hotspot like many other islands in the Galapagos region, so a random boat ride was unlikely. The sun continued to rise in the sky, filling me with warmth for the mission ahead. I knew that I needed to eat as much as I could before I left and warm my cold-blooded body as much as possible before climbing into the frigid Pacific waters. I had seen the black spiny marine iguanas do this many times before, but they had a tail for swimming and a more streamlined body than this old tortoise. I couldn't likely walk along the bottom of the ocean back to the research station.

I decided that my best course of action would be to head southeast to the coast and see what I might be able to figure out along the way. Looking to the east where the sun was rising I headed due south. I knew that would be the best place for me to 'swim' to the next small island of Marchena. I knew that Marchena was southeast from Pinta and that the Charles Darwin Research Station was due south from there. My thinking, depending on how things went, was to try to take a straight shot to Santa Cruz Island, but I could always head toward another island if I stayed toward the center of the Galapagos island cluster. I had no intention or desire to float out to sea.

I started my slow and steady descent toward the southern shore. I could be there in a few hours. As I walked under some dried plants, I looked for something that could help me float. The shrubs I found were mostly thin, cracked sticks that had no chance of supporting my weight. I saw many larger prickly pear cacti, but I had no idea if they floated. I knew I'd only get one shot on this trip. Maybe I could walk down to the shore and stay there for a few days. I didn't know whether it was better to risk a trip now and possibly sabotage the whole mission, or stay here on Pinta Island and do my best to direct the others.

While I trudged southward I figured I'd check in with Stella who was just getting ready for her long 20 day swim to meet me at Pinta Island. She was back in good spirits.

"Thanks for the pep talk last night George. I've decided that I am going to go where no Steller's sea cow has gone before...to the Open Ocean!" Stella exclaimed.

"Well, have fun with that. I guess that I'll be seeing you on day 23 then. Maybe you can even set a Steller sea cow speed record too. Do you think you can hit 11mph?"

"I'll see what I can do George. No promises though. I don't want to pull a muscle. I'm not a dolphin, so don't even ask me to try one of those crazy flips," she said.

"Do you have any pointers for a beginning swimmer? Maybe something your mommy taught you?" I joked.

I knew it was a rhetorical question, but it livened both of our spirits. I told her to be careful and that I'd check-in at the end of each day before going to sleep to see where she was. I didn't tell her my thoughts about waiting for her to arrive to carry me across the ocean. I didn't want to discourage her from what she was doing. Astuto's words about not telling everyone everything came to mind, and I was beginning to see what he meant.

I quickly checked in with the Southern Triad, and they were still attempting to get to their rendezvous point. It seemed like things were coming together very smoothly for them. Stephen had found a bottle half-buried outside the lighthouse, and Moana didn't have much to say, as usual. Benjamin was still on the boat, full of unshakable confidence. If all went well they might be here as early as day 27. It almost seemed too easy; five of us making it to Pinta Island within 27 days.

After talking with Eldey and Astuto, I decided to get in touch with the last two members of the mission who I had not yet spoken with, "Martha and Boomer, can you hear me?" I said, sounding like a scientist on his radio back at the research station. "I was wondering how the first three days have been for you two?"

To my surprise, I could hear them *and* see them. I knew that if I asked, I could speak with more than one creature simultaneously, but I didn't know that I could actually *see* them. In my mind, I could see each of them from the other creature's eyes. It seemed perfectly natural, but it was an eerily strange feeling at the same time. Maybe this is how that chameleon thing felt seeing the world.

"We're here George. We say we're here because we've been together since the first day. Our old ranges overlapped quite a bit more than we remembered. It's nice to be back here again and see so many people. You see George, we sometimes have trouble sitting still for a long time, and we get kind of restless," Martha rambled.

"Really, Martha? *You* are having trouble sitting still? I just can't imagine that," I laughed. Boomer echoed my laughter.

"Oh George, you are such a joker. That's one of the things we love about you. We can't deny the facts. We definitely have a little trouble focusing and staying still, but we don't think that will be an issue. You see George, we're passenger pigeons and the cities are full of pigeons. Sure we look a little different, but people haven't seemed to notice me or care that we have a slightly different colored body than the pigeons around me. As female passenger pigeons, we're also a little more 'blendable' than if we had chosen our flashier orange and blue male counterparts," Martha explained.

Martha's pluralistic talking made communicating confusing, so I was glad I could see she was actually with someone else while rambling on and on about *we this* and *we that*. I had a theory that

I wanted to test for my sanity. I asked her to fly away from Boomer just for fun so that I could see exactly where she was. As she flew up into the air, I could see Martha taking flight from Boomer's perspective on the ground while simultaneously seeing the world below the flying passenger pigeon.

In the distance was what appeared to be New York City, whose skyline I had seen on tourists' shirts over the years at the CDRS. I asked her to fly toward the city, but once she left Boomer's visual range my ability to see through their eyes faded; leaving me only with the ability to hear each of them. I asked Martha to fly back to Boomer, and after a few moments, my vision grew less and less hazy until I could see both birds clearly. I decided not to let them know about this shortcoming in my communication, but I carried on with the conversation about how they were doing.

"How is everyone else doing? How's Eldey and Astuto and Stella..." Martha began.

Trying not to appear rude, I cut Martha off, "Everyone is on the move now. Things are going well. Eldey says he expects the Northern Triad to be here by day 20 of the mission. You might be the first to meet me on Pinta Island."

Realizing that Martha could talk to me for the entire 37 days left in our mission, I decided to redirect my questions toward the heath hen, "Boomer, how are you feeling about the next leg of your mission? Any idea of how you might cross 2,500 miles of land to reach the Pacific Ocean?" I asked trying to get him involved in this so far one-sided conversation with Martha.

"I'm just hitting my groove. I know that we will have Eldey with us which is very reassuring. He is the main reason that I came on this mission. As I said back in the Garden, I believe that the people can change, and they did try their best to protect us heath hens long ago. I want to make sure that I repay their attempted kindness and set things right. Plus I can't wait for them to see some new dance moves I've put together since I last danced in my lekking grounds in Martha's Vineyard. I've had eighty years to work on these new moves, you know." Boomer said bending over and inflating his orange neck pouches while doing some kind of backflip.

"Yeah, I've been working on my dance moves too; all three days I've been extinct. I was going to do a head bob to the left, another to the right, and then spin a full circle in under two minutes. What do you think?" I asked.

Being fast-moving birds, Boomer and Martha laughed at this thought.

"I realize that Martha can search around and be the eyes for our team since Eldey can't fly, and I can only fly a short distance. I will have to stay out of sight and save my passion for dancing until our *big moment* with you on Pinta Island. As far as how we'll travel, I haven't given that much thought. Eldey is the thinker in our group, so I'll just relax and listen to his advice," Boomer stated rather humbly.

"George, do you know when Eldey will make it to us?" Martha asked excitedly.

I told them that Eldey had hoped to join them near the mouth of the Hudson River sometime today. They were both elated about this and asked me if I could talk to him to find out his exact location. That seemed like a very good suggestion, especially since I had now ventured down to the beach of Pinta Island and wanted any reason to stall what needed to take place for me.

"Eldey can you hear me? I'm talking with Boomer and Martha, and we were all wondering how close you were to the Hudson River?" I asked expectantly.

"Hello, George. I figured that I would be hearing from you soon. I should be arriving near where the rest of my triad is in about three hours. The swimming has gone rather smoothly. It is the long walk ahead of us that will be more of a challenge. Martha and Boomer, I would like you to make your way toward the Hudson River to meet me. Martha, you can probably fly a little more freely than Boomer and me. For one; I can't fly at all, and Boomer and I don't blend in well with the current animal population," Eldey explained.

"Oh Eldey, we can't wait to see you. We're on our way right now to find you. Boomer can hide somewhere close by, and we'll keep an aerial lookout for you. How has your trip been? We can't wait to talk to you about it. Tell us. Tell us," Martha said excitedly.

"How about we do this Martha? I will tell you all about the past three days over the next 27 days while we're traveling. Right now, I'm eager to get back to swimming so that I can be with you and Boomer," the great auk said panting slightly from apparently swimming all morning.

I told them that I was going to try to figure out my long distance trip. I ended the conversation, and everyone was upbeat and sounded confident which made me a little more hopeful.

Then I looked out at the ocean. It was a long way to Santa Cruz Island, and I couldn't muster up the courage to start swimming yet. I placed one toe in the cool water and a shiver ran up my spine; partly from the temperature and partly because this water might be the undoing of my species. It could be the second time I went extinct in three days. How many other creatures could say that?

Chapter 11:

LUSADÉ

I didn't want to bother Eldey again, but I needed to get his advice. Eldey didn't seem annoyed but rather seemed to have been awaiting my call.

"George, it's so nice to hear from you again. I know that you still have a lot of things going on in your mind. You are probably down by the ocean right now, wondering how in the world a 200-pound tortoise is going to swim back to the CDRS. I bet you are even wishing you were a great auk at this moment," he said with a tension breaking laugh.

"Eldey, you seem to always know exactly what to do and never seem to worry about anything. I must be honest. I am beginning to doubt that I can do everything you are expecting of me. I don't want to let you down, but you realize that tortoises sink, don't you?" my voice cracked.

"George, we all have our doubts, but we cannot let those doubts control us. We must instead move forward in hope. If we focus on our fears and doubts, we will risk stealing hope from others. George, you are the glue that will keep this group together. I *do* worry what will happen if we fail but staying in that mindset won't help move us forward, will it?" Eldey asked.

"I guess not. I find it hard to believe that you fear anything Eldey. You are more of the glue of this mission than I am. I have to keep asking you for help don't I?" I sighed.

"Oh George, you do not see that as much as you fear to drown as all tortoises do, you are unique in that you truly *fear to be alone*. It is hard for you to ask for help because you have been on your own for so long. You fear to be close to others, for fear of losing them like you lost so many family members long ago. You fear to let me and the others down like you have been let down so many times in the past," Eldey said in a fatherly way that cut me to the core.

"I have plenty of fears, but I also have *faith*. Faith is trusting in the things you cannot see or do not understand and moving forward despite that. I believe in you and the others, just like I truly believe in the people. My biggest fear is that we will never again be able to live in peace and harmony with the people. I also fear Lusadé and what he is capable of," Eldey said.

"I'm glad you believe in me Eldey because I'm not sure I believe in myself. Even as I look at this ocean in front of me, I'm not sure I have the faith to try to cross it," I said gazing south out over the sparkling blue water. "What exactly is Lusadé capable of if you don't mind me asking?" I asked not knowing if I wanted to know the answer. A different conversation would at least take my mind off the deadly waters lying before me.

"The scary thing about *him* is that I have no idea what he is capable of doing. Since we left the Garden, serpents have always had a bad reputation," Eldey explained.

"Well doesn't he deserve his bad reputation since he led the people into eating the fruit from the forbidden tree?" I asked sternly.

"As you might know from other apparently straightforward questions, the answer is complicated," Eldey stated. "The best way to explain this is not to go back to the beginning in the Original Garden as you might expect, but to go back to our final days on the Ark before going forth and multiplying for the second time."

"That doesn't make sense. Didn't the serpent cause problems in the Original Garden that led to the curse that led to the corruption on earth that led to the Great Flood?" I asked.

"Let me explain, George. I do not know everything like you and many other creatures think. I am a finite animal like everyone else. Just because I am called the great auk, that doesn't make me great. I was once close friends with Lusadé before he took that name almost as a punishment unto himself; a mixture of insults he had heard from others since leaving the Original Garden. You see, once we left the Original Garden, we all had only vague memories of life there and how pure and simple it was in the beginning. No one knew exactly what happened other than what you and the people know from the stories. For instance, I don't remember strolling along the clear brook talking with Adam about the beautiful weather," Eldey explained.

"Oh, I figured that was some ability you had that I lacked because of going extinct ahead of schedule," I said more to myself than to Eldey.

"Now let me try to fill you in on what happened from my limited perspective. On the Ark, life was simple and good, almost like the Garden. The animals and Noah's family lived in harmony. Noah's family treated every living thing very well. Other than lacking the ability to speak directly with the people, life was virtually perfect. When we found out what post Flood life would be like with the people, many animals began to panic, realizing that our short-lived "Ark life" was a façade that would soon fade.

Lusadé and I both had a heart to help the people. I think Lusadé had an even bigger passion than I did to set things right, since he was constantly blamed for all of the corruption in the world in the first place. True the curse stemmed from the action of the people, but every creature including the people blamed the serpent," Eldey clarified.

"Wait, so you're saying the serpent was *not* responsible for the people's eviction from the Garden?" I interrupted.

"Yes, he was ultimately responsible for his actions in the Garden, but what exactly happened before the event with Eve is something I am not clear about. As I said I am not omniscient, I just know what I heard," Eldey said humbly. "I think I need to back up. Lusadé and I debated how to best help the people throughout our last days on the Ark, until..." Eldey's voice cut out like when he spoke of his family's death at the hands of the bird collectors on Eldey Island.

"What happened?" I asked.

"Things changed after the dove returned, carrying the well known olive branch. The flood waters had abated, and we could go forth and multiply. All of the creatures lined up expectantly by the great door to the Ark. The enormous ramp was slowly lowered, and I motioned my mate forward toward our new life. Then I turned toward Lusadé and his mate, Silvia, who began slithering down the ramp too. There was great excitement and hope in both our hearts. Even though we did not know exactly how we would help the people, we knew there was a chance for a fresh start."

"So you were friends with the serpent? Then why do you and the others fear him so much? Can't you simply talk to him now and let him know that we're planning to help him by setting things right with the people?" I asked hoping it might be that easy. "I mean, I could probably contact him."

"If the story had ended there, that might be a possibility, but it was on that massive ramp leaving the Ark, where all our hopes and plans unraveled. As we were walking down the ramp, Noah and his family members were helping all of us out of the Ark. As you can imagine it was a little chaotic after a year in snug quarters, and everyone wanted off of that boat. Amidst the chaos, Ham, one of Noah's sons, accidentally stepped and crushed Silvia's head under his sandal. I saw it happen, as did Lusadé," Eldey said, his voice distant.

"Oh my!" I gasped.

"Lusadé and I rushed to Silvia to see if there was anything that could be done, but it was too late. Lusadé was devastated, and he did not want to leave her side. My mate and I stayed with him as he grieved the loss of his mate, but we knew there was nothing we could do to ease his pain. We simply wept with him. My mate and I dug a shallow grave with our beaks and buried Silvia at the foot of that ramp. We grieved for six days with Lusadé," Eldey said sadly.

"That is terrible. Did Noah's son, Ham, know what he had done?

What did Lusadé do after the loss of his wife?" I asked, trying to be sensitive.

"In all of the hustle and bustle of 'exodusing' the Ark, Ham did not realize anything had transpired. Ham also had his problems soon after leaving the Ark with his father Noah. The people did not know, and it was honestly a simple, tragic accident. Lusadé struggled to make sense of what he should do. Something in him seemed to change that day. Our conversations about how to save the people turned into how he could see Silvia again. I told him that we had an obligation to help the people in this new era, but he said there had to be another way to help the people *and* his mate," Eldey explained.

"I could not leave him there so soon after his tragic loss, so I kept my mate on Mount Ararat as long as possible, but we needed to eat and find our place in this newly reset world. I told him that we needed to 'go forth' soon, or we would die. That was a poor choice of words to use with a creature who could no longer multiply," Eldey confessed.

"That was when the idea hit him to go back to the Garden at that very moment. He had no mate, so his extinction was assured. He thought that if he went back to the Garden he might be able to set things right there. Like you, he went extinct voluntarily. He was the first to do so. The problem was that he soon realized in the Garden, he could never be with his mate. He would be alone in the Garden as the sole ambassador of his species for all time. He could not live with that, so he decided to come back here. That is when he realized that he could communicate with other animals for 40 days if he sought them out," the great auk explained.

"That explains how you knew about the *40 day rule* and why you were so sure that I'd be able to lead this mission. It doesn't quite clarify how the post-flood death of Lusadé's mate links to the happenings in the Original Garden," I reminded Eldey.

"After Lusadé returned from his brief stint in the Garden, he contacted me with a new plan he had thought up to save the people. He thought that he could go back into the Garden and find a way to "reset the Original Garden", setting right his reputation and the events in the Original Garden which even he did not fully understand. I told him that while he was in the Garden, my mate and I had settled far from Mount Ararat, but I would help him however I could. For whatever reason, he was able to communicate with me. We could use that to our advantage. I could be with him in a way; assuming he made it back to the Original Garden," Eldey continued.

Feeling like I would never keep up with all of this, I ventured another question, "So let me get this straight; after his mate's death on the ramp of the Ark, Lusadé chose to go extinct like me, and then came back here, and then formed a plan to go back to the Original Garden, and reset history itself?"

"Yes. That is exactly what I am saying. I was trying to help the people keep things as close to perfect as possible in the post-flood days, and Lusadé was trying to go back to the Beginning to help the people that way. It did not seem possible, but I wanted to support my friend in any way I could while he mourned his fallen mate," Eldey said.

"I'm assuming that when he went back into the Garden; that he found a way back to the Original Garden of Eden since you said his story started *on the Ark*. What happened when he went back then?" I asked.

"At first Lusadé would openly communicate with me daily. About the 35th day, Lusadé told me that he had done it! He never communicated exactly *how* he did it. I had often searched for a way to the Beginning myself when I was back in the Garden after my extinctions, but never found it. Lusadé told me that he had grown legs when he returned to the Original Garden and that he had seen the man and his wife, Adam and Eve, walking in the distance earlier in the day. He said that he located the two trees of the Garden, so he could stake out the area and make sure nothing happened."

"If he found the tree where the people were to eat the fruit and curse the world, why didn't he succeed?" I asked, astonished by what I was hearing.

"Lusadé wanted to make sure that no serpent in the Original

Garden did anything to bring the curse upon the people. He admitted he did not know who to be looking for exactly, but he vowed to let no creature talk to the people without him being there. He told me what it was like to be with Adam and Eve in the Original Garden and how at peace he was. I began to grow excited by the possibility that if he had made it back to the Beginning, maybe he could reset things from there," Eldey explained.

"Wow. That is amazing!" I blurted.

"I am not clear what happened in those last few days, but he began to withdraw into himself. Lusadé told me that he had been talking to someone in the Garden who seemed wise, and this someone told Lusadé that if he ate the fruit of the tree of knowledge *before* Adam and Eve, he would know *exactly* what he had to do."

"So he met an angel or something in the Garden?"

"I am not sure who he spoke to, and I do not want to even venture a guess. He never told me, but that was when Lusadé's plans to reset things began to unravel and inevitably fulfill the long foretold prophecy. When I asked him what was going on, Lusadé said that he now saw a flaw in his plan. Seeing the man with the woman happy every day, made him realize that if he reset things in the Original Garden, he would never again be *with* his mate. Things would appear perfect for everyone else, but he was afraid he would be alone and miserable for eternity. As you know George, when you choose to go extinct you are not as at peace as other animals in the Garden. Lusadé ranted that creatures should have more of a role in the Garden than trying to help the man. He reminded me that was what the woman was for. I did not know how to console him so soon after the loss of his wife," Eldey said exasperated.

"On what was the 40th day, the last day I was able to communicate with Lusadé, things completely fell apart. It was almost like he was fighting with himself; partly concocting revenge on the people and partially wanting to help them. At least that was what I think happened from his rantings. He talked to me, but it was more of a window into his internal monologue. Eating the fruit from the tree of knowledge did not help him know the best thing to do. The tree of knowledge made him aware that he did not know everything," Eldey confessed.

"That's what happened to the people when they ate from it too wasn't it?" I asked, trying to recall the specifics of the story.

"Yes. One of the last things I remember him telling me was that if he could not have Silvia back then the man and woman did not deserve to live happily ever after either," Eldey explained. "I pleaded with him to think things through, but he said he had made up his mind. I told him that if he did not change the past, the future would play out the same way, with him losing his mate all over again. He said he would rather live a year *with his mate* aboard the Ark, than to live forever in the Original Garden without her. That day I lost my best friend, and we all lost what could have been."

"That is terrible. So have you seen or heard from Lusadé since?" I asked

"No, but we do hear about things that he has done. I know that he still despises the people. The problem is that he loved his mate and feels justified in his actions. He blames the people for his mate's death under the foot of Ham even though it was an accident. Blinded by his hatred, Lusadé doesn't see that his selfish, spiteful actions against the people were just as much to blame for his mate's death as Ham's misplaced, curse fulfilling step. "

"I almost feel bad for him," I said sadly.

"So do I, George. So do I. I blame myself for not being able to do more for him. This is a burden that I must bear. I am hoping that this mission will somehow bring peace between him and the people. He might even be able to tell us how to return to the Original Garden and reset things there. I know that we have not seen the last of Lusadé, but I hope we can still accomplish what we are here to do," Eldey said more hopefully.

"One more question if you don't mind," I pressed.

"Go ahead," Eldey said, regaining his composure.

"If Lusadé went back to the Original Garden, and no serpents left the Ark other than him, why are there so many snakes in the world today? I mean you said he couldn't *go forth and multiply*," I said.

"Like I said George, I do not know everything. Remember to view things more globally. Not all serpents are created equally; meaning there are over 2,700 species of snakes in the world today. You cannot label all serpents *evil* because of the bad choices of one individual. The people tend to group them all together and hate the entire serpent family. Do not think like the people George. Lusadé is like Pat, Nessie, and you. He is an individual trapped here, facing extinction in its truest sense. The only difference is that Lusadé does not seem to want to go back to the Garden as you do," Eldey said before parting.

Chapter 12:

TAKING THE PLUNGE

After my conversation with Eldey, I needed to take some time to think. I hadn't checked in with Astuto today, but I knew he could handle himself. I'd talk to him tomorrow. My brain couldn't take any more deep thinking, so I decided to check in quickly with Stella before finding a place to rest for the night. Day 3 was not my day to make the 75-mile swim. I still had 37 days left and was content to wait upon Stella's massive back to transport me across the Pacific Ocean. Of course, I didn't let her know that when talking to her. She was nothing but positive and excited to be overcoming her fears about the Open Ocean. I thought it was okay to let her believe that I was doing the same. Stella had only seen a few passing fish, a seagull that perched on her back for a while removing some crabs and parasites from her blubbery sides, and a ship sailing in the distance.

After bidding Stella good night, I turned in myself. I glanced at the sun setting in a smattering of reds and oranges in the western sky. Yep, somewhere directly south was the Charles Darwin Research Station, my home away from home, and Fausto. I wondered what he would think when he saw me again, a Lazarus species.

I dreamt about the research station and how Fausto would read to me and sing songs on his guitar. I awoke to feel almost confident about the mission at hand and about what I must do...once Stella gave me a ride. Until then I'd be the operator, sitting on the beach talking to my new found friends.

I decided to check in with Astuto to see if he had come up with a plan to swim over 6,000 miles across the ocean. Selfishly, I had hoped he might inadvertently give me some insight into my situation.

In his usual direct, non-empathetic tone he told me that his hopes of hiding on a plane or a boat would be harder than he had thought. Mauritius hadn't forgotten the dodo. In fact, there were dodos posted all around. He joked that he knew how Bigfoot felt. Astuto was a celebrity in his hometown, which made blending in impossible. He told me that he had spent the whole night concocting a plan and now he was ready to act.

"Is there anything I can do to help you out?" I asked, expecting a blunt no.

To my surprise, Astuto replied, "Yes. I will need your help to get to the Falkland Islands in time without being captured. I have no desire to be paraded around by the people or placed in some zoo. I'm not photogenic, as you have pointed out. I prefer to have my picture painted," he said, trying to skirt the fact that he had just asked for help.

"What can I do to help out since I'm literally on the other side of the planet with only the ability to communicate with you and the other animals?" I asked sarcastically..

"That's exactly what I need you to do George. I need you to communicate with the other animals for me," Astuto said.

"You mean to do another *all call* as I did before? But you told me that *all calls* were dangerous. What made you change your mind?" I asked, wondering what he was planning.

"No. No. No, Tortoise. That wouldn't be good for our mission at all. We don't want to give Lusadé any idea of what we're planning or where the members of the team are right now. That would be bad. Plus..." he said hesitantly. "Plus, I don't want the others to know that I need... that I need help getting to the Falkland Islands."

So this must be the old dodo bird's fear; being thought of as dumb and incompetent. Feeling bad for Astuto and honestly wanting to help him, I asked what I could do.

"Now no one knows how you can communicate, but it seems that you can call those that you want. I was thinking about any *natural* ways I could get to the Falkland Islands, and I came up with one possible solution. This might sound crazy to you but hear me out," Astuto said, sounding less than confident.

"Okay, what do you need?" I asked, trying to reassure him.

"I need you to do a specific 'all call' for any *orcas* close to Mauritius," Astuto said.

"You mean that you want to talk to a killer whale?" I said almost mockingly.

I tried to figure out what the dodo had in mind. Just once, I'd like to come up with a great idea for someone before they did. I always seemed to be leading them toward a great idea, but never actually gave one.

"Yes, here's my thought. I will travel by orca from Mauritius to the Falkland Islands," he said matter-of-factly.

I must have laughed out loud because he hesitated before continuing, "It has been done at least once before, so it's not as unrealistic as it might seem. By my calculations, traveling at thirty miles or so an hour by orca, I should reach Strong on the Falkland Islands in 9 to 10 days; getting me to him on day 14. We could reach Pinta Island by day 20 or so. Of course, we'll need to get a second orca to transport Strong, but they swim in pods so it should be pretty straightforward," Astuto said more to himself than to me.

"Wait. You said you've done this once before?" I asked, trying to picture a dodo bird surfing on a killer whale.

"No. No. No. Not me Tortoise. A *person* did it long ago. Of course, he was only in a whale for three days, and my trip will take three times as long, but I think it can be done. Maybe I should add a day or two to my expected arrival date. Expect Strong and me to be there by day 22. Yes, expect us then," Astuto said with growing excitement over his wisely improvised plan.

"Okay, Astuto. I will see what I can do. Are you sure you don't want me to contact a toothless, baleen whale of some kind? I mean, how do you know the killer whale, won't... won't kill you?" I asked.

"The killer whale is the fastest of the whales and as I've said many times Tortoise; time is of the essence. I don't want to waste a moment. I've found that just when things seem to be going smoothly, disaster is right around the corner. I have over a week in the belly of a whale to think about. Now Tortoise, please contact an orca for me. Tell the orca to meet me in Port Louis on the western side of the island. I'm not far from there now. I'll be looking for some leaping or splashing near shore as a sign of my escort," Astuto said, hurrying me along.

It was awkward to call all orcas near Mauritius. What I noticed about doing this, was that I could sense them and call them, but they couldn't give a verbal reply like the members of my mission. I told Astuto that I had tried to contact them, and had put the notice out for an escort. He thanked me and said he was going to make his way down to the shore. I guess that was the biggest thanks I was going to get from him. I guess the softer side of Astuto was gone once again.

"Before I go, I was wondering how you planned to get to Santa Cruz Island. Have you already begun your swim?" Astuto asked.

"Uh. I've been contemplating that for the past day or so, and I was thinking about waiting for Stella to come to pick me up around day 18 or so," I said, trying to underestimate her arrival day.

"No! No! No! You can't wait that long Tortoise! There is too much for you to do during that time. You must contact Fausto as soon as possible, to complete your part of the mission. Without involving a person, we can't complete our mission even if every member of every triad makes it to Pinta Island. I'm afraid to say that you must find a way to do it soon, or we will fail to reset things," Astuto said firmly.

I didn't want to discuss what I had to do with Astuto, so I bid him good luck and looked back out at the sea lay before me. How? I hadn't seen a ship in the past two days, so that wouldn't be my saving grace. I decided to walk a little further down the coast to see if I could find any better options.

As I crested a small rocky outcropping, I looked down in the water. There, in a slant of golden rays of sunshine, was a rather large log. I cautiously crept over to the massive log which might just be my way to cross the ocean. There were a few gnarled branches for me to balance on. I wasn't sure if this tree had come from the island or whether the current had brought it ashore. Either way, I knew this log would be my cruise ship.

I looked down at the log and felt the pit of my stomach roll like the ocean before me. I spent some time by the log trying to muster the courage to push it out into the sea and start my adventure. I thought how a creature like Benjamin would love a thrill like this. Even Astuto's idea of riding inside of a killer whale was painted with excitement. I had no desire to climb onto an unstable log and go sailing. Tortoises simply weren't created for flight, for swimming, or for sailing. Dry land was our domain.

I decided to stall once more, checking in with the members of each triad one last time before possibly drowning. The Southern Triad was still on pace to meet up in New Zealand tomorrow, day 5. Little Stephen had floated his bottle across the ocean to D'Urville Island. He was running as fast as possible to meet up with Moana. Moana seemed to be waiting for Stephen in Nelson, but she said, "I will go get him." And she was off again sprinting over the New Zealand terrain. Benjamin was full of optimism and still hiding out aboard the ship.

The Northern Triad had just come together and didn't have much to report. Eldey's plan was for them to get on board a train from New York City to Los Angeles which he estimated should take about three days, putting them on the west coast of North America by the end of day 7.

The one thing that I was taken aback by when talking with the first *completed triad* was that I could hear, see, and *feel* them. It was a strange sensation, but I could feel what each member was feeling. I had a perfectly blended picture of all three creatures in the Northern Triad from all three perspectives. This must have been what it felt like for the others when I was back in the Garden with them. I decided to say nothing about it for the time being.

The Scattered Triad was also doing well. Astuto was waiting impatiently on his killer whale escort. Strong was trying to locate a good place to meet up with Astuto and an orca without being spotted. He explained that there weren't any trees on the Falkland Islands, so he had to sneak around at night or hide out in the tall grasses. He seemed eager to be back with the people. He had seen several dogs on the island, which was also a comfort to him; reminding him of his time sailing with Captain Strong. I have to admit I envied Strong's bond with his captain. Stella was the last creature I checked in with, and she was still confidently making good time. *Slow and steady wins the race* was her mantra that she dedicated to me, the tortoise.

Everything seemed set. Everyone was scheduled to arrive well ahead of schedule, and everyone was in good spirits about their part of our mission, except me. Day 5 would be my day to complete my other mission, the swim. I took one last look at the blue water in front of me and shouted at it, "Tomorrow, you are mine!"

I nestled next to my log and collapsed into a dreamless sleep. Toward dawn, I was awakened by a small whisper, *You should stay here on the island. It's not worth risking your life to make it to Fausto. There must be another way.* I pushed this voice to the side, dismissing it as a post dream memory like the giddy goat I snapped at a few days before. Whatever it was, it didn't help bolster my courage.

I didn't want to give myself a chance to reconsider what I was about to do, so I took a few steps back and ran at the log as quickly as I could. As a tortoise, I made up for my lack of speed with brute force. I was a natural battering ram. After my seventeenth or eighteenth log ramming, it began to move away from shore. I instinctively, or anti-instinctively, stepped onto the midsection of the log where there were several branches to use for balance. I had no idea how long I might be adrift, so I wanted added stability. I had no desire to sink to the bottom of the ocean.

To my surprise, it seemed rather easy, and I thought it might work. I shifted my weight a little too quickly. My heart started racing, and I could feel a very real sense of fear take control. Even though I probably only floated a few hundred feet, I must have already broken the longest solo voyage by a giant tortoise. I was fighting my fears when a small voice again seemed to speak to me, *It's not too late to turn back. What will happen if you slip off of this log? It's not worth the risk.* The voice was no lingering dream, but something else. It continued. *If you die, the mission will surely fail. It's better to be alive and wait for twenty days than to let everyone down and die now."*

I again dismissed those thoughts. I floated south, or what I thought was south and within a few hours, I spotted land to the east. I assumed that it must be Marchena Island. Since things were going so well, I decided to bypass the island and head straight to Santa Cruz Island, the CDRS, and Fausto. I had figured out that if I supported my bulky shell and back legs on the tangled branches behind me, I could use my front legs as heavyweight paddles. The thought of Astuto surfing on a killer whale must pale in comparison to seeing a tortoise paddling a log across the ocean. Maybe a long lost relative of mine paddled their way to the Ark after all.

At this rate, I might be at the Charles Darwin Research Station in a few days. Then I'd have to cross the island on foot which might take several more days. Okay, I had to be honest with myself; it might take a week, putting me there around day 16 or so. That still was not too bad.

I looked off into the distance toward a growing noise that sounded familiar. I went to shift my weight slightly because a puny wave had pushed me to the side. I overcompensated and began to lose my footing. A second, slightly larger wave buffeted my log. The last thing I remember was that I was frantically grasping for branches and trying desperately to hold on. I knew that in between the islands I had no chance of holding on very long. A third wave flipped the log over, and I held onto it with all my might. The cold ocean water began taking its toll on my cold-blooded body. I knew it wouldn't be too long before it would all be over.

"I'm sorry Eldey. I have failed you. I hope that you can still reset things without me," I said hoping Eldey heard.

I heard two voices before sinking into the depths of the cold Pacific, one saying; *Hold on George,* and the other saying; *You should have listened to me*. Things began to fade as the ocean laid claims to me.

Chapter 13:

LOSING HOPE

I felt terrible. My body ached, and my head was throbbing. My thoughts were foggy, and I tried to make sense about what had happened. The first thought to enter my mind was that I felt like I did when I woke up from a nightmare. But waking up implied I wasn't dead.

Slowly I opened my eyes, and I could see home. Not my Pinta Island home, but my enclosure back at the Charles Darwin Research Station. I saw the two female tortoises that I had left five days ago when I went extinct. It seemed like a lot longer than that. I began to wonder if I had again dreamed up the whole thing, but the sign outside my enclosure read, "Lonesome George - extinct June 24th, 2012."

I raised my head off the ground and slowly looked around. I saw some of the local scientists talking in the distance. One of the men in khaki shorts and a blue floral shirt pointed over to me, and there was a jovial stirring amongst the people. They rushed over to my side flashing bright lights in my eyes. One woman put a stethoscope to my neck to listen to my breathing. There was a lot of excitement, and at first, I wondered why. Then I remembered that I had been extinct, and now the people were viewing me as a Lazarus species, raised from the dead.

Amidst the pushing and shoving of scientists, I saw Fausto. I wanted to call out to him, but I remembered that I had been told to only talk to Fausto. I would have to wait for my turn to talk to him. Until then, I would just tolerate all of this unwarranted attention. As soon as things settled down, I would contact the Northern and Southern Triads to see how their reunions were going.

The scientists wanted me to eat something, but I wasn't interested. I had a lot to do and wanted them to leave me alone. I snapped at the one who drew blood from my leg. I guess I was still just an old grumpy Pinta Island tortoise to them. I wanted to scream but instead controlled myself, hissing incessantly. Finally, everyone left me alone to go sort through all of the data they just gathered at my expense. Fausto was nowhere to be seen, so I figured that I'd check in with the others.

"Northern Triad, do you have a minute to talk?" I asked..

By my calculations, Eldey, Boomer, and Martha should be heading west on a train by now. Eldey had made their mission seem pretty simple, as long as they weren't spotted. I knew Martha would be safe and Boomer looked like several other types of prairie chickens, but Eldey was a three-foot-tall great auk. It would be a lot harder to hide him in broad daylight.

I had forgotten that when I talked to a whole triad at the same time, I could feel their emotions, see, and hear them. It was like having a three-way vision, but somehow my brain could sort it all out. I could see a concerned look on their faces and asked them what was wrong.

"We were really sad, but now we're really happy all at the same time," Martha rambled.

"We thought you were dead George. We haven't heard from you for over a week. It's day 14," Boomer explained.

"It's nice to hear from you George," Eldey said. "Things are going very well for the Northern Triad. We traveled by train without incident. It was a little tough to get on the ship headed toward Pinta Island, but thanks to Martha's flying ability keeping us informed, we made it. The three of us should arrive on Pinta Island by Day 18.

"Wait. You're saying it is day 14?" I asked, trying not to sound panicked. "I ran into a little trouble with my 'swimming' trip. Just so you know I air quoted that," I said trying to regain my composure.

"I am so glad you are doing well. We are going to try to get a little sleep now, but keep in touch George, and good luck on your mission," Eldey said with an unfinished tone in his voice.

I wished them all a good night and apologized for my unavailability the past week. I told them that I had made it safely back to the CDRS. They were elated to hear that. After ending the conversation I called Eldey to see if he had more to say or if I had misunderstood him.

"George, I am glad you picked up on my tone. I need to talk to you. I have a bad feeling about things. It is going well for us, but I am not sure how the others have been faring without your support," Eldey said in a tone more serious than I'd ever heard him use.

"Eldey, I'm sorry. I didn't mean to let you down. I was on a log paddling to Santa Cruz when a wave knocked me overboard. I'm not even sure how I got back to the research station. Apparently, I just woke up after a week of unconsciousness," I said solemnly.

"George, you have not let anyone down, especially me. I am very proud that you even attempted the swim. I thought you might try to wait for Stella, but that would not have left time for what you need to do before the 40th day. I think that you still have time, but we are cutting things kind of close. I have full faith in you. I would love to talk more with you, but I think it is pertinent that you see how others are doing. Whatever happens, you and six of us must be on Pinta Island in 26 days," Eldey said before heading to sleep himself.

"Southern Triad, this is George. I wanted to apologize for my absence and see how things are going for your triad," I said hoping they were halfway across the Pacific by now.

"Things have gone 'south'. Pardon the expression," Stephen said, trying to lighten a bleak situation.

"Not good. Not good," Moana said with fear in her voice.

I didn't hear from Benjamin and began to fear the worst. Had she been killed while I was unconscious? Why did Moana say *not good* twice? That really couldn't be a good thing. I tried to think about how to approach this situation in a way that would benefit the group. I could only *hear* them, so that meant they were *not* together. This was problematic for two reasons; one, they weren't together, and it was already day 14, and two; it would take them 20 days to reach Pinta Island assuming all went well. I didn't know what to do. I decided to talk to them one at a time to piece together what had happened in my absence.

"Stephen. Stephen, can you please let me know what happened? I have been unconscious for the past week. It doesn't sound like things have been going the best for the Southern Triad either," I said trying to mask my anxiety.

"Well, when we last spoke with you things were going smoothly. I had floated across the ocean to D'Urville Island, and Moana had swum 1,500 feet to pick me up because I wasn't able to carry by heavy bottle the length of the island to use again. I'm too small and have very minuscule wings you know," Stephen said, trying to keep the truth as light-hearted as possible. "That's where things started to fall apart. We reached the city of Nelson just as Benjamin's ship was pulling into the harbor. Moana and I hid the best we could in view of the ship. Around dusk, we saw Benjamin leave the ship, and we met up with her."

"It sounds like everything went well up until that point. What happened?" I asked.

"The trouble came when we were boarding the ship that was to carry us to Pinta Island. We snuck onto a cruise ship heading toward the Galapagos and were on our way to the cargo hold. It was a very stealthy operation until we got to the cargo hold itself. Moana looked down into the blackened hole and panicked. It was everything we could do to keep her on the ship. When she panicked, Moana backed into a stack of crates, knocking them over. One of the people heard us and came to see what was happening. We were all in danger of being captured. Without hesitating, Benjamin jumped out of the shadows yipping and growling at the man in the blue uniform with the badge," Stephen explained.

"So Benjamin was captured trying to save you and Moana? Why

aren't the two of you together now?" I asked, wondering if maybe they had all been captured and were in cages traveling to be studied as we spoke.

"The man in the blue uniform called for more people to come. Benjamin growled at them and bounded toward the opposite side of the ship away from us. All the men aboard had heard the news of a thylacine sighting back in Tasmania before their ship set sail for New Zealand, so they instantly knew what they were seeing. It seemed like they genuinely cared about seeing Benjamin and took great care to be as gentle as possible capturing her. Benjamin told Moana and me that we both had to make it. With Benjamin being captured, most of the people on board stayed topside presumably observing her. Moana blamed herself for what had happened and ran off somewhere up into the hills surrounding Nelson before the ship set sail. I tried to catch her, but it's hard for a tiny flightless wren to keep up with a twelve-foot tall moa, bent on fleeing," Stephen said. "I don't know what to do George. I don't know what to do."

"Benjamin never answered when I called the Southern Triad, so I'm assuming the people must have put her to sleep to run tests. I can imagine how overjoyed they are to see a thylacine in their midst after a 76 years hiatus. I mean you should see the scientists here at the research station celebrating my rediscovery after a 5-day absence. Moana seems very distraught over what had happened. Why don't you let me try to speak to her and see if I can convince her to join you?" I said trying to keep things positive.

Doing the mental math, assuming everyone else could make it back without Benjamin and Moana, that still gave us seven others and myself. I hated the thought of having others not make it. I was beginning to see why it was so important to have brought three extra animals on this mission.

"George, the fact of the matter is; I must depart for Pinta Island within the next two days or I might not make it there in time. I figure that the previous ship that discovered the thylacine, must be sailing her back to Tasmania as we speak. Now, I'd love to sail my bottle 1,500 miles back to Tasmania to rescue Benjamin, but I know that isn't the most important thing right now. There's a boat that leaves for the Galapagos Islands from Nelson in two days. If you can't convince Moana to be at the boat by then, I will have to leave without her," Stephen said remorsefully.

"I will see what I can do," I said, not sure of how I was going to do that.

Before I contacted Moana, I touched base with Eldey to let him know that his premonition was correct and that we had one member who wouldn't be making it. Eldey, always looking at the positive side of things, said he was just glad that Benjamin was alive. I told him that I would check in with the Scattered Triad after I spoke to Moana.

Eldey reminded me to be gentle and to try to approach the giant moa with sympathy and to do so slowly. Even though I usually excel at doing things slowly, I realized that when it came to talking to others, I was neither slow nor consistently compassionate. All I was thinking about was that I only had two days to convince the giant moa to join Stephen or lose her from the mission.

"Moana, I know that you can hear me. I wanted to let you know that I am here for you if you want to talk," I paused to see if the conversation would be that easy. "I know you are a creature of few words. There were years that I spoke to no one because I was a bitter old tortoise. I was angry and very self-focused. I wasn't able to see the big picture. I'm asking you to give me a chance to help you. We need you to be part of the big picture Moana," I said ending my horrendous motivational speech.

There was nothing said for a long time, but since this was Moana, I waited a long time before finally saying, "I'll be in touch, Moana, but you only have two days until Stephen's ship sets sail for the Galapagos. Leaving any later than that might mean neither one of you would make it to Pinta Island on time. Take care, my friend."

I didn't know who I should contact first in the Scattered Triad. I decided that I'd check in with Stella first because she was so chipper and in high spirits before my near-drowning.

"Stella, how are you doing? I figure you should only be a week away from Pinta Island," I said optimistically.

There was a longer pause than I was used to with Stella, and I began to fear the worst. Then her timid voice spoke angrily, "George, you left me! Why did you leave me? You promised to check in with me *every night* before you went to bed! How could you forget about me? I needed you, and you left me!"

Her words hit me like a tsunami because I understood that I had broken my promise to her. At the same time, my anger began to overcome my compassion because I had almost drowned crossing the sea. There was a battle raging within me, but I managed to gain control of my anger and err more towards compassion.

"Stella. I am sorry. I didn't forget about you at all. I had some *complications* on my journey that prevented me from talking to anyone," I said slowly to make sure I said things the way I wanted to.

"You mean you have been asleep, hibernating or something for nine days?" Stella asked with a mixture of concern and anger.

"I don't think I slept the whole time, but it's a little fuzzy. Tortoises are a little slower than other creatures you know, especially when swimming in cold water. I must have blacked out or something," I said, stretching the truth a little bit.

"I'm sorry to have jumped to conclusions, George. Please forgive me for my judgments. I have just been very scared without you, and I have had to stop along the coast several times. I think I should reach Pinta Island around day 28 or 29. I'm sorry that's later than you thought, but I've been struggling to keep going south. I saw a great white shark on day six and panicked. I've been hiding out in a small bay since then, but I will start swimming right now. Will I talk to you later tonight then?" she asked, trying to pump herself up for another long Open Ocean swim.

I assured her that I would indeed check-in unless I decided to hibernate again. Next, I checked in with Strong, the Falkland Island Wolf. He reported, "I am simply waiting and surveying the people of the island at a distance. I will sneak toward the docks in the town of Stanley and wait for Astuto in the giant shipwreck near Christ

Church Cathedral."

"Okay. I'll let Astuto know," I said.

"George, please let the orca know to look for a large orangish brown and gray church. You probably shouldn't mention to the orca that there's a whalebone sculpture in the courtyard of the church. I don't want to spook the whale away from Stanley," Strong explained. As always, Strong was a creature of detailed planning and action.

"I'm sorry I've been out of touch. I had trouble getting back to the CDRS." I explained.

"I understand completely. I will be awaiting your orders once Astuto reaches the rendezvous point. I have scouted out the path to the airport and calculated that Astuto and I should be able to catch a flight to Santiago, Chile. The LAN airplane takes off every seven days from what I can tell. The next flight leaves the Falkland Islands in two days, but we could also fly out in nine days if need be," Strong relayed.

I wanted to relay what Strong had told me to Astuto and to see how his whale ride was progressing.

"Astuto, I wanted to see how close you were to the Falkland Islands. Strong is waiting for you in the town of Stanley somewhere along the eastern coast of the Falkland Islands," I said, hoping to avoid a rebuke for not checking in sooner. "Strong said to meet him in the wreckage of a large ship that lay off the coast outside of Christ Church Cathedral."

"I'm not exactly sure where I am. I can't see anything inside this blasted whale," Astuto said bluntly. "This orca can swim quickly but hasn't been swimming in a straight line. From what I can tell from our few stops along the way, we should be arriving at Stanley within a day or two. Although I don't think there was any choice in my transportation method, I can't wait to rid myself of this horrendous fish smell. I am *not* a fish eater, and can't wait to step on dry land again."

"How have you been able to survive in the belly of the whale? I mean it doesn't seem physically possible," I inquired.

"I'm not in the whale's belly. That would be absurd. He's been holding me in his mouth the whole time, and I'd rather not talk about what I've been eating. Thankfully we were able to stop on a small island off the coast of South Africa for a break and to get food. That put us back a day, but it was a much-needed stop. This orca is a very energetic creature, with all the leaping and flipping, but I think we have been moving toward our goal," Astuto explained.

"I don't even want to venture to guess what you've been through," I said trying to picture the cranky old bird stuck in a whale's mouth. "I will check in tomorrow and let Strong know to be expecting you."

Chapter 14:

LUSADÉ'S FIRST STRIKE

The next morning, day 15, I checked in with the Northern Triad who were still progressing south at a good rate. Since they were aboard a cruise ship, they had made more stops along the way than Eldey had anticipated. Whenever they stopped, the three birds would have to hide from the people who jostled the cargo around below deck.

Stephen was still waiting aboard a ship that would leave the next morning. He was very concerned that Moana wasn't coming back, and I felt like I had to be honest with him.

"Moana has refused to answer my calls. I can sense her presence, but something seems to be keeping her from even giving me a one-word answer," I told Stephen.

"Moana is soft-spoken but has never been a rude bird. Something isn't right," Stephen stated.

"She seems to be ignoring me for some reason, and I'm not sure why. I will try one last time in a little bit to try to convince her, but it looks like you may have to face your journey on your own, Stephen," I said regretfully.

I figured I'd check in with her later, but I was eager to hear whether or not Astuto had made it to the town of Stanley yet. To my surprise, the old dodo had done it! He had completed the 6,000 miles trip from Mauritius to the Falkland Islands via orca. Although he complained that even after several dust baths he wouldn't even be close to removing the fish smell from his plumage, he was in good spirits. Strong spotted the orca in the distance and motioned it toward the wreckage where he was hiding.

Suddenly while talking with both Strong and Astuto, they both burst into view. I was still getting used to the fact that when two members of the triad got together I could see as well as hear. At first, all I could see was the shaggy wolf standing on a plank of wood from behind a set of small white teeth. It took me a second to realize that I was seeing things from the inside of the orca's mouth. Simultaneously I could see the dodo stepping out from the massive whale's mouth. Astuto touched his bulbous beak to the orca's nose, apparently thanking him for the ride. Astuto, knowing Strong had spent the past two weeks scouting out the two miles between the wreckage and the airport, walked over to the wolf and asked about the next phase in the plan.

Strong explained his plan, "In a few hours the sun will set, and we can make our way to a secure location at the far end of town. There aren't many places to hide in this region of the island because the people cut the grass. There are risks of meeting in the only city on the island, but it was also the best places to stow away aboard the flight to Santiago, Chile which will cut our remaining travel time in half."

"So I may get to fly after all," Astuto laughed.

"Twice actually. We can then find a second flight from Santiago to Baltra Airport in the Galapagos near the CDRS. If all goes well George, Astuto and I may be with you in a few short days," Strong calculated.

I wished them luck and told them I'd check in the next day to see if they made the flight. I knew that I had to somehow convince Moana to get on the boat with Stephen before the ship set sail. From what Stephen had told me, I had to convince her within the day.

"Moana? I can only imagine what you are going through right now," I sighed, "I just wanted to tell you that what happened to Benjamin was not your fault. She was trying her best to protect you and Stephen. Benjamin saw the value of saving two for the loss of one. Did you know that Tasmania's seal has thylacines on it? The people there love her and will take good care of Benjamin. She is a national treasure to them. Isn't the whole point of this mission *to help the people see the error of their ways and reset things*? I believe Benjamin is in the perfect position to do just that," I said pausing.

Suddenly I felt a wave of terror come over me and a shiver ran down the length of my shell. I could vaguely see Moana's outline looking down the hill toward what I assumed was the port of Nelson, New Zealand. How could I be *seeing* Moana? Benjamin was on a boat, presumably unconscious headed back toward Tasmania, and there was no way tiny Stephen, the little flightless wren, had the time or ability to travel that far. No. There had to be someone else there with Moana, but who?

"Moana, I think there is someone there with you. Can you see anyone? I think you may be in danger. Something doesn't feel right," I said, losing my composure.

There was still no answer from the massive bird, and all I could see from her point of view was the port of Nelson off in the distance. Judging from the back and forth shaking, Moana seemed to be wrestling with whether to head back or not. She had to know that Stephen's boat would be leaving right after sunset. Didn't she care? I just couldn't get through to her. Something was blocking my ability to communicate with her...or *someone*. Not knowing for sure scared me the most.

That's when I decided to speak to the stranger. "Why are you following my friend around New Zealand? What do you want with her?" I blurted out Astuto-like.

There was a long pause, and I wrestled with what to say. I tried to think positively like Eldey always did, but I had my doubts because of the underlying sense of dread I had by this potential new member of our mission. Maybe another animal like Inca, the Carolina parakeet, who Eldey tried to keep from coming back in the Garden followed us here to help with the mission. Maybe he had found two more animals to secretly join us as a fourth triad? That was a nice thought, but that didn't make any sense. Plus, why would I have this uneasy feeling if someone else was *joining* us? That's when the thought hit me, *what if this was Lusadé?*

At the thought of his name, a voice entered my head, "Have you considered what you're doing? Moana has *all of the information* now and has made a better, more *informed* choice."

"What have you done with her, Lusadé? Why can't she hear me?" I asked, assuming this new voice was more than likely the serpent Eldey had warned me about.

"Oh, she can hear you," the serpent replied, "but she no longer will be swayed by your lies. She knows that she can never repair things between us and the people. It's not for us animals to do. We are not, and will never be *a helper suitable* enough for the people."

I remembered what Eldey and Astuto had said about trying to talk with Lusadé alone, so I broke my communication with him before I could hear what else he had to say. Moana's image faded as Lusadé's communication was broken off, but as her perspective faded I thought I could see a dark figure slithering over the horizon.

Lusadé's statement about my lies echoed in my thoughts. *What if he was right? Should I have listened to him just a little more?* I knew that Eldey and Astuto hadn't told me everything. Was my ignorance bliss or were they simply using information gaps to persuade me? No. I knew I couldn't think like that. They were trying to help me and the people. What could Lusadé do to me since he was obviously in New Zealand, and I was safely 6,000 miles away in the Galapagos? My thoughts quickly returned to the giant moa, who was struggling with something Lusadé had said to her.

"Moana, listen to me, you need to get back to the port now and rejoin Stephen within the hour, or you will be stranded all alone in New Zealand. I don't know what the serpent said to you, but you cannot believe him. Remember that *he* is the one who has been cursed, not you," I pleaded. "Moana, answer me this; why did you run away from the ship and Stephen in the first place?"

"My fault. It was my fault," Moana finally replied. "Benjamin gave her life to protect me because I was scared. Saving people won't fix everything. I know that now."

Now, this was a longer statement than I'd ever heard from the giant moa, but her words were drowning in complete anguish over what had happened. I didn't know how to respond; with compassion like Eldey or bluntly like Astuto? I decided to respond like myself and hope for the best.

"Moana, can I be honest with you? I'm no good at this; being a leader and all. I hated being alone for the past 40 years, but I was so comfortable with it. All this communicating and leading is the hardest thing I've ever done. I'm not wise like Eldey or Astuto. I can only offer to help you along the way the best that I, a simple Pinta Island tortoise, can," I pleaded.

There was another long pause. I knew I still had a lot to do at the CDRS before the triads began arriving. "Moana, listen. I don't know what Lusadé told you, but I do know that if you don't at least try to get on that ship soon, we are down to only eight animals. You are important to this mission Moana. Please consider what I've said. Think of Stephen who needs you and think of Benjamin who sacrificed herself for you. Don't let her freedom be sacrificed for nothing," I said a little more firmly than I intended.

After a responseless pause from the giant moa, I was about to end my communication. I again felt someone pushing into my thoughts. It was a strange feeling to be the one being *called*. Maybe someone from one of the other triads needed me? Maybe I could hear them in their times of need? I still hadn't figured out all of the nuances of my communication abilities.

This presence didn't make me shiver or feel terror like Lusadé seemed to. I knew from Eldey and Astuto's warnings not to talk to Lusadé. Seeing Moana doubt the entire mission so much should have given me more apprehension about talking to another possible stranger, but curiosity killed the *cat* as the people always said, *not* the tortoise. This tortoise was safe here. So to celebrate metaphorically 'killing a cat' for Stephen's sake I responded simply, "Who's there and what do you want?"

There was a pause of reluctance, but then a cautious female voice filled my thoughts, "This is Pat."

"You mean, Pat from Eldey's last mission to try and save the people; as in Bigfoot?" I asked, taken off guard.

"Yes, George, the very same one. I'm sorry that Eldey has tricked you into coming on this foolhardy journey. I wish I would have known his intentions to involve you, so I could have tried sooner to contact you," Pat explained, struggling with a pang of underlying guilt presumably for my very existence.

"Why would you have tried to stop me from trying to reset things with the people? Isn't that what you always wanted too, a Garden-like world alongside the people? Eldey didn't trick me at all. Eldey and Astuto gave me a choice to join or go extinct at my appointed time," I clarified.

"That *is* their trick George, to make you believe you have a choice, and then they manipulate you into risking the safety of the Garden and your very existence for a mission that can't possibly succeed," Pat explained.

"What do you mean it *can't succeed*? If we can get everyone to Pinta Island in the next...," I stopped myself mid-sentence realizing I didn't know anything about Pat or if she was even on our side. I hesitated to try to craft my words more carefully.

Taking my pause as a possible conclusion to our conversation, Pat took the initiative to keep the conversation going, "George you know he will do everything in his power to stop you don't you? Lusadé knows things that Eldey won't tell you. That's why your friend Moana will no longer risk herself for your foolish mission. She knows that if she joins the little wren, more creatures will be hurt, punished, or worse...just like the thylacine."

How could Pat know these things about members of our mission? How did she know what happened to Benjamin when I couldn't even talk with her? My mind began to swim with thoughts of anxiety and dread. Perhaps Pat had more information that I needed to consider. Eldey had been clear not to talk to Lusadé, but he hadn't said anything about Pat.

"You know that Eldey takes complete responsibility for you being trapped here, don't you Pat? He blames himself for not preparing you better for your mission. Eldey hopes that if we can succeed in our mission that you and Nessie can return to the Garden safely *with* us," I said, trying to soothe Pat's distrust of Eldey.

"Eldey has returned to save me?" Pat said rather shocked. "I thought he had forgotten about me."

"Pat, Eldey cares deeply for you. Trust me when I say, he has never forgotten you. He has been desperately looking for a way to rescue you since you fled from the man on the horse that day in the woods. I don't know what the serpent has told you or what you think you know that I don't, but I do know that *you* are a central reason for this whole mission," I reassured her.

"I don't know what to say. Eldey left me here, alone, and Lusadé has at least tried to help keep me safe. He has protected me from the people. And Eldey... he stopped talking to me after forty days of fleeing from the people in the woods. He left me to fend for myself, my very existence when I needed him the most. If Eldey did care about me so much George, why would he leave me all alone?"

"Pat, Eldey didn't have a choice. After forty days of being back here, we lose the ability to speak with others," I explained.

"What?" Pat retorted.

"It's true. That's why it's so important that we get everyone who is a part of this mission to..." I paused to consider what to tell her. I realized that I needed to tell her the truth, "to Pinta Island by day 40. If we don't, I too will lose my ability to talk to you and the others. Eldey didn't *choose* to leave you alone, but he lost the ability to help you which is why he's here risking a third extinction to save you. It's part of the 'rhyme and reason' here Pat. I can't tell you what to believe, but I ask you to carefully consider who *truly* cares about you; Lusadé who has a track record of deception, or Eldey, a friend who returned to get you back to the Garden safely."

Pat seemed to be at a loss for words and didn't respond except to say she needed some time to think about what I had just told her.

I ended our impromptu conversation feeling overwhelmed

by yet another unexplained piece of this puzzle. I had never considered contacting the other 'boomerang' species, but I decided it would be best to keep this, like Lusadé's earlier promptings to myself. This conversation made me wonder if I should contact the other boomerang species who I hadn't talked with yet, Nessie, but I decided against it for now.

Chapter 15:

BALAAM'S TORTOISE

Moana never made it to the ship before it set sail at the end of day 16, so our mission did hang in the balance. Stephen was apprehensive about 'flying solo' on his long journey, but he understood that was his part to play without his massive escort. He had asked me if I thought he should try to go find Moana before the ship set sail, but I said he was already pushing his arrival. Stephen, always the optimistic one, said he was ready for a challenge and would do his best to get to Pinta Island on time.

I made sure to check in daily with Stella as she slowly and steadily moved further south. After my return, she was again in high spirits, and it was nice to talk to someone so upbeat, even though the conversation was veiled in my uncertain confidence. She had a bubbliness about her that helped me take my mind off things.

"George, I'm starving. There's not much seaweed out here in the Open Ocean, but this intermittent fasting is giving me a more streamlined figure. I feel so "fast", after fasting, like a dolphin. You know what I could go for right now?" Stella asked happily.

"An orange fruit from that tree in the Garden?" I asked.

"That would be lovely, but I was thinking of a nice sea cow steak and bread smeared with blubber butter," Stella laughed. "Those sailors always said it was delicious."

"That is so wrong and disturbing Stella. What's wrong with you?" I retorted. "I guess you think I should desire a nice bowl of tortoise soup?"

"Now that's just wrong George. Everyone knows creamy blubber butter far exceeds turtle soup!"

"Thanks for always cheering me up Stella. Take care and see you soon," I said before turning my attention to the next triad.

By day 17, The Northern Triad was also traveling slow and steady, but for different reasons. Eldey said they were all faring very well because Martha could easily slip out and gather food for Boomer and him. Their leg of the journey seemed to be going off without a hitch. It was probably because they had Eldey as their leader. I wished I was on a cruise ship leisurely heading south. But no, I was here.

When I couldn't hold it in any longer I asked, "Eldey, what do I have to do exactly? I'm still not clear. The research station is full of scientists poking and prodding me all day, and I have only seen Fausto a handful of times. There are people with cameras everywhere as well, so I don't know how I'm supposed to accomplish anything."

"George, you are doing great, and being a great auk, I know 'greatness' when I see it. I could not do everything that you have so far," Eldey said, surprising me.

"What do you mean? You are the wisest animal I have ever known, and I feel like I keep making mistakes. It seems the only thing I'm good at is failing. Eldey, we've already lost two animals on our journey because of *me*. If I hadn't fallen off that log trying to be a hero, I could have helped Moana get on that boat and prevented Benjamin from being put in some zoo. Don't you see, this is *my fault*," I said, feeling a tear roll down over my cheek.

That tear caused a big ruckus with the scientists, who made a big deal about it. They said it almost seemed like I was sad and crying. All that did was lead to more testing and prodding. The cameras zoomed in on my face, and I heard the news people saying they thought I was shedding tears of joy after my miraculous Open Ocean rescue. Soon after that, I noticed posters with my tear-filled eyes springing up around the CDRS.

Eldey sighed and in a calmer more soothing tone than I've ever heard stated, "George these things are not your fault in the least. If anyone was to take the blame, it would have to be me."

I didn't understand how Eldey could feel that those two losses could be his fault. I was the one who had failed a majority of the Southern Triad, not him. I could barely stand the pain that resounded in Eldey's voice at times and wanted to end our communication, but I knew I needed Eldey's direction.

Seeming to pick up on this fact as well, he continued, "George, I know you think that I am such a stupendous leader, but I know you will lead us well over the second half of our mission. You must find a way to communicate with Fausto, and do it soon. Indeed, we are down two animals, but we can still complete the mission to 'reset' things between us and the people. It is not over in the least. Even if we lose one other animal, tragic as it would be, our mission still has a chance. I will not let you be stuck here like Nessie or Pat, George. I vow to do everything in my power to set things right between the animals and the people. I vow to keep my promise to keep you safe as well."

Feeling a little more confident I redirected him to my original inquiry, "But Eldey, what do I need to do? I just don't understand. What would you do if you were me?"

After a slight pause, Eldey replied hesitantly but honestly, "I am not exactly sure George."

Well, that was *not* the answer I was expecting or hoping for. Apparently, leading by leaving out details, was something Eldey *did* believe in. I felt my anger begin to rise again because I was risking my life and extinction for nothing. Maybe Pat was right about Eldey after all.

"What do you mean, you don't know!?" I yelled at Eldey in frustration. "Eldey, I almost drowned! I am risking my entire species' existence! For what? I could have just waited in loneliness for another 23 years at the CDRS. But no; I let you talk me into this...this foolhardy endeavor because you can't just let the people slip into a dismal existence that they deserve!" I said, feeling an avalanche of self-pity taking over.

"George, I know that you are upset and understandably so, but I assure you, our efforts here are not in vain. Will resetting things with the people miraculously fix every wrong between us? No. That's not for us to do. We cannot remove the curse, but we can try our best to help them see the error in what they are doing to themselves and species like ours. When I said I was not exactly sure, what I meant was, I do not know everything like you keep assuming. I have just experienced more than you over a much longer period and have spent countless decades trying to find a way to help the people. It cost me, *my family... twice*. I know what it means to sacrifice too, George!" Eldey responded uncharacteristically harshly.

That got my attention. I had never experienced Eldey be anything but compassionate toward the people and to me. I guess I never really thought he felt any resentment toward the people for what happened during both of his extinctions because he never expressed it. All at once, I again felt an uneasiness flood my thoughts. I didn't know who was trying to enter my thoughts, so I pushed them out.

"I'm sorry Eldey. It's been a very difficult few days, and I feel guilty for the loss of Moana and Benjamin. Your Triad is doing so well compared to the others, but I still feel like a total failure," I said grievously.

"George, you do not see that you *are* a failure in some regards. Being a great leader is doing your best *despite* your failures and your circumstances. The responses to those situations are the burden that any good leader has to bear alone. By *that definition*, you are one of the best leaders I know. I have failed many times. Remember I have failed six times so far, and I am sure I will fail again," Eldey stated.

"Six times?" I inquired.

"Yes, once with my mate, then my egg during my return from extinction; once with Nessie, then with Pat, and now with Benjamin and Moana. Those losses are ultimately on me because I believe so wholeheartedly in what we are trying to accomplish, that I convinced creatures like you to join me. I have no power to make you do anything that you do not want to. I can only direct you to the best of my ability, and regardless of what you think, my ability is far from perfect," Eldey confessed.

Seeming to sense a need to return to my original question, Eldey turned back to my current dilemma. "George, I believe that you need to talk with Fausto tonight before he leaves the research station," he said.

"But how do I do that? It's not like I can just walk over to him by the railing of my enclosure and say, "Hey Fausto, why don't you sit down? We need to talk."

"Why not?" the great auk replied with a questioning pause that made me reconsider my sarcastic response.

"You make it sound so easy; like there is a rhyme and reason to everything," I said.

"There *is* a 'rhyme and reason' to everything George as we tried to explain to you earlier. You just have to try to understand what that rhyme or that reason is. No one ever gave me a scroll or a manual about how to return from the Garden to rescue the people. These are things I have figured out over time after studying how things work. I mean, did you ever think that you would venture into the Garden of Eden or find out that many of us were actually *on the Ark* with Noah? I am guessing the answers are no. You see George, we only have to look carefully to see what is truly possible and what is not," Eldey explained.

"Where should I look? I'm back at the Charles Darwin Research Station, in a hopeless situation. I've come full circle," I confessed.

That's when it hit me. I was trying to think about this whole thing in the wrong way. I was looking at my situation too narrowly. It wasn't about a Pinta Island Tortoise swimming across the Pacific Ocean or about an old tortoise who needed to jump the fence and type up some sort of note to Fausto. I needed to take a step back and *look for the rhyme and reason; what was possible and what was not.*

"That is exactly right George," Eldey burst in, "You asked me how I know so much, it is because I have learned to look for hope in times of hopelessness. It is not all about you, and it is not all about me. It is about so much more than either of us George. Do I know exactly what you need to do? No. But I do know that it is possible for an animal to talk *with* a person."

"But how do you know that? That's what I'm still missing," I said, eager to understand this crucial piece of information.

"Well George, there are two times that I know of where an animal actually did talk to the people. The first was the serpent's speech in the Original Garden...," Eldey stated.

I interjected, "But in the Garden, animals can hear one another's thoughts and talk. I don't think it works that way here."

"Are you sure?" Eldey asked again, making me doubt my logical answer.

"Well, when you ask like that, I guess my answer should be *no*," I replied hesitantly.

"Have you ever heard of Balaam's Donkey, George?" Eldey asked.

"Can't say that I have," was my only reply.

"Well George, besides the serpent talking with the woman in the Garden, there is another lesser known story about a person long ago, named Balaam who was hired by an evil king to bring a curse upon a blessed group of people. Balaam knew that he could not curse someone or something that was blessed, and he could not bless something that was cursed. That is part of the 'rhyme or reason', I spoke of earlier," Eldey explained.

"But how does that relate to a talking donkey?" I interrupted.

Eldey, back to his composed self, didn't acknowledge my rude interjection.

"All I know from that story is that Balaam's donkey spoke to Balaam and saved the man's life. So, George, I am hoping that when the time is right you too can speak to Fausto, as the donkey did to Balaam. You have to help open Fausto's eyes to what is happening around him so that he can help us," Eldey said.

"But how is Fausto supposed to help us? That's what I don't

understand," I stated honestly.

"George, I know you will know when the time is right, but that is a question I cannot answer. All I do know is that a speaking animal is possible, and we need the people to be involved in our mission in some way," Eldey admitted. "Noah was asked to build a gigantic boat. Maybe you can have Fausto build some kind of boat or house for all of us all once we arrive to Pinta Island"

"Build a house? Really?" I laughed. "Maybe I'll ask Fausto to build us a little lighthouse for us on Pinta Island... for Stephen."

Eldey echoed my laughter because he knew how his suggestion had sounded. He wrapped things up by saying, "The biggest part of all of this is *faith*, George. You have to have faith, as do the people. If we lose hope and faith in what we are doing, the future will truly be lost. That is why Lusadé is so dangerous. He has a knack for twisting the truth to make things seem to be something they are not. He feeds on fear and chaos, which cannot coexist with hope and faith."

I mulled over what Eldey had said, but so many things just didn't make sense to me. I decided to check in quickly with Astuto and Strong to see how things were going. They were still hiding out in the wreckage of a ship just off the coast of Stanley in the Falkland Islands. Strong peeked his head out of the wreckage to show me the town. They were on what appeared to be some sort of cargo ship which was half-sunken off the nearest pier. There was an old dock of some kind jutting off to the left with three support braces standing above the water. Strong swung his head to the left and walked me through his plan.

Strong explained, "I will swim Astuto to the earthen pier over there past the large orange building. Then we'll have to stealthily cross the street and hide behind the large stone wall in front of Christ Church Cathedral."

I remembered the cathedral from Strong's earlier orca directions. I thought I could even see the whalebone arch he had mentioned. I listened but was amazed at how deeply he thought through things. My daily plan was to walk to the waterhole. Walk to food. Take a nap. Strong's type of planning was so specific and thought out, but for some reason he respected my input as leader of this operation.

He asked, "Do you think it is wiser to hide deeper into the town of Stanley or hug the less populated coast?"

I tried to confidently say farther from the town, and Strong thanked me for my input; saying that's what he had been thinking too.

Strong said he planned to wait in the wreckage until nightfall and head toward the airport. He emphasized that if they missed this flight, they'd have to wait for another week in the wreckage. There were no other flights. In theory, they'd still be here with me in plenty of time. I wished them luck and thanked Strong for all of his reconnaissance. I told him to watch out for Astuto who wasn't too thrilled with the chilly Falkland Island weather.

Now that I had done my daily check-ins with the team, I realized that I had intentionally been putting off the very thing I had to do; *talk to Fausto*. Even thinking about it emphasized the ridiculousness of the idea. Eldey had said that it would take hope and faith to accomplish our mission, so I tried to muster up either. I looked across my enclosure and saw Fausto sitting amongst the other scientists obviously discussing me and my apparent emotional outburst of tears earlier. Not only was I now deemed a Lazarus species, but I could demonstrate some human emotions, or so I had heard them say earlier.

I waited for the sun to begin setting and watched as the scientists and guests to the CDRS dispersed. I hoped that Fausto would stop in to see me before he went home for the night. Right when I was sure that he had forgotten me, I saw him jump the fence with a plate of food and slowly walk toward me.

"Hello there big guy," he said in his usual reassuring voice. "I'm not sure quite what to call you yet, other than a miracle. I don't think you have any idea how special you are, my friend. I just wish you could have been here a few weeks ago to meet George before he… before he passed away," Fausto said remorsefully. "He wasn't even that old as far as tortoises go, but I believe he died of a broken heart. I hope wherever you came from, we can help you be happy here at the CDRS."

I raised my head toward Fausto who took a slight step back, probably not sure if I would snap at him or not. Just as I was thinking Fausto didn't recognize me he remarked, "You know; you look so much like George, not just because you're a Pintie, but because you look like George's twin. It's amazing! But I don't know what to call you. I can't just call you George, because George was the name of my dear friend. I hope that someday you will be my friend too," Fausto said slowly lifting his hand toward my outstretched head.

I wished that it was as easy as Eldey had said; just strike up a conversation with Fausto. But how to begin?

"Would you like me to play you a few songs? They say that music soothes the savage beast. Now a nice-looking tortoise-like yourself isn't that savage or much of a beast, but I'd like to believe George liked my guitar playing. I guess I'll never know whether he did or not," Fausto said, "Maybe if you're a good tortoise, I'll read you a story tonight," Fausto said, walking over to get his dingy, yellow guitar.

"Can you read me the story of Balaam tonight?" I unintentionally burst out as soon as he sat down to begin tuning his guitar. Fausto's response was priceless. He dropped his guitar, jumped up, and looked around completely caught off guard.

"Who's there?" Fausto shouted. He must have thought someone had broken into the research station. He hopped the fence quickly, looking around. Then he cocked his head and looked right at me with a puzzled, yet intrigued look.

"Did you hear that Miracle?" he said looking right at me.

Did Fausto just name me Miracle? That name was way too cutesy for me, and I figured I should answer the man before he had a heart attack.

"I'd prefer if you just called me George if you don't mind," I said looking right back at him.

Fausto seemed surprisingly unphased that a tortoise was

speaking to him. All he said in response to my request to be called *George* was to repeat what he said earlier; that he couldn't call me George because that honor belonged to a dearly departed friend. Fausto simply sat back down and finished tuning his guitar. There had to be a million questions swimming around in his head like; *How is this possible? Maybe this talking tortoise will make me famous? What should I say back to this amazing creature? Maybe we can sing a duet together?* Nope. Nothing.

Fausto simply raised one finger to tell me to wait and walked back to the research building. He came back with the book he often read to me in his hand, and simply opened a third of the way through the book and began reading the story of Balaam to me.

I desperately wanted to understand the 'rhyme and reason' within this story that gave Eldey such faith. The story unfolded with the prophet, Balaam, on his way to visit some evil king when an angel appeared in the road. That part echoed what Eldey had described to me earlier. For some reason I couldn't understand, Balaam couldn't see the angel, but the donkey could. The donkey lay down in the road, to avoid the angel, but Balaam lashed out at his donkey three times.

The donkey opened her mouth and replied to Balaam, "What have I done to you that you have struck me these three times?"

I did take note that the donkey was struck *three* times, which was one of those important numbers. Balaam threatened to kill the donkey. So typical of the people I thought to myself, but I continued listening carefully to every detail.

But the donkey pleaded, "Am I not your donkey, on which you have ridden all your life long to this day? Is it my habit to treat you this way?"

At that point in the story, Balaam's eyes were opened, and he saw the angel wit the flaming sword, waiting to destroy him. Balaam then went and did what he was sent to do.

After reading the story, Fausto simply looked at me, kissed the top of my head, and said he'd see me in the morning. It was as if after listening to the story of Balaam's donkey, and realizing we had just spoken had left us both speechless. I began to think about what I would say to Fausto tomorrow when he came back. What if tonight's conversation was the only time I could speak with him? The 'rhyme and reason' of the story seemed to explain that Balaam's donkey never spoke again. That fact didn't seem encouraging.

I knew sleep would be hard to come by that night, so I checked in with Stella who could only laugh at my lack of confidence after having just spoken to a person.

"Only you, George, could have such doubt after literally talking, with words, to Fausto in your enclosure," Stella mocked. "I mean, I would have loved talking to Dr. Steller and telling him to sketch my good side before he ate me."

"As always, you have a knack for words when being eaten. Maybe you should see a doctor," I joked back.

"I did. And then he ate us all," she replied.

"You have issues Stella, so many issues," I responded.

"That is probably true, but it seems you have solved one of your biggest issues, because you just did the impossible and talked with your human friend," she stated.

I knew she was right. I remembered then what Eldey had said about fear blocking out faith and hope. I knew I could either be hung up on myself and all my shortcomings or focus on the fact that things were moving forward despite myself.

"Well, I won't be telling Fausto how nice I'd taste with some salt and pepper, but I will be thinking about what I *can* do next. Thanks as always for cheering me up," I said.

Chapter 16:

BUILDING MY LIGHTHOUSE

Sometime in the middle of the night, I realized that although I had checked in with Stella to see how her journey south was going, I never checked back in with Astuto and Strong to see if they had made it to the airport.

I contacted the two of them early in the morning. All at once, I could see that the weather had drastically gone downhill since we last spoke. A large storm was coming through, dropping a mixture of sleet and snow on the two creatures. Astuto didn't look too happy and was struggling with the cold climate and with traveling in the dark.

I noticed that Astuto was traveling directly behind Strong; beak clamped on the wolf's tail. In this way, they were traveling back from the airport. They were in what appeared to be a cemetery of some kind running through the icy rain back toward the public jetty to where their boat wreckage hideout was located. They'd have to wait there for another week until the next flight was to take place. If there was bad weather again next week two-thirds of the southern triad might not make it to Pinta Island by day 40 either. I pushed that thought to the back of my mind. *Maybe they could find another whale escort or something if they missed their flight,* I thought to myself trying to maintain a positive outlook on the situation.

Strong said that they could have taken *Snake Street* instead of cutting straight through the 1982 Memorial Wood and the cemetery, but that seemed to be too ominous given the possibility of Lusadé appearing. He also clued me into the fact that there were still several minefields that were a danger leftover from a prior war between two warring countries on the Falkland Islands. Thankfully he could sniff them out and avoid them. Strong explained this was another reason why the usually proud, do-it-myself Astuto, had agreed to hold onto the wolf's tail as they traveled.

As they continued running, I noticed a colorful glow lighting the sides of what Strong referred to as Ross Road. I took in the beauty of the city covered in icy snow; grateful for the tropical weather that existed in the Galapagos. As a tortoise, I feared freezing to death as much as drowning. As we were conversing a bright light illuminated the distance like a fire. Like a moth to that flame, Strong and Astuto headed straight toward the light, shadows bouncing off the short fences that lined the street. As they approached the cathedral, everything was shrouded in a veil of orange glow emanating from the courtyard where a large arch stood.

"The Falkland Islands used to be an important center for whalers. The four posts of that glowing arch are four whale rib bones," Strong explained.

I knew that whalers had discovered many of the islands in their pursuit of whales long ago. Many species, like my own, were affected by them long ago, and this monument showed that they had left their mark in the Falkland Islands as well.

I watched as Strong and Astuto walked along the hedgerow, still taking in the intense glow from the underside of the whalebone arch. They walked up to a wooden fence, glancing up and down Ross Road before heading back to the red and orange storage shed.

At this point I told them to be safe and that I'd check in every day or so to see how things were going. I reminded them to stay together because I had no idea where Lusadé may be lurking. I didn't mention the fact that I had spoken with the serpent several days ago, but still in the fiery orange glow of the cathedral, I couldn't help wondering what Lusadé was up to? I figured, being a reptile, he'd have to stick to the more tropical regions for an ambush which is why he started with Moana in New Zealand.

Before I allowed Lusadé to enter my thoughts, I turned my attention to what I needed to do today. Once Fausto returned, I needed to have him do something. I still had no idea what that something would be, but maybe he would know. Maybe he would never come back. Maybe he would refuse to help me. No, if I knew Fausto he would come back today, bright and early, and ask a bunch of questions.

To my surprise, Fausto didn't show up the first or second day after I had spoken to him. I was beginning to worry that he wasn't going to show up at all. I contemplated trying to talk to someone else like Edwin, the director of the research station. I didn't have a lot of time and every moment put me closer to day 40, but I decided to be patient and wait.

Finally on the third day; day 21, as the research station was closing, Fausto came over to my enclosure, placed his index finger to his lips. Then he walked over and discussed something with a few lingering scientists, shaking their hands as they left for the night. A small news crew walked over next to my enclosure and filmed a short interview with Fausto, wherein he explained that "the blood samples did prove that I was a Pinta Island tortoise." He stated that this was, in fact, an exciting finding. He was again hopeful that there may still be a female Pintie out there somewhere and that the CDRS would be resuming their search for a mate for me.

Fausto shook the hands of the film crew and walked them to the CDRS exit, locked up for the night, and came over to my enclosure with a wooden crate. I wondered what I should say or if I could still say anything. Eldey's 'rhyme and reason' speech was ringing in my mind; what if like Balaam's donkey I could only speak once or if I was also limited to just three sentences? I had already used up two of those possible sentences *three* days ago. There were so many things to consider. This next sentence might be my last. Maybe I was overthinking things? Maybe I was under-thinking things?

Fausto came into my enclosure, flipped over the wooden crate, and sat down next to me. He placed a hand on my shell and kissed my head. All he did was look at me and then showed me the book in his hand.

"What story would you like to hear tonight, Miracle?" he said, smirking at me.

Now I didn't want my possibly last sentence to be, "Call me George," so I blurted out, "My nine friends and I need your helping building a lighthouse on Pinta Island in the next 19 days to save the world's people and animals and please call me *George* again, not Miracle."

I knew that the last sentence was a long one, but I wanted to make sure I got everything out that needed to be said. Then came the real test; I tried to speak again. But to my great disappointment, nothing came out but a hiss. So the rhyme and reason thing held water. I was glad that I had listened to the story of Balaam carefully and hadn't said more the first night we spoke.

I felt a wave of fear come over me. Had I failed? I tried again to speak once more, but nothing came out except for a slight hiss. Fausto seemed to be able to sense my frustration and said what I had feared.

"George, my friend, I think your ability to communicate with me, as miraculous as it was, has been lost. I was thinking about the story you had me read the other day, and I must say that I didn't know what to make of things. I'm sorry I kept you waiting, but I needed to do some soul searching. I mean, *you* asked *me* to read a story about a talking animal, while you, an animal, were talking to me. It was a lot to take in at first," Fausto laughed.

All I could do was look at Fausto and nod my head.

"Wait. Can you still understand me, George?" Fausto asked.

I realized I could still understand him, and he could tell my response to his questions. Was there still a way for me to communicate with him without actually talking? Fausto looked at me curiously. I could tell he was also trying to make sense of our new communication glitch.

"Let's try something," Fausto said, looking into my eyes. "I will ask you a few questions, and you nod your head for *yes* and shake your head back and forth for *no*."

I think Fausto realized how ridiculous his basic instructions sounded to me; an animal who had just spoken to him.

"You said I need to make a lighthouse on Pinta Island in the next 19 days to save the world," he stated as more of a question.

All I could do was nod my head. I just wished he would ask one question at a time. That's when I had a communication thought of my own. I knew I couldn't talk with Fausto directly, but what if I could write him notes in the sand? After all, I had been mapping the three triads' movements on a map I drew in the sand before my infamous 'swimming lesson'.

"Okay, George. We are going to need to take this one step at a time," Fausto said to me.

I nodded to him again and looked around to find a twig. I took a few steps toward the closest shrub and picked up a small branch in my mouth. I slowly spelled out the words in the smooth dirt, "Slo n steady wins the rays, rit?" I looked up at Fausto expecting to see astonishment that a tortoise was writing in the sand.

He simply looked at my writing and rewrote my message under my original. "I see we need to work on your spelling George, but I appreciate your sense of humor. And to think, people always thought you were just a tortoise," Fausto said, smiling at me.

I realized my spelling would slow down our process a, so I drew Eldey's original map of the three triads' trek for Fausto to see. I knew I couldn't explain everything to him in detail, but I was hoping that he might understand the basic idea of the plan. I drew the creatures involved in the mission the best that I could. Even though I was a talking, swimming, heroic tortoise, my artistic skills were definitely lacking.

Fausto could pick out the dodo bird, thylacine, and great auk right away. He thought the Steller's sea cow was a large Caribbean monk seal, but it was in the Pacific not the Atlantic. He got the idea. I looked up at him waiting to see how he was processing everything scribbled in the dirt before him.

"Let me see if I got this straight. You are working with nine other animals all over the world to save it?" he inquired.

I nodded my head. Maybe this wouldn't take as long as I thought.

"These dotted lines show the path each animal must take," he said, studying my masterpiece carefully, "and you are all trying to get to your homelands to build ten lighthouses?"

I shook my head and placed my clawed foot to my head. I realized that I needed to be patient with Fausto because without him I knew our plan couldn't reach fruition.

"Okay, let's try this again. So these animals are not headed to their homelands," he said, scratching his chin.

I carefully drew directional arrows pointing each creature's path toward *Pinta Island.*

That shed light on the plan for Fausto because he replied excitedly, "Oh I see. All of these nine animals are starting there and heading... heading here?"

I nodded, writing, "And...?" in the dirt trying to keep Fausto thinking.

"And they are meeting you on Pinta Island for some reason to see the lighthouse you want me to build?" Fausto concluded.

I realized that this wasn't a perfect translation of what I was trying to communicate, but it was close enough for now, so I simply nodded and smiled (well smiled on the inside).

"Wait! I think there's more to this plan. There must be something special about these animals with whom you are working. Let's see, you have a dodo bird here, meeting with a dog here to the east of what looks like South America. Wait! Wait! I think I'm beginning to understand this part. Wait here, George. I will be right back," Fausto said, skipping off toward the research station.

I didn't have much of a choice about waiting there, since I was in my enclosure. If I could just leap over the fence like Fausto, I would have done so years ago I thought to myself. I would just wait there because we tortoises love just waiting around. Fausto came back carrying a large rolled-up paper and his laptop.

"Okay, let's see. We both know a lot of these animals since you've been the rarest animal on the planet for so long. The dodo bird is here on Mauritius," he said circling the island, "... the thylacine is here in Tasmania below Australia and the dog..." he said, running his finger down the east coast of South America until he came to the Falkland Islands. "Okay that would make this a Falkland Island wolf?" he said looking at me for assurance.

I nodded my head and drew a smiley face in the dirt with my foot for fun. I knew that the people loved their smiley faces from all of the shirts I had seen over the years at the CDRS.

"George. Are you saying that you are working with nine other *extinct animals*?" Fausto asked.

I again nodded, pointing my foot toward the "and...?" already drawn in the sand.

He was able to figure out that the great auk, passenger pigeon, and heath hen were traveling across North America and that the thylacine, giant moa, and with some added prodding and patience, the Stephens Island wren were making their way to Pinta Island.

Although he finally figured out that the seal near Alaska was a Steller's sea cow, he didn't understand how it fits in with the dodo bird and Falkland Island wolf which weren't even close geographically. As always Fausto seemed content to carry on with what he could figure out instead of worrying over those things couldn't. I could see he had a lot more faith than me.

I added a smiley face on Pinta Island next to a 'self-portrait' of me. I added the number *40*. It wasn't too bad if I do say so myself, but in all honesty, tortoises are a little easier to sketch than a lot of my colleagues. Next to the smiley face, I doodled a frowny face and the number 41.

"So what you're saying is that if we don't finish building our lighthouse on Pinta Island by day 40, something bad will happen?" Fausto asked.

I nodded slowly. Failure did seem like a definite possibility now that our time was half of what it was when I started. It hadn't been working out as I had planned, and I again thought about Moana and Benjamin lost from our mission. I could feel that ever-present regret setting in, but thankfully Fausto cut in before it overtook me.

"Well George, if bad things happen on day 41, let's get this light-house built and get your friends here as soon as possible. We better get started," Fausto said, preparing himself for the next 19 days.

Fausto told me that he was going to copy my sketches onto his world map so that he could remember everything we had talked about. He put the number 21 on the top of the map and put the number 41 there also with a frowny face.

"That's to make sure we don't get too close to that day. We can do this George! I'm going to go get some supplies and figure out how to get this lighthouse made. You stay here and do whatever it is that you need to do. I will try to check in every day to let you know how things are going," Fausto said, kissing me on the nose before leaping the enclosure fence for the night.

That could have gone better, but it could have gone worse too. I had somehow communicated the plan to Fausto without words. Feeling a little more optimistic, I decided to check in with Stella one more time before heading to sleep for the night. She seemed in high spirits and had made good progress over the Open Ocean. She had been using her long swim to construct a comedy routine.

"George, you want to hear a few jokes I've been working on?" Stella asked.

"Do they involve how good you taste on bread because I still think that's disturbing?" I stated.

"No. No. Nothing like that, even though we Steller's sea cows do taste delicious. Here goes the first joke. Ready? What's black and white and only knows the first three letters of the alphabet?"

"I'm not sure. An illiterate zebra?" I guessed.

"No. You get an *a-b-'C cow'*!" she laughed.

"That has got to be one of the worst jokes ever. I'll still go with the illiterate zebra." I replied.

"Okay. One more. One more. What do you call a sea turtle cov-ered in cement?" she asked.

"An a-b-Cement turtle?" I asked.

"No. It's you! Get it? Because you sink like a rock," Stella laughed.

Between Stella's disturbing sense of humor and Fausto's

optimism, I had no choice but to feel a little more hopeful myself.

Chapter 17:

SLOW AND STEADY PROGRESS

I never thought this mission would be easy, but I never dreamed that I'd be sitting here exactly where I was just 23 days ago, alone with these two female tortoises back in the same enclosure at the CDRS. I didn't know if I'd be able to communicate with Fausto today or even over the next several days. I was confident that he would do everything in his power to construct some sort of lighthouse on Pinta Island. Honestly, I didn't even know why I had blurted that out. A lighthouse was a far cry from anything like an ark, and I wasn't even sure whether seven of us would make it to Pinta Island in time to do whatever it was we had to do.

I checked in with the team and not much had changed. The Northern Triad was still en route, but their cruise ship was still broken down somewhere off the coast of Mexico. Eldey said he had heard some people saying things would be moving again soon. From what Eldey had said many passengers on the cruise ship had been enraged due to the ship breaking down and had requested a refund. Many people wanted to leave the ship, making it a dangerous time for the birds. People were constantly getting luggage and supplies out of the storage area where Eldey, Boomer, and Martha were hiding.

Stella was still in good spirits and by her calculations, she would be on Pinta Island by day 29. She had even asked whether I thought she should try to find the broken cruise ship and pick up the Northern Triad.

"I don't think it will be very easy to hide a thirty-foot sea cow with two birds surfing on its back," I joked.

Stella laughed out loud and replied, "It would only have to be one 'surfer', Boomer. Eldey could technically swim himself to Pinta Island and Martha could easily make the flight. Being a partridge, Boomer is the only 'distancely challenged' of the three."

"That is true, but I still think you should meet me on Pinta Island. If need be, we can always have Eldey and Martha make the trip solo and have Boomer take the next ship or orca available. I know they are trying to stick together right now, and once they get moving they should be here in 4 days or so," I said.

"Orca? Do you mean *killer* whales? I don't see how those guys can be of any help to us," Stella stated with a mixture of horror and apprehension in her voice.

"Well one helped Astuto cross 6,000 miles of Open Ocean in record time, so I think they're safe," I blurted out.

A wave of guilt hit me as I realized I had accidentally broken my promise to keep Astuto's whale escort a secret.

"A killer whale helped Astuto across the ocean?! Well, I know orcas are bad news to us Steller's sea cows, and I hope to *not* see any on my trip to you," she said.

Stella still didn't like the idea, but returned the conversation to the trip at hand, "Okay then I'll keep connecting with my inner tortoise. Slow and steady wins the race, and I'm sure glad about that because we, Steller's sea cows, are not fast at all," Stella said chuckling. "Talk to you later tonight before bed then?"

"Yep. As always. If you don't hear from me you can assume I went for another swim," I said, returning her hearty laughter.

Astuto and Strong were still keeping a low profile on the wreckage off the shore from Stanley. The next flight to leave would be in three more days barring any additional bad weather. Strong was very mission-oriented, and Astuto was not happy at all. He said he was freezing his tail feathers off, and would never again leave tropical Mauritius if he ever got back there.

Next, I wanted to check in with the Southern Triad, knowing that only Stephen was still part of this mission. Stephen was somewhere aboard a cargo ship in the Pacific Ocean. He was chipper as usual. He joked about being the easiest animal to remain hidden because he fit in just about every nook and cranny. It was the first time in his life he was glad to be so small.

I retorted, "I'm actually the easiest one to hide because everyone can see me, but they didn't realize it was *me*; well, except for Fausto of course."

"That is true. I'll just keep playing hide and seek with myself until I arrive on Pinta Island," he said.

I had been trying for quite some time to get in touch with Benjamin, but I hadn't heard from her since she had been captured and taken back to Tasmania. I decided to try again because I didn't want her to feel like I had forgotten about her. Benjamin was constantly on my mind because she was interacting directly with people against her will. I wondered how she was faring.

"Benjamin, I was just wondering if you were doing okay at the Hobart Zoo? I haven't heard from you in a while and ..." I started, not expecting a reply.

"George. It is great to hear from you," Benjamin interjected happily.

"But... I...," I stammered.

"What? You thought I had gone extinct again and that the people had done something bad to me?" Benjamin mocked. "You know me. They can't keep a good tiger down, at least not a Tasmanian one."

"I'm sorry for stammering. I just didn't expect to hear from you since you've been out of contact for so long. I wasn't sure what to think happened. Stephen and Moana said you had been captured and that was the last I heard from you," I explained.

"Speaking of my team, when are they expected to arrive with you on Pinta Island? I hope I gave them enough time to get somewhere safe with my little diversion back in New Zealand. I mean Moana is enormous you know," she said laughing.

I was still taken aback that Benjamin was in such good spirits. Maybe she had been released back into the wild or found some other way to escape. Benjamin seemed as confident as ever, so I figured I should just ask what had happened to her.

"Moana *is* a whopper of a bird," I stated, wondering if I should tell Benjamin about Moana's disappearance. After considering the options I began, "Stephen should arrive here on day 36 last I heard, which should give us plenty of time to get things around." I hesitated, "Moana on the other hand...she won't be making the trip."

"What? Did something happen to her? Was she captured like me or is it something worse? You can tell me, George," Benjamin prodded with a hint of worry in her voice.

"She is fine as far as I know, but she ran away into the New Zealand hills after you were captured. She blamed herself for getting you captured. Moana just kept blaming herself, and..." I hesitated.

"And...?" Benjamin prodded.

"And I think Lusadé got to her somehow. Moana kept saying that *she knew the truth and things had been explained to her*. I'm not sure what happened exactly, but she hasn't spoken to me in days," I explained.

"I see. And how are you doing with everything George?" she asked.

I had been so worried about caring for others and not thinking about myself, that I didn't know how to respond.

My pause allowed Benjamin to continue, "I know Eldey had warned us not to be alone too long because Lusadé would pick us off one by one. Speaking of which, you've been alone most of this mission. Lusadé hasn't gotten to you has he?"

This question caught me off guard, and I didn't want to say he had tried to sway me several times. I thought I was fine and didn't want to get into all of that, so I skirted the question stating, "No, not at all. Now tell me, what happened to you and why are you so optimistic?"

Benjamin explained what happened during her capture but most of it was a blur. She thought she must have been tranquilized or something before she was taken back to Tasmania.

"I'm staying in an enclosure the people are building for Tasmanian devils. The enclosures here are so much nicer than those back in my zoo in 1936," Benjamin explained.

"It's nice to hear they've improved the Hobart Zoo since then. You know I was in my twenties while you were there," I quickly calculated.

"Actually, the Hobart Zoo was closed the year after my extinction due to financial reasons. That probably explains why the last thylacines were so neglected in our last days. I am staying at the Tasmanian Zoo in the city of Launceston. There is plenty of space to roam and each enclosure is lined with pristine white or green fences. It's so beautiful here and there are no cages. Even the food is carefully prepared for us each day," Benjamin explained.

"Being a tortoise, I've never been kept in a cage, but a short wall makes escaping impossible," I stated.

"I have no desire to escape. I've been given celebrity status throughout Tasmania the day I was captured, and the world as a whole seems to be taking notice. People are lining up outside my enclosure from the zoo's opening until well after closing every day to see *me*! I have officially been deemed a Lazarus species, George. It's been amazing," Benjamin declared.

I wondered what would happen next for Benjamin since she was the very last thylacine in Tasmania. Would she simply die of old age and go extinct again? I didn't want to ask her about her opinion on that and squelch her excitement.

"You have no idea how genuinely grateful the people of Tasmania are to see me. I had no idea what it would be like myself. My face is all over posters, shirts, and hats. They feed me gourmet food every day, and it makes me wish I had come back sooner as a Lazarus species. I always feared being neglected and abused back into extinction, but this; this is more than I could have dreamed of George. Is this what zoo life has been like for you?" Benjamin asked giddily, assuming I shared her positive outlook on my enclosure.

"Well, I guess I did...I mean do have celebrity status here at the research station, but it's always been a position I've hated. I guess I never really looked at the positive side of things here. I've never been neglected. I *am* famous, and my name has been on shirts, hats, and posters for years. I guess I've always been so focused on going extinct and self-pity that I never took the time to think of everything the people have been trying to do for me. I mean they had been searching the world for me to find a girlfriend and offering money for her. Yeah, I guess it hasn't been that bad here now that I think of it," I reflected.

"I'm enjoying life right now George. I'm not sure what the future holds for us after the mission is over, but I wish we could just stay here forever," the thylacine said dreamily.

"I'm glad that things are going so well for you, and I'll be sure to pass the good news on to the team. I'll be sure to let Stephen and Moana know you're in good spirits about being captured," I said, closing out the conversation.

"George, I have renewed confidence in the people, and I wish you and the rest of the team the best of luck. One last thing before you go; be sure to let that stubborn moa know, that I'm *happy* I was captured. It is truly a blessing. Who knows, it might benefit the team in the long run. Tell Moana I said to stop wallowing in self-pity and get on the next ship to Pinta Island. Tell her not to make me come over to New Zealand and drag her sorry self there myself," Benjamin scolded sarcastically.

I told her that I'd pass along the message as soon as we ended our conversation. Benjamin told me that she wouldn't feel upset if she didn't hear from me in a while. She understood that she was no longer directly a part of the mission, but she'd do her best to motivate the people of Tasmania to help us.

I was apprehensive in contacting Moana, partially because I was mad at her refusal to follow my orders as the leader, and selfishly I didn't feel like dealing with someone that didn't matter because she was no longer a part of our mission, but I realized that I needed to contact her and at least keep my promise to Benjamin to relay her message to Moana.

"Moana, I just wanted to give you an update from Benjamin," I said half-heartedly. I could feel Moana's presence, but I didn't expect much of a conversation from her. Even when she was 'talkative' she barely spoke at all.

"How is she?" Moana's voice chimed in.

"Benjamin wanted to relay that she is happy that she was captured," I said, trying to predict the moa's response.

"Happy... that she was caught?" Moana stuttered.

"Yes, you see the people of Tasmania are treating her like a national hero of sorts. They have a pristine enclosure that serves three filling meals a day. Benjamin said she couldn't be happier," I explained.

"Really?" Moana retorted. "Are you telling me the truth?"

I was half insulted by her lack of trust, especially because I was so honest with her during our last conversation about my inadequacies as a leader.

"Yes, I'm being honest. She said that several of the people at the zoo right now were wearing t-shirts with her picture on them. The people of Tasmania love her!" I exclaimed.

"I... I don't know what to say, George. I have been too upset to do anything since we last spoke. I'm ashamed of myself. I have failed you and everyone," she stated solemnly.

"You didn't fail everyone Moana. Benjamin wanted to thank you for making her famous again. She also wanted to relay to you that you'd better get your monstrous backside onto a boat and head to Pinta Island soon, or Benjamin would come to New Zealand personally and drag you here," I said.

I waited for her reply to this order from her former teammate. Benjamin had been the brains and the strength of the Southern Triad. I knew Moana was a bird of few words and relied on others like Benjamin or Stephen to guide her. If only her confidence was half as big as her body.

"Okay. I will do it," Moana replied.

This took me off guard, because it was so straight forward.

"Do what?" I asked.

"I will take the next boat to Tasmania. I can't make it to you in time, but I can be famous like Benjamin. I can be on a shirt too. The zoo sounds fun," Moana said.

This was an odd development because it didn't help our mission at all. Moana was too far away to make it here in time, but still, she was willing to get on a ship again, braving the claustrophobic cargo hold, to go to Tasmania Zoo with Benjamin.

I had to wonder how the people of Tasmania would react to a twelve-foot bird *from New Zealand* showing up there, 500 years after it went extinct on a totally different island. I imagined the Guiness Book of World Records people deeming her the 'world's largest emu'. The people would have to wonder what in the world was going on; with two extinct species showing up in the same short period; a Tasmanian tiger being captured in New Zealand and a giant moa being captured in Tasmania. I guessed the resurrection of the Pinta Island tortoise wasn't going to be the biggest news story after all.

"I want your help. I want to believe, but it's hard because of what the serpent told me," Moana said hesitantly, but honestly.

I wanted to ask her what Lusadé had told her exactly, but I thought there might be a danger in knowing too much. It seemed better to *not* know all of the details.

I simply replied, "Moana, of course, I will help you. I never gave up on you, and I was just hoping that you wouldn't give up on you either."

"Thank you, George. Thanks for not giving up on me," Moana stated.

Not much happened over the next few days. The Northern Triad was still stranded on a broken cruise ship. Stephen was making slow and steady progress toward Pinta Island, and Moana was still trying to figure out which cargo ship was heading toward Tasmania. For obvious reasons, she was unable to sneak around the port as easily as Stephen or Benjamin had been able to.

I was excited that Stella would be here in about four days, so I wouldn't be so alone here in my enclosure. Fausto visited me once, smiling from ear-to-ear, and giving me two thumbs up. I simply nodded to him as he gathered some supplies and a can of what appeared to be green paint.

Strong and Astuto had spent the last week hunkered down in the wreckage off the coast of Stanley awaiting the next plane's departure from the small airport there. Strong said that he had checked the weather report posted outside the airport and the skies were supposed to be clear for the next several days. The sleet hadn't been an issue for them lately. Astuto had said it was the shortened days of the southern winter that were starting to get to him.

Just the thought of the sun only being up for five hours a day and of snow was hard for a tortoise-like myself to fathom. I had seen pictures of snow of course, but being an equatorial tortoise I didn't know what that was truly like. Maybe I'd have to hibernate or something. I had heard that other tortoises around the world had to do that at times, and a four-month nap didn't seem all that bad.

"So how has the old bird been doing the past week, Strong?" I asked, knowing the answer.

Always a creature of positivity and planning, Strong replied, "Astuto is doing very well. This isn't an easy place to survive at times. I mean when the people first arrived on the Falkland Islands, we wolves greeted them with all skin and bones. During the winter months like these, food has always been hard to come by."

"What have you been eating if there's not much to eat?" I asked.

"Thankfully times aren't quite as tough as they were back in the day. The people here tend to throw out quite a bit of food. I didn't know dodos were able to eat such a varied diet, but Astuto has graciously tried everything I've brought back to him in the wreckage except for some chicken."

"I told him that eating chicken seemed a little too cannibalistic for me," Astuto explained, smirking. "You know it's not so bad here, and I am appreciative of Strong's hospitality."

It was at this time that I realized Astuto was wrapped up in several sweaters, socks, and what appeared to be some sort of reddish-orange coat.

"Astuto, I never knew you were so fashionable. If I didn't know any better, I'd almost confuse you with the people," I joked.

This prompted an uncharacteristic laugh from Strong and

Astuto.

Strong again covered for Astuto, "I guess that'd be my fault. We, wolves, are colorblind, and I guess I didn't consider color clashes when snatching random clothes from around Stanley." Strong regained his mission focus and added, "I was trying to be a good host and to make sure that my partner was as comfortable as possible so that he'd be ready for the next leg of our mission."

"What is the next leg of your mission?" I asked, trying to remember what day it was and exactly what day the next flight left the Falkland Islands. "Does your flight leave tomorrow then?"

"We'll be headed north shortly. I can't wait to get where it's a little warmer. If I had known we'd be so far south in the middle of winter for this long, I might have opted to join the Southern Triad and ask Moana to join the Scattered Triad. I mean she is one shaggy bird. With all that poof, she'd have to be warmer here than me," Astuto said, apparently trying another joke.

"We leave base camp in a short time to make it to the airport where I believe we'll be able to easily sneak aboard the plane. I've been scouting out the town since I arrived here, and as I mentioned there is a place called the 1982 Memorial Wood. We can use it for cover and then weave through some of the taller grasses. Unfortunately, we can't take as direct a route as I would hope for because there are still *minefields* around the town from a war the people had here thirty years ago," Strong reminded me from our earlier conversation, laying out his plan.

"People! Sometimes I wonder why we're trying to help them at all. It seems that they will always return to their old ways, fighting against one another. I wonder if they will ever change...," Astuto said half to himself, before cutting off his words.

Regaining his composure he continued, "I apologize. I think the short days are getting to me. That is no talk for a member of our mission. I know there is nothing we can ultimately do to set things totally 'right'. I just hope the people appreciate the sacrifices we're making for them."

I could sense his enthusiasm quickly fading like the southern winter sun, so I wanted to redirect them toward the positive results Benjamin was seeing since arriving back in Tasmania. They were both excited to hear that the people were so receptive to having a thylacine back.

"Benjamin had told me that one old couple had stopped by her enclosure and upon seeing her they wept for joy. The elderly couple apparently could remember how devastated the state of Tasmania had been when the original Benjamin was found dead in her enclosure due to exposure that last cold night," I reported.

"In a few days when everyone is here with me on Pinta Island maybe the people will throw us a celebration. Who knows Astuto, maybe you'll see people wearing a shirt with your beautiful face on it," I mocked.

"That would be something unexpected," Astuto said seriously. "I just hope that they are excited to see us and that things come together once we get there. By the way, how are the others doing?"

I hesitated but decided that Strong and Astuto weren't as prone to worry as some of the others. I explained that Moana wouldn't make it in time, but the others should be arriving before day 40. Even though the Northern Triad hadn't moved in quite some time, I explained their desire to wait a few more days before Eldey started his swim and Martha her flight. They were still hoping to get the cruise ship working so that Boomer could make the journey south without needing a whale escort.

"Well, I hope no one else ever needs to have to do that again. Of course, I'm grateful for the ride here, but I'm glad that my next transport will be man-made and not reek of rotten fish," Astuto joked.

I wasn't sure why he was so happy. Maybe it was a little cabin fever on his part or maybe just the fact that his visit to the Falkland Islands was almost over. The two began their journey toward the airport. There were a few people out and about as they ventured forth.

Strong said, "We want to try to keep out of sight if possible because even though there are a few sheepdogs on the islands and other neutered dogs, no strays are allowed to roam freely. I overheard people saying that was against the law in the Falkland Islands. It shows that the people here are trying to protect the native species here now."

I was again impressed by just how well planned the wolf was. He seemed to have thought of everything and learned so much during his stay. The only things I'd been able to explore over the past 25 days were my old stomping grounds on Pinta Island and confirm the fact that tortoises were not made for swimming.

As the two wound their way through the town, I would watch as Strong would scour the upcoming section of road or forest, come back to wherever he had stashed Astuto, and tell him exactly where to run and hide next. For a fifty pound bird, Astuto was able to run with a sort of grace that I wouldn't have expected.

In this stop-and-go way, the two made their way across Ross Road, zigzagging through the less-traveled roads of the town. I was intrigued watching the way Astuto submitted to Strong's wisdom and mapping of the town. I honestly didn't take note of many specifics about the town until just before they reached the safety of the 1982 Memorial Wood where they could begin weaving through the footpaths away from the main roads.

The road that led to the footpath read *Snake Road*. I felt a shudder run through me at the sheer mention of a snake in a similar way I noticed it had affected the creatures back in the Garden. I noticed that Astuto had the same reaction. If Strong had noticed it, he didn't let it deter him from the mission at hand. Soon they were passing the lighthouse on the way to the airport.

Upon arriving at the airport, I noticed three people were moving around the white building. There was a sign above the red door of the building which read, *Welcome to Stanley*. Above that, there was some sort of symbol with a white sheep on it. Next to the red door, there was a sort of wagon, with what appeared to be a blue cage on it. The three people were loading boxes and bags in this wheeled cage. I wondered if Strong would climb into that cage or if he'd somehow sneak directly onto the plane.

I saw Strong look briefly at the loading wagon but thought twice about it. The plane was not a small one but was in no way a large jet like I had seen flying over here at the CDRS. The plane was bright red with a horizontal blue stripe running the length of it. *FIGAS* was printed vertically on the plane's tail. Strong had explained that FIGAS stood for Falkland Island Government Air Service. The wolf seemed to have figured out everything about how Stanley functioned. There were two propellers on the front portion of the plane, and I didn't see where Strong and Astuto would be able to hide until they reached the plane.

As the three men were loading the plane I could see Strong's ears go back and his muscles tense every time the people went into the building as if he were willing himself to make a break toward the plane. There was a lot riding on this moment. If they were both captured before they made it to the plane, the results for our mission would be devastating because we'd only have six of us left.

Just as I was about to ask what Strong had in mind, I noticed the three people go into the building for more bags, and at that very moment Strong and Astuto sprinted toward the plane. My visual was of Strong running with great speed toward the back tire of the plane, with Astuto in hot pursuit. They had done it! They made it to the plane without being spotted.

It seemed like forever before the three men unloaded the cargo from the blue wagon cage into the back of the plane. Most of what I could see of the three men loading the plane was from the knees down, but when they walked further away I could get a sense of who was in charge of flying the plane, and who was simply helping to load the cargo. The man who I assumed was the pilot wore shiny black shoes and a uniform that the other two lacked. I saw the shiny shoes walk right in front of the tire which hid Astuto and Strong. I watched as the shiny shoes walked past the wing and climbed into the front door.

Within a few moments, there was a sudden loud whirling as each propeller began spinning. Astuto let out a startled, hoarse squawk that seemed to be drowned out by the noise. I noticed that another pair of shoes from one of the cargo crew began walking around the plane. He stopped at the front tire and kicked it, then walked to the larger rear tire and kicked it. I had to hold my breath as the shoes rounded the plane, and I watched from both Astuto and Strong's vantage points as the shoes closed in on their hiding place.

Both creatures huddled as close to the tire as possible, as the man drew back his foot. He hesitated and stopped. He knelt quickly and looked down. I thought this was the end. To my surprise, he turned away from the tire. I saw him tie his shoe and then stand back up apparently unaware of the wolf and dodo hiding inches away. He kicked the tire. It seemed like forever. Seemingly satisfied that everything was ready for takeoff, the man moved away from the plane. I'm glad a third member of the Scattered Triad wasn't there, or I might have *felt* one of them having a panic attack.

Strong glanced around the tire to see if the coast was clear when he noticed the cargo loader person pointing to the pilot's window and then back to the tire where the two creatures were hidden. Had the person seen Astuto and Strong crouched down behind the tire after all? Were the people planning to capture them as the Tasmanian crew had with Benjamin? It was my turn to fght off a panic attack.

I watched as the man ran back to the airport building. He emerged with a pump like the ones they used here at the CDRS to inflate flat tires. I realized that Astuto and Strong hadn't been spotted, but Strong must have been thinking they had.

I saw him mouth something to Astuto who lunged quickly for the step which led into the back storage part of the plane. From Strong's viewpoint, I watched as Astuto mistimed his jump and his lead foot slipped. He tried to regain his balance using his stubby white wings, but I could tell he wouldn't make it. Somehow Strong managed to hurl his entire wolf body into the puffy white plumage of Astuto's feathered backside, hurling them both in just as the crew member came to inflate the tire.

Astuto and Strong wiggled their way behind the cargo and under some supplies in the back of the plane. Once they were squared away, I gave us a moment to regain our composure and lower our heart rates.

"Well Strong, was that exactly what you had been planning all week?" I joked.

"Something like that. That's why it's best to be over-prepared in these types of situations. The most important thing is that we've made it aboard this plane and have gotten that much closer to Pinta Island and the rest of the team. Eldey had said it wouldn't be easy, especially for us," said the mission-minded wolf.

"I guess you're going to get your wish after all, Astuto," I said.

"What wish is that? That I'd be able to go somewhere a little warmer and sunnier than this crazy island? No offense Strong, but we dodos aren't built for your part of the world," Astuto said.

"Astuto, you know I'm a big fan of warm climates, being cold-blooded and all, but that wasn't what I meant. I meant that you are getting your wish of being the first and only dodo to get his bulky fifty-pound frame off the ground and 'fly'," I said air quoting the final word like so many of the other Garden animals tended to do.

I made a little mental note to ask one more trivial, quagga type question later; when I was alone with Astuto or Eldey. I wanted to understand why all the Garden creatures enjoyed air quoting so much. It did seem a little excessive at times but oddly therapeutic.

According to Strong, they would only be taking a very short flight across the island and catching a special flight to Santiago, Chile. He said that during his extra week prowling around the airport he realized that Stanley airport wasn't the international flight center. Actually, according to what he had overheard some scientists talking about, there usually weren't any international flights this time of year. But a few Chilean scientists had luckily booked a flight back home after a several month excursion to study the Magellanic penguin population on the islands.

I had stayed with Astuto and Strong until they transferred to a second plane at the international airport a short distance from Stanley. This was a relatively simple transfer because the crew was so busy helping the Chilean scientists with their equipment.

Strong said, "The scientists are flying straight back to Santiago instead of making the usual refueling stops taken by most tourists' flights. Since they were the only ones on board and were willing to pay a little extra, the pilot was happy to oblige."

I wondered how in the world one wolf could find out so much in just a few weeks.

"This flight should take about seven hours, and then we'll have to figure out how to maneuver around a more highly populated airport. Then we must take the one-stop nineteen-hour flight from Santiago, Chile to the airport on San Cristobal, another island in the Galapagos a short distance from where the Charles Darwin Research Station is located. In theory, we could be to you by the 28th day," Strong continued.

The next day began a day of hope; with a quick check-in with Stella. She was still in high spirits and said she'd have to pick up the pace because she didn't want to be beaten to Pinta Island by a fat flightless bird. It was hard to know exactly where she was since she was swimming across the Open Ocean. I told her that if I had money to bet, my money would be on her to be here first. I reminded her that I probably wouldn't be on Pinta Island to meet her since I was still on display at the CDRS. She said that she'd keep a low profile once she arrived.

Benjamin was still living it up like a celebrity at the Tasmanian Zoo and Moana had remained true to her vow to overcome her claustrophobia and headed to Tasmania. I told her that I was proud of her for making it aboard a ship by herself, especially down below deck. I knew it wasn't easy for her to do. I asked her what she intended to do when she arrived in Tasmania. She quoted one of Stephen's favorite little flightless bird sayings that she'd have to 'wing it' which was ironic for Moana because as far as I could tell when I had been with her, she didn't have any wings to speak of.

Stephen was still safely hidden in a nook in the cargo area of the ship and would slip upstairs at night to find some scraps of food. As usual, he was chipper and hopeful about his 'small' part in the mission. He said that the only trouble that could hamper his mission was if a cat snuck on board. The little wren was aware that many cargo ships kept cats onboard to catch any stowaway rats or mice, but he hadn't seen any yet.

Maybe I was finally getting the hang of this leading thing. Sure it hadn't been perfect, and there had been a few minor losses, but soon we'd be together. I couldn't wait to check in with Eldey to let him know the good news.

"You will never believe it; in three days we'll have three creatures safely on Pinta Island. Half the mission will be over! That means once the three of you arrive, we'll have seven of us here and things can move on to the next phase," I said joyfully to all three members of the Northern Triad.

"We are so happy to hear about that George!" Martha blurted out rapidly.

I couldn't help wondering if *we* referred to the Northern Triad, or the passenger pigeon herself. Her way of talking still threw me off when it was out of context. "Martha, it's really good to hear from you again."

I still couldn't get over how real it was talking to the only completely intact triad. It made me be able to connect with them in a deeper way than I ever knew possible. My only hope was that I would make it back to the Garden with them to experience it for myself. That's when a small voice of doubt seemed to try to enter in, *What if you don't make it back?* I again shunned the voice and focused again on the members of the Northern Triad.

I could sense the excitement in all three animals with my report, but Boomer was more withdrawn and less confident than I had ever seen him. I was wondering if he might feel like a failure, since he was the main reason Eldey and Martha had stayed waiting on another cruise ship to Pinta Island for so long. There wasn't any way for the heath hen to get here without a ship or plane.

"Boomer, have you been working on any new dance moves for the cameras once you get here? You know that all eyes will be on you, and you will have to give the best dance performance of your life to wow them. From what I've always heard, people in 1932 would come from all over the world to see you strut your stuff at your lekking grounds in Martha's Vineyard. You don't want to disappoint the people do you?" I said, hoping to refocus him.

At this challenge to his birdhood, he took a deep breath, lowered his head, extended the long feathers of his neck above his head, puffed out his wings, and blew out those orange balloon things on his neck. For such a plain-looking partridge, this radical transformation was amazing. He went from a plain brown and white chicken type bird to an elegant dancer. Boomer put everything he had into his dance, leaping into the air, stamping his feet at an unbelievable rate, and making that distinct booming sound.

"Okay, okay. I guess you win. That is pretty good. I think a choreographed dance number between you and me is kind of out of the question since I'm quite a bit slower than you. I don't suppose you can do that dance in slow motion?" I asked, trying to keep things light-hearted.

At this unintended challenge, Boomer did a spectacular slow-motion version of his previous dance. I could have simply watched him dance the whole day, but I had a few things that I wanted to talk directly to Eldey about, so I bid Martha and Boomer farewell.

"Eldey, there have been a few things I've been meaning to ask you, but I keep forgetting because I'm either taking pictures with tourists here at the research station or taking swimming classes," I said.

"George, as I have been telling you all along there is a 'rhyme and reason' for everything. You simply need to try to understand it. I want to echo what Astuto and I told you before, we are not any smarter or better than you or any other animal. We simply have learned some of the 'rules' for this world we live in," Eldey explained.

I wished he wasn't always so humble, and just once he'd admit he was, in fact, the wisest animal amongst us, but I doubted that would ever happen. Upon sensing his air quote of 'rules', I had to clarify why in the world all of the Garden animals did this, even to the point of absurdity.

"Eldey, this might seem like a random question to start with, but I have been noticing a weird custom of the Garden animals since the day we met that I don't understand," I stated.

"What is 'that' George?" Eldey said as if knowing what I was thinking.

"Haha," I laughed knowing that he knew what my question would be. Not wanting to be predictable I asked, "Why is it that you all only eat vegetation?"

This threw Eldey off because he stammered and then regained himself, "Well George, you see this is how things were in the Garden before the serpent's deception."

Deciding to probe a little more into this question before actually asking about the air quoting, I continued, "Well, I've seen Strong and Benjamin eating some sorts of meat since they returned. Why aren't we vegetarians now?"

"This is one of the questions that I do not have a definitive answer to George, especially since we are the first creatures that I am aware of to ever return as a 'triad variety pack', and not simply three of our own species," Eldey admitted honestly. "Now on to your real question about why we *air quote* so much," he said, pausing to simulate air quoting..

"For someone who does not know any more than anyone else you are quite astute," I replied, not intending the play on words with the dodo's name.

"The air quoting is a safeguard measure of sorts that the Garden animals created soon after the Original Garden fell apart due to Lusadé's mingling. You see George, one of the punishments for the serpent's deceitful ways was his losing his legs and being forced to crawl on his belly. Because of this, we realized that there was only one way we could communicate, that Lusadé couldn't. That was by air quoting," Eldey explained.

"Because Lusadé doesn't have any arms or legs to do so? Oh, I guess that makes sense, but *why* do you do it? I've seen people do it in conversations at the research station, but I haven't been able to see a pattern in when or why you Garden creatures do it," I explained.

"There is not a specific time we do it exactly, no true 'rhyme or reason' because it is something we animals created. It helps us pause and reflect. It is almost like a splash of cold water or a loud noise. It simply makes us more alert to what is taking place around us. It's a way to focus. Plus, it is a lot of fun and helps us not to take ourselves too seriously. If you have noticed, even Astuto does it from time-to-time," Eldey said, pausing to give me time for a question before continuing his explanation.

"You see George, this is simply a way for us to keep ourselves grounded and focused. When times get stressful we tend to lose our focus, which can lead to losing hope if we stay there too long. Air quoting and taking time to laugh in response to our trials was one way we found to renew our hope. We know it doesn't solve our problems, but it can help us take a step back from our situation and focus on the positive. That's why we do it so much, especially when you might be perceiving stressful situations. It's not that we don't care about the problems we're facing or are taking them lightly. We are trying to help refocus ourselves and others in our group to see the big picture, so we can move forward in faith. I probably should have mentioned this tidbit to you earlier in the mission, but I figured since we cannot see you until we reach Pinta Island, it was not of primary importance. A second reason we air quote is that it is a way to signal each other in case Lusadé does attack. He has a way to make each of us doubt ourselves and what we know to be true. The serpent is crafty which is why the other animals wanted a subtle way to communicate, should the need arise," Eldey explained.

"Wouldn't Lusadé figure that out because he is so perceptive?" I asked.

"Perhaps, but using this form of sign language gives us a 'leg up' over the serpent," Eldey laughed.

I laughed too, "That was a terrible joke Eldey. Plus you can't air quote with just one leg up."

"I guess you're right about that George, but you see how you are a lot more positive and carefree now even though we have a mission to accomplish? Keep the faith my friend, and we can overcome any obstacles that we have to face," Eldey encouraged.

I updated Eldey on Strong's plan to hop from plane to plane to get here sooner. I also explained how Astuto was enjoying his new-found wings. Eldey seemed pleased to hear about his friend and knew Strong would do his best to get Astuto there safely.

Upon hearing that Astuto and Strong could be arriving within a day or two Eldey said, "It seems that you will not be lonely anymore then, 'Lonesome George'."

"I guess you're right Eldey. I must say that today has probably been the most exhilarating day of my life. I'm filled with hope and a sense of joy I've never had, at least not here. There was a moment back there in the Garden, but it's like everything is at peace. I can't wait to see you all," I said giddily.

"And you have every right to feel that way, George. You are taking this mission upon your back and it is excelling because of *you*," he paused letting that sink in. "I know leading is difficult, but I truly feel blessed that you are the one leading us."

I knew there was something else I needed to ask Eldey but was apprehensive to even talk about it. I felt like my concern needed a second opinion. "Eldey, as things stand right now in about 3 days we will have the entire Scattered Triad here with me. Stephen will arrive around day 36, giving us five. I hate to say this, but as the leader, I need to consider the possibility that you might not be able to find a ship to the Galapagos in time. If you swim here and Martha flies down the coast, we could have seven of us here *without* Boomer. I hate to even mention this, but if it means being able to complete the mission to help the people, then it's something to consider... isn't it?"

There was a Moana-like pause before Eldey replied hesitantly, "That is something that I have been wondering as well. I would hate to leave Boomer behind. There is a great chance that we would be able to have eight of us on Pinta Island by day 36 when Stephen arrives, but we also have to consider that Stephen's boat might be delayed. Then we could have six of us there and no way to finish the mission."

"So what are you thinking then Eldey? I trust your judgment more than anyone else's. You've been at this leading thing much longer than I have. I understand your point about risking the mission and ending with six of us, but I don't know which decision is best?" I replied honestly.

"I am not sure either George, but *six* is a *bad number* and does not help us complete our mission. I was hoping that this boat would be fixed soon. From what Martha has been able to find out by scouting around the port that we are currently docked in, we are about a six-day shot to Pinta Island, assuming we do not sleep. We may be rested from our stay here in La Paz, Mexico, but I think the actual trip would realistically take seven or eight days. Some quick math says that we would arrive on Pinta Island by day 34 or 35 if we left tomorrow morning," Eldey explained.

"Oh I see, that's a little further away than I had thought you were, but that still gives us five days to get things ready," I retorted, trying to keep things light and optimistic, which at that moment was more difficult than I thought. "How about this? If the people can't fix the boat by tomorrow morning, I will do an 'all call' and get a whale or dolphin to escort Boomer south as I did for...," I paused remembering my already broken promise to shield Astuto's secret Jonah-like trip, "...like I know it can be done because of the whole 'rhyme and reason' thing. Right?"

"Very good George. You are starting to think more deeply about the 'rhyme and reason' of things. As much as I do not like doing an 'all call' that might be our best option. I wish I was just a little bigger and I could take Boomer myself, but I fear that I could not swim fast enough to make it to Pinta Island in time," Eldey said.

"Then it is settled. To play it safe, I will find an escort for Boomer. I'm just not sure what animals travel between La Paz, Mexico, and Pinta Island," I explained.

"It is another 'rhyme and reason' thing, George. *We* animals *can* travel outside of our normal realms, but creatures here are not as willing to do so. I mean right now somewhere flying over South America; there is a dodo bird. Let us look at what we know. Maybe you can ask Fausto tonight what large ocean animals swim that route, maybe during the migration."

"That sounds like a plan. I will see what I can do," I said.

"Do not worry about us, George. We will figure things out. I will send Martha out to see if she can find out more about what is taking place on our ship. You probably should check in with Astuto and Strong to see how things are going in Chile. We look forward to hearing from you tomorrow morning. I will prepare Boomer for tomorrow's possible 'adventure'," he air-quoted, snapping me out of the growing pessimism.

There wasn't anything to truly be concerned about. The Scattered Triad would be here in two days. Fausto was working on building a lighthouse for us on Pinta Island. Stephen was safely crossing the Pacific, and the Northern Triad was doing quite well. What was there to worry about?

I checked in with Strong and Astuto to see how things were progressing, and they were on the next plane that was taking them from Santiago, Chile to Guayaquil, Ecuador. This flight would be landing soon, but the biggest obstacle for a dodo and Falkland Island wolf would be in Guayaquil. There they would have a ten-hour layover before the second flight to San Cristobal, one of the eastern islands in the Galapagos Islands.

"You will be leaving in about ten hours, so I'll check in with you tomorrow before you take off from Guayaquil to join me in the Galapagos. Then we will just need to figure out a way to get you from San Cristobal to Pinta Island," I explained.

Strong seemed shocked to hear this, "You mean that we're getting on the wrong flight to the Galapagos? I thought I had double-checked our itinerary to make sure it was correct."

"You did a fine job, Strong. You did not make a mistake. You see the airport into the Galapagos Islands from Ecuador lands on San Cristobal Island. There are thirteen large islands and three smaller ones that make up the Galapagos Islands. The airport is on San Cristobal. I am at the Charles Darwin Research Station on *Santa Maria Island*. We all need to make our way to *Pinta Island*, which is a more northerly island."

"I didn't realize that the Galapagos Islands were so far apart. Pardon my ignorance. The Falkland Islands are much easier to understand, just two big halves," the wolf explained. Regaining his stoic composure he added, "Do we need to stop by any of the other islands there to pick you up lunch or something?"

I had to laugh at Strong's ability to be serious and joke at the same time. "No. All you need is to show up with that old dodo bird, and that'll be more than enough. I'll serve you both lunch when you get here."

That was a busy day, but overall encouraging. Everyone was in high spirits. All of that talk about lunch made me hungry. I knew that we tortoises could last many months without food, but this was ridiculous. Where was Fausto? Just as I was beginning to worry about him, he showed up with an arm full of various vegetables for me.

"Good news George! Things on Pinta Island are coming along very well. I have to admit, I don't understand what's going to happen when your friends arrive, but I'm excited to meet them," Fausto said, looking around as the visitors to the research station wandered to the exits for the day.

He looked around again and motioned me over to some thicker brush off to the corner to plot out everyone's whereabouts. I picked up a stick in my beak and pointed to the outline of Stella and drew a 29 in the sand, but he had already written that down. Then he pointed to the silhouette of the dodo and wolf and I put a 27.

At this updated number, Fausto turned giddy and looked at me exclaiming, "George, you mean to tell me that at this time tomorrow I will see a real dodo bird and a Falkland Island wolf?"

I nodded and drew a smiley face in the dust.

"How are they getting to Pinta Island? I mean a dodo and a wolf can't swim around South America, can they?" Fausto asked.

His hesitation at their ability to swim 3,500 miles showed that he had faith even though he had no clue about the 'rhyme or reason' of what we were doing. I shook my head and to the best of my ability drew an airplane.

"They are on a flight to the Galapagos? So that means that they will be arriving in San Cristobal tomorrow?" Fausto asked, trying to figure everything out for himself.

I nodded my head, and he asked when their flight would be arriving. I drew '10:00 am' in the sand, and he pointed to the smiley face I had drawn.

"Well then, I will have to be there to greet them then won't I?" Fausto said grinning.

I didn't know how to respond to this inquiry, so I just looked at him as his brain tried to map out a plan.

"I'm supposed to get all of these creatures to Pinta Island including you right?" he asked.

I nodded, and he continued, "Well you might be a little more of a challenge, but I think I can take a boat to San Cristobal tomorrow morning and pick up your friends. Do you think you can let them know that I will be there?"

I nodded again pointing to the smiley face in the dust with my stick.

"Tell them that I will be wearing my...," he paused, pondering how to make himself distinguishable to my friends. "I will wear my blue *Lonesome George* shirt and a yellow hat. I will also be carrying a green bag with wheels to try to carry them in. Let's see, a dodo weighs about fifty pounds; add a small wolf and maybe eighty pounds or so total. Yeah, my green bag ought to do the trick."

Fausto stayed a bit longer then departed for the night. After a quick check-in with Stella, I laid my head down feeling good about the day's events as I drifted off to sleep. While I knew I had to be level headed, the excitement of seeing some of my friends welled up in me. It was at that moment, I had realized I did view this ragtag bunch of extinct animals as friends, true friends. I was no longer alone. Little did I know how short-lived this time of hope would be for me.

Chapter 18:

STRIKE THREE

Day 27 marked the most emotional day of my entire life; worse than the day I lost my mom in the Last Raid, worse than the day I realized I would never see another of my kind. This day marked the end of things. The end of hope. I just wished I would have seen it coming. I would have been more diligent to stop it. Maybe if I hadn't let the calm days and giddiness of seeing my friends cloud my careful pursuit of helping the three triads arrive safely, I would have been more prepared.

Terror. Sheer terror was what woke me up. At first, I thought that I must have been having some sort of nightmare like I did after my family was smuggled away, but this was different. This felt wrong and scary on a level I never knew possible. I felt panic and anxiety overwhelming me. I couldn't quite place it, but then I realized that my terror had a name, and I involuntarily spoke its name before I could think, *Lusadé.*

Just saying his name sent shivers up and down my spine, but my heart sank when I heard an eerie reply. "George, I told you that your mission would not and should not succeed. There are so many things that you don't understand. I know you think that I am the bad guy here, but that simply is not true. I can not let you do this thing for the people," the serpent hissed.

"I really don't know what you're talking about. We are trying to set things right between us and the people. This is the only way that we know how to do that," I replied.

"But George, you don't understand what's at stake here do you?" Lusadé continued.

I realized that the less he spoke to me the better. I knew there was a danger in talking to him at all, but I had a deep need to understand what he knew or thought he knew.

"What is it that you want from me, Lusadé? Why don't you want us to succeed? Why won't you help us?" I pleaded with the snake.

"George, this problem with people won't go away. Don't you see that? There's nothing *you* or *I* can do to change that. Trust me I have tried. You will only make things *worse* for us. Every time things are reset for the people, their relationship with us gets more traumatic. Don't you see, there will be *added curses* if you do this thing. This resetting that you and the others are planning is dangerous. I can only imagine how much *worse* things will be for us," Lusadé pleaded.

I could feel myself wanting to know more... needing to know more. I longed to know what he knew and what he saw long ago when he was able to somehow return to the beginning, to the Original Garden. But I also knew I needed to end this discussion soon before he had a chance to lead me astray like he had done to Moana.

"Lusadé, I know that *you* have a problem with the people, but I want to help them if there's even a chance. Can't you see that it's already over for my kind, but if there's any chance that I can keep another species, even one other animal from feeling the loneliness that I did for so long, I have to do it," I shouted.

"I see. So your mind is made up then, and there is nothing I can do to sway you? I guess the lines have been drawn then. I hope it is worth you risking your life and your very existence for what you *believe* is right George. I know that what's happening in Tasmania with the thylacine is encouraging to you, but trust me that the people cannot be trusted. Just when you think you can trust them and put your hope in them, they crush your dreams. They can't help it, but that's simply the rhyme and reason for how things are with them. I guess we must both do what we feel is right George. I'm truly sorry for what I have to do then," the serpent said with a seemingly sincere tone.

Suddenly he was gone. There was no sleep for me that night. That conversation left so many questions racing through my mind; troubling questions. *Was there truth to what he said about adding a new, worse curse?* Until the Ark, it seemed the people and animals interacted in apparent peace. *Could the people really be trusted?* This had been a question I had for so long. Being an animal on the Galapagos, I was supposed to be trusting, but history with the people had taught me differently. Lusadé's last statement about Benjamin's successes and Eldey's rhyme and reason were the most troubling. *How did the serpent know about these things unless he had been able to somehow listen in on the conversations I had had over the past 26 days?* This must be Lusadé's strategy; to breed fear and confusion long enough to stop the mission from going forward.

His parting statement echoed within every fiber of my body, "We must both do what we feel is right. I'm truly sorry." *What did he mean by this?* A sense of dread filled me as I realized how serious this situation was. I was now fighting, not only the people and the forty-day time limit, but the serpent himself. The fact that he apologized for what he was about to do was the most troubling thing of all.

After a sleepless night, my body was alert, but my mind was tired. It was hard to focus. I didn't know whether to let the others know about the impending threat or keep it to myself until there was a reason to panic. Before I could decide which triad to contact first, I could again sense a presence. Since there was no accompanying shiver, I assumed it could only be Pat.

"You must be careful because Lusadé would do *anything* to stop the people from having any peace. Beware and be aware. He is the master of deception and lies and will only do what moves his agenda forward, " Pat cautioned before fading out of my mind.

I still didn't know whether she could be trusted or not. I figured Pat felt the same way about me. There was something about being so vulnerable that made it hard to know who to trust.

I spoke with Stephen and Stella to start the day and was about to check in with Eldey when *it* happened. Every hope I had unraveled at *that* moment. The terror of last night exploded in the depths of my being. Without me asking to hear from them, Astuto and Strong burst into full view. Something was wrong and at first, I couldn't place it. I could hear and see Strong and Astuto huddled behind some luggage, but I could also *feel* their thoughts like I could when a complete triad was together. That wasn't right, and I suddenly knew why. Someone else was there with them.

The impending threat must have eluded them because Strong and Astuto were feeling a sense of excitement, with the knowledge that in just a few hours, they'd be in the Galapagos Islands with me. They were discussing what to do when they arrived in San Cristobal. I hadn't told them about Fausto meeting them at the airport, which ended up being for the best.

I still didn't understand the 'rhyme or reason' for why Lusadé was able to apparently listen in on my conversations. Was there something I didn't know that he did? I knew of all creatures, the serpent knew more about what could and could not be done, even more, than Eldey or Astuto. Astuto had warned me when I called for the killer whale escort that Lusadé might be able to hear me, but no one knew if Lusadé could hear my other communications. I racked my brain trying to make sense of it all, and the only two guesses I could make were; my orca escort call had opened all communication, or Lusadé could only listen in to conversations with an intact triad, which is why he was able to directly quote parts of what Eldey had told me. I just wasn't sure, but that seemed to be the least of my worries at the moment.

I felt Strong and Astuto brace for takeoff. Maybe I was worrying about nothing. I mean even if Lusadé was trying to thwart our mission, he was still a finite snake; smart yes but not magical. Magic definitely wasn't something that fit everything's 'rhyme and reason' scheme. Maybe I was able to feel their emotions because they were closer geographically.

I decided that the best course of action would be to simply tell Strong and Astuto about my interactions with Lusadé the night before. I knew those two were some of the most level-headed animals on this mission. At first, both of them expressed concern for me, asking many good probing questions to see if Lusadé was able to get to me and add doubt that wasn't there the day before.

"I am sure that you will continue to lead us the best you can, George," the wolf said, trying to encourage me. "Just be careful not to let him get to you. He is a craftier creature than any of us. He thinks in ways that don't make sense to us."

"You know that Lusadé will try his best to get you to doubt everything we've been telling you," Astuto said, trying to refocus me. "He has a hidden, tainted agenda that you don't. Lusadé is seeking revenge for the death of his wife, and that clouds his judgment. You have to keep this in mind, as he talks to you. He has been trying to get back at the people since the beginning and will stop at nothing until he has accomplished that. His hate runs much deeper than yours ever could."

"Thanks, Astuto, but I'm scared for you and Strong because I feel a growing sense of dread but for you," I said hoping that what I was saying made sense to them.

"We will be fine George. I will make sure of that," Strong said, sitting up straight.

"Remember that you can't trust Lusadé. If something happens to one of us, we will simply return to the Garden, but you and Lusadé are staking your entire existence on your missions. You both can't succeed. Be assured that if he needs to choose between you and his own existence, he won't hesitate, and you can't either," Astuto said, trying his best to be firm and encouraging.

"I know, but it is something I don't know how to do. I mean, I've hated the people, and even other animals for so long, but I couldn't possibly take a life. That's exactly the opposite of what I'm trying to accomplish by leading this mission," I pleaded.

"We will be fine. We're almost to you, well at least to the Galapagos. We'll make a plan to thwart his attacks once we get there. There's one thing I have to admit, and it's hard for an old fuddy-duddy like me. I was wrong about you. I have to admit that Eldey was right to choose you to lead this mission. There's no one else I'd rather have leading us. I'm grateful that *I* have had a chance to follow *you*, George.

Astuto had used my actual name, not *Tortoise*, but he called me *George*. I didn't think he even knew what my name was, but Astuto had actually said he appreciated the way I had been leading. Maybe things weren't all that bad. Once they got here, they would help me lead the final stages of our mission.

"I can't wait to be with you soon and tell you that in person. George, there's one thing I've been meaning to tell you...," Astuto's words cut off abruptly.

It happened in a blur. I could see and sense a wave of panic as Strong turned toward Astuto with a look of sheer panic on his face. There, wrapping himself around and around Astuto was a large, olive green snake with yellow splotches. The serpent peered straight into Strong's eyes and consequently straight into mine. It was like the serpent was staring straight into my soul, and I didn't know what to do.

Without hesitating, Strong leaped into action, sinking his teeth into the side of Lusadé. The snake simply coiled its massive body tighter and tighter around the dodo, leaving only Astuto's head and white rump exposed. Strong's counter-attack was in vain. I could hear Lusadé's laughter and feel his sheer pleasure as his grip tightened around Astuto.

"Please Lusadé. There's got to be another way. We could work on a plan together," I pleaded frantically, flailing for some kind of counterplan that might alleviate the snake's attack. "Maybe we could go back to the beginning, the Original Garden, and find another way *together*. You did it once, so you must be able to do it again. Just tell me how you did it, and I will help you. Please, Lusadé, think about what you're doing."

I felt nothing but panic from friends and pure, unadulterated hate from the serpent. Just as I was about to plead with him again,

I heard a bone-crunching pop and the *sensation* of panic ended sharply. I was left with only my eyes and ears on the situation. I was frozen in a whirlwind of disgust, anger, and disbelief about what just occurred. I watched as Strong took a step back from the serpent who turned toward the wolf. I feared for the worst, but Lusadé simply slunk through a vent in the plane and was gone, leaving me in darkness. I could now only hear the Falkland Island wolf, who for once seemed to be without a plan.

My mind reeled, but I knew I needed to act quickly to save the wolf and in turn our mission.

"Strong, are you okay? Are you injured? Please tell me you were able to get away in time," I pleaded.

"I am fine George, given the circumstances. Lusadé seems to have vanished, but I will keep my eye out for him," Strong said, as if he didn't believe it himself.

"Do you think you should try to let the people flying the plane know about Lusadé? I mean, maybe if you barked and led them to the snake, they could capture him and end his threat to our mission," I said, hoping that this could be the case.

"I don't think I can do that George. Think about what you're saying. Even if I were able to let the people know about the snake, I would be captured as well. I would gladly sacrifice myself for the mission, but as I understand it we'd be down to only six creatures left. We would have stopped Lusadé, but he would ultimately have beaten us," Strong explained, trying to keep his composure and keep mission minded.

"I understand what you're saying, but *you* are in danger Strong. If he is able to ...," I trailed off catching my words before I spoke them. I feared to say them out loud in case Lusadé could hear my conversation. If the snake knew the whole mission now depended on the Falkland Island wolf on the plane *with him*, he might be a little bolder. "Just take care of yourself, Strong."

I tried to be calm and logical, but my mind was reeling by what had just taken place. Astuto was *dead*. I couldn't let myself dwell on this fact. There was so much still riding on me, and I had to keep the mission going until it was over, one way or another. I simply told Strong that Fausto would be waiting for him at the airport and described what Fausto said he'd be wearing for the pickup. Strong reminded me that it might be a little difficult for him to spot Fausto in a *blue* shirt since he was color blind, but he would do his best. I told him to look for my lovely picture on Fausto's shirt.

I wanted to simply curl up in a ball and weep, but I knew that wasn't an option. I knew logically the mission *could* still succeed, but I was heartbroken with no one to share the weight of my burden. Of course Strong knew first-hand the horror of what had just occurred, but I didn't want to jeopardize his safety by talking with him. I still didn't know how Lusade seemed to know so much about pieces of my conversations with the others, so contacting Eldey seemed to be an unwise option too.

There was no one to lead me through this. I was again alone, all alone. But this was far worse than any loneliness I had ever experienced at the CDRS; far worse than the days after the Last Raid or the Starving Time. I had to remain alone *by choice* to protect the others. My mom's last sacrificial moments flashed in my mind, and I finally understood why she hadn't simply fled and saved herself that day.

In this confused state of emotion, I again felt a familiar, *unsummoned* presence enter my thoughts.

Pat's voice simply said, "I am so sorry George. I didn't think Lusadé would take things this far." And then as I'd grown to expect, Pat faded without allowing me any follow up. I pleaded with her to talk to me more, not knowing if that was a wise choice or not, but she refused for some reason.

Isn't there anyone who I can talk to? I thought. That is when a new presence filled my thoughts. It was not a terrifying presence like Lusadé, but one similar to Pat. I figured that this could only be the one 'boomerang species' I hadn't been in contact with yet.

"Nessie?" I asked.

Almost before I could finish speaking her name she rebuked me in a harsh tone, "I hope you're happy with what you have done! You are playing with forces you do not understand George."

"What do you mean? What don't I understand? I am on a rescue mission to fix things between us and the people, to save other animals from extinction, and save *you*. Isn't that a good thing?" I responded.

"If there was any chance of success, then what you're doing might be admirable. Even if you are able to succeed in gathering your forces to reset things on the earth, which you aren't, the consequences would be catastrophic for all involved. Don't you see that every cleansing comes with a *price*?" Nessie hissed a little more serpent-like than I would have preferred given what had just taken place with Astuto.

"What price is that Nessie? My life? I know that my own existence is on the line, just like yours, just like Pat's, but I'm willing to at least make an effort which is more than I can say for you," I yelled, losing control of my emotions.

"How dare you say that I *refused to make an effort*? I was the first to try this foolish mission of Eldey's. I've been trapped out here for so long, unable to return to the Garden, and unable to finish the mission because it is impossible. People have hunted my kind for millennia. I have seen countless other giant species tracked down by hunters or what they used to call knights. *They* romanticized *our* deaths, the demise of countless dinosaur-like species, saying we were fire breathing monsters. *They* are the real monsters. *They* painted those similar to me in such a bad light that we had no chance to survive," Nessie explained.

"I'm sorry to hear that. I understand ..." I said.

"You understand? Do you understand what it's like to be hunted for being a monster, judged by your appearance as not deserving to live? Do you truly understand that? Ha. You're a pathetic tortoise! The people laugh at your kind and mock you. You have no idea what it's like to be hated, my dear tortoise," Nessie continued.

"Not all people are the monsters you paint them to be either. Are you saying that they all deserve to die? Wouldn't that be following in their judgmental footsteps? If that's the way you think then you're no better than the knights who used to hunt your kind, are you? There are good people out there, like Fausto or even the little girl you met that day by the loch; people who can protect you and would help you if you let them," I said.

"I'm not a cute and cuddly thylacine at some zoo in Australia. I was created to be massive. The consequences after the Great Flood have added spikes and sharp teeth to my form which only makes it harder for people to even consider trusting me. I tried George but to no avail. In their eyes I will always be a threat, a monster," Nessie hissed.

"There's got to be a way to save all of us Nessie. It doesn't have to end like this. Eldey is trying to..." I interjected but got cut off.

Nessie lashed out, "Don't give me your Eldey sob story like you did Pat. Whether Eldey feels bad about what he did to us or not is of little consequence to me. The only choice I have now is to try to survive. If you or I die, it's all over for us, forever. If those Lazarus species like Astuto die, they simply return home to their perfect, happy little world in the Garden. You and I don't have that luxury, George."

"But Eldey said when we get all of us to Pinta Island, we can reset things. You, Pat, and I will be able to return safely to the Garden," I explained.

"Do you believe that George? How many times during your journey has Eldey been wrong? How many times has he told you that he was unsure about what to do next? He admitted that he doesn't know everything. He is just guessing!" Nessie said.

"You have to *trust* that this will work, Nessie," I said.

"Why should I trust anything? Even if your little resetting plan works, and the world is cleansed between us and the people, the fact remains that you and I will still be in constant danger. Not to mention, that there *will be* a greater curse to try to survive. It's hard enough surviving now, but an additional curse will be an eternal death sentence for us George," Nessie fumed.

I was now wrestling with my own doubts. Nessie seemed to have explored the reality of our circumstances in ways I had never considered over the past few weeks. My faith had been blind from the beginning, and I could feel my faith slipping.

"What would you have me do then, Nessie?" I asked, unsure of myself.

"I can't and won't tell you what you should do. I am not Eldey, and I am not Lusadé. I am simply saying you need to consider the *reality* of your circumstances and choose a side. As for me, I'm joining the side that needs to win for me to survive eternal extinction," Nessie said with finality.

I had lost Astuto because of not being willing to compromise with the serpent and now had apparently made another enemy in Nessie. I had no idea where Pat's allegiances fell, but I couldn't do anything except withdraw into my shell and doubt everything.

Chapter 19:

PRESSING ON

As hard as it was to do, I vowed to keep positive and keep the day's happenings to myself. Fausto stopped by that morning and could tell something was bothering me. He even brought me some prickly pear from Pinta Island to try to cheer me up. I tried to fake excitement.

We went back to our meeting place before the research station opened for tourists. He pulled out his map for a quick update. I walked over to the low vegetation and snapped off a small twig in my beak to use to write. I slowly and meticulously wrote out, 'big and fast oshen animals neer heer?'

Fausto was momentarily confused by my random question, but as always, he tried his best to answer my question.

"There are a few large ocean animals around the Galapagos. The sperm whales are breeding now. There are always a few orcas around eating seals. There are some dolphins. Every once in a while there are a few humpbacks or blue whales that come through."

I scrawled in the dirt, *fastest?*.

"Let me see. According to the internet, humpbacks go eight miles an hour, blue whales can travel about twenty miles an hour, and orcas can travel about thirty miles an hour," Fausto said looking at his laptop.

I was temporarily confused because the orca that had carried Astuto from Mauritius wouldn't travel to the Galapagos Islands.

I thought a humpback whale might be good for Boomer because they were both show-offs, but at eight miles an hour, he wouldn't get here until day 37. A blue whale or orca could get Boomer here in six days, by day 33. I figured that I would go with what had already worked for this mission so far, the killer whale.

I drew a 'smiley face' in the dirt to let Fausto know that he could stop his web browsing. He pulled out his map for the daily location/time frame update. Stella and Stephen's arrival time frames remained unchanged. With my writing twig, I pointed to La Paz, Mexico on the map and to the great auk and passenger pigeon to show Fausto they should be arriving on day 32. Then I drew a killer whale in the sand which Fausto didn't quite understand. I pointed to the heath hen and scribbled day 33. At this Fausto scratched his head and told me he'd take my word for it.

"I'm taking the research station's boat out to San Cristobal now to pick up the dodo and Falkland Island wolf," Fausto said enthusiastically.

At the mention of Astuto, I put my head down in the dust and slowly shook it side-to-side. Fausto must have realized something had happened because he came over and rubbed my head, the way he did when he used to try to cheer me up in my lonely days.

I pointed to the silhouette of the dodo on his map and drew an X over it. Fausto realized what I was implying, and he simply said, "I am sorry to hear about the loss of your friend George. I will do all I can to pick up the wolf."

I pointed to the previously doodled smiley face, trying to show my appreciation for all that Fausto was doing to try to help me.

"Does this friend of yours happen to have a name George? I don't want his first human interaction in over a century to be disappointing," Fausto said.

I scribbled Strong's name in the dust, and Fausto nodded. He bent down and gave me a kiss on the head before jumping back over the fence.

I knew I needed to keep things moving forward. I checked in briefly with Eldey, Martha, and Boomer hoping there would be good news about the ship, but there was no such luck. Martha had heard people saying that the repairs could take another week.

I had no choice now. I needed to find Boomer another ride to Pinta Island. I asked the three of them whether they all wanted to travel via whale or whether they thought it would be best to divide and conquer. I told them that another animal had recently traveled by orca, but I kept the specifics intentionally vague, not wanting to break my promise to Astuto.

I didn't tell any of them, not even Eldey, of what had happened to Astuto on the plane. Even though the whole mission now depended on Stephen and Boomer's safe, timely arrival, I didn't want to burden the group with those particular details. If Eldey could sense something bad had happened since yesterday, he chose not to ask.

"Gee George, we think it'd be great to ride inside a whale together. We are ready whenever it gets here. This is all very 'Jonah style' isn't it? After all, we know it's safe since another creature just did it. We're just glad we didn't have to try it out first," Martha rapidly shared.

Just the mention of Astuto's whale travel by Martha almost opened the flood gate of sorrow, but I managed to hold it together. Boomer had come to the same realization that Astuto had earlier; he had to submit to his limitations. A heath hen was simply not made to fly or swim long distances. I think Eldey would have liked to swim to Pinta Island, but his protector instinct seemed to override his desire for comfort.

"We will await the arrival of our whale transportation then George. Hopefully, you can find us something 'roomy'. At least it will have the pleasant aroma of fish," Eldey joked.

At this, I noticed Eldey's joke had caused Martha and Boomer to cringe slightly. Apparently, like Astuto, they weren't fans of fish.

Even though Eldey was a little apprehensive about doing an animal 'all call' again because of Lusadé, I prodded him in that direction, knowing Lusadé had somehow been listening in to at least parts of what had been said anyway. I found a pod of killer whales off the coast of La Paz that was willing to transport the whole Northern Triad. I told the lead orca in the pod to sneak into the harbor at nightfall after a majority of the people were asleep. The Northern Triad understood why they needed to wait for nightfall, but I knew they were eager to get moving again.

Fausto had managed to talk to Edwin, the organizer of the CDRS, and convinced him to let me roam around on Pinta Island until they could possibly locate another Pintie. Edwin was reluctant at first, but after Fausto discussed the idea of placing some kind of tracking chip under my skin, Edwin agreed. Fausto had explained that the tracking chip would allow him to know if there was any change in my location or if I went for another swimming lesson.

I was excited to hear that my transport back to the island would be rather simple compared to the others. Fausto seemed to be able to accomplish anything he set his mind to do. I was excited that I'd soon be reunited with my friends, who I had been talking to, but hadn't actually been with in over 33 days.

Fausto had been able to find Strong rather easily at the airport. Apparently stray dogs had become a problem on San Cristobal in recent years, so a mangy Falkland Island wolf running around the airport didn't draw too much attention from the people there. From what Fausto and Strong said, it was a happy reunion, even though they had never met before. Fausto simply whistled and called for Strong, and the wolf ran to his waiting arms. After fastening on a collar and attaching the leash, the two simply walked back to the research boat and headed back to see me.

Fausto had to convince Edwin and the other people working at the research station that I needed to be less lonely, so he had found me a *friend*. At first, I thought the idea would backfire, but Fausto explained that he had heard there was a tortoise and a hippo that had been reported to have bonded, so it wasn't as absurd as it sounded. When Strong was put in my enclosure, we walked over to one another, doing the social sniffing and scanning that the people expected. Edwin said he thought the idea was ludicrous, but he'd allow it for one day and one day only.

The next morning when the people arrived and saw Strong and I snuggled up under a tree together, the people *oohed* and *ah-hed*. No one ever suspected that my newfound companion wasn't simply a mutt Fausto found, but an extinct relic from the Falkland Islands, 3,500 miles away. Being with Strong lifted my spirits immensely. The others were really excited to learn the people were so receptive to Strong and me.

I arrived on Pinta Island early in the morning. Fausto brought Strong along, keeping him on a leash, to appease Edwin and the other scientists who had fought so hard for the removal of goats and other feral wildlife from my pristine habitat.

Stella had been so motivated to be first, that she had actually arrived on Pinta Island earlier than expected. She had found a small inlet in which to hide from passing boats until I could arrive. Fausto had taken her some seaweed and cabbage that he had skimmed off the top of my food allowance to avoid drawing undue attention to what he was doing. We were all expectantly awaiting the arrival of the rest; the Northern Triad and Stephen.

The Northern Triad arrived on Pinta Island next. Of course, there was great excitement when the pod of six orcas arched out of the air to mark their arrival to the island. It really was a sight to behold. Stella fought her natural fear of killer whales to help escort them into the shore where our motley crew had been hiding. I was so impressed by the transformation I had seen in that sea cow. When we first met she was so scared of everything and so unsure of herself, and here she was escorting a pod of killer whales. Showing her sense of humor by mimicking an orca, she dove down as far as her massive body would allow before breaching a good three inches out of the water.

The largest male orca came ashore and opened its massive toothy mouth revealing the entire Northern Triad, instantly doubling Pinta Island's extinct animal population. Boomer was the first to fly out and land. He even did a little victory dance to mark the occasion. Martha said something about needing a bath and rolled around in the dust. Eldey waddled out of the massive whale's mouth and walked around its head. Looking into the leviathan's eye, he bowed to show his gratefulness for the ride. The orca shook its head up and down, making some clicking noises.

I asked the orcas if they'd be willing to swim west to find the cargo ship that carried Stephen. Whale escort seemed to be the safest way to go, and it would save Stephen the trouble of finding his way to Pinta Island from wherever the cargo ship dropped him off. The large male nodded and swam with his pod to pick up the seventh and final member of our crew.

The six of us huddled next to the shore and exchanged greetings, but I felt uneasy. I knew it wouldn't take long for everyone present to realize that Astuto was missing. He was the outspoken know-it-all of the group. There was no way he wouldn't be boasting about making it halfway around the world in the time it took Eldey to get his triad a much shorter, easier distance to Pinta Island.

That's when the weight of the burden I had been carrying alone, hit me full force. For so long I had withdrawn, happily hating everyone and everything around me. But now I felt a sadness for the great grief I was about to unveil to the group. As I struggled to find the words, I saw some of the creatures looking around taking a headcount. I felt sick to my stomach, and I didn't know how to gently deliver this massive blow to our joyful reunion.

Martha was the first to verbalize what everyone else was thinking, "George, we thought you had said that there'd be seven of us here today. We only count six of us and that one person who has Strong on some sort of dog leash. Why is Strong on a leash?" Martha yammered. "Where is Astuto? We figured he'd be here making fun of us for being so slow, but we don't see him anywhere and he's never been one to be shy, you know…"

Unable to hold the truth back any longer, I blurted out the sad truth, "Astuto is dead."

I had often wondered what pure silence would sound like. It was deafening. For that moment, everything including the waves on the shore seemed to die. The previous hugging and joy had instantly morphed into shock and weeping. Strong let out a sad, heart-wrenching howl which he must have been bottling up for my sake. Fausto couldn't comprehend exactly what was happening, but he bent down and hugged the remorseful wolf.

Martha was speechless, and I saw the dire look in everyone's eyes. I tried my best to explain what had happened and why I thought it best to keep Lusadé's attack from them until they arrived. This seemed to offend many of them, and I noticed that Stella wasn't able to look me in the eye.

Eldey was the first to utter any words and didn't have much to say other than, "Thank you, George, for leading us the best you could. I know holding this burden by yourself was not a decision you made lightly. You had the mission in mind."

I couldn't find words to say. Strong was unable to fill in the details because he was still whimpering inconsolably in Fausto's arms. I looked to Eldey for help, but he had no great words of wisdom to offer.

I felt like I had succeeded in my goal to lead this mission, but at the same time, I felt like I had failed everyone. It was too much. I joined the blubbering group of animals, weeping for our fallen comrade. Not much was said the rest of the 34th day. It was a day of remorse and sorrow.

I tried to bring myself out of my misery by speaking the *truth* to myself. Benjamin and Moana hadn't made it to Pinta Island to be with us, but they were being celebrated by the people of Tasmania. Astuto was no longer with us, but he *was* safely back in the Garden. I knew we couldn't mope around Pinta Island for the next two days waiting for Stephen's arrival. We needed to do something. I decided to give us a short time to grieve for our friend, but then we had work to do. Time was of the essence, as Astuto had so often pointed out to me.

I had to drag myself out of my self-pity and sorrow and lead these animals to the end. I debated whether to try to be the comforting friend or return to my blunt old self. I decided to step outside my comfort zone and tried a third approach that I had learned from my fallen friend.

I moved slowly over toward the group sulking by the shoreline. In my best 'Astuto voice' I called them into action, "Why are you all so sad? Don't you know that I am back in the Garden awaiting your return? You have a mission to do, and it's not over yet. Time is of the essence. Blah, blah, blah. You know I know all of your names, and I could sit here saying nice things to each and every one of you, but I'm not going to. Get up and wipe your eyes. We got 'work' to do."

I thought I had blown it and should have been more sensitive, but the air quoting at the end of my mocking tribute to Astuto got a smirk out of Stella and a few others.

Returning to my normal voice I continued, "Listen, we do have work to do, and we can't wait here doing nothing until Stephen arrives tomorrow or the next day."

During my motivational speech, my back had been to the shore, so I was startled by a gust of wind and spray that hit me in the back of the head. I instinctively withdrew into my shell, but I heard Stephen's small voice say, "Did someone mention my name?

Chapter 20:

FACING THE LIGHT AT THE END OF THE TUNNEL

It was time for action. What exactly that action was supposed to be, I didn't know. We now had seven representatives here on Pinta Island, but no one including Eldey knew what we were to do next. We met and brainstormed, but none of us had ever done anything like this before. But I realized one of us *had* done this before.

"Eldey, I think you might have an idea about what we need to do. I mean you were present during the last 'resetting' with the people," I said, turning my gaze to the great auk who was looking at me blankly.

"I don't understand what you're getting at George?" Eldey replied flatly.

It was nice to finally be one step ahead of Eldey. I asked, "What I mean is; the last time things were 'reset' between us and the people was on the Ark right?"

"Okay, I think I see what you are getting at. I was there, but I am not aware of what the plan was other than get into the boat with your mate, close the door and wait seven days for the floodwaters to come. I do not see how that is going to help us now since there is no sign of impending rain. I need to remind you, George, that a great flood cannot happen again; it's part of that whole rhyme and reason thing," Eldey explained.

"Maybe there was something Noah or someone in his family

did to prepare in the days leading up to the Great Flood. Do you remember any details that might be helpful to relay to Fausto?" I asked.

"Noah simply built the Ark and gathered the animals up. He tallied and documented each pair that went into the Ark and made sure every one of us was properly cared for. My mate and I had roomed with Lusadé and his mate during that year on the Ark. I do not think Noah had a specific reason for that. I do not recall anything else that the people did specifically before the Great Flood. Even the directions for building the Ark itself were more of general guidelines. Most of what Noah and his family did was simply done by faith using what they did know, and what they did not understand they improvised," Eldey recalled.

"I thought that there was some simple answer *on the Ark*, but I guess I was wrong yet again," I sighed. "I guess we should ask Fausto to see the lighthouse he's been diligently working on for us. Once we see it, maybe we'll understand what we need to do next."

Eldey nodded his head. I decided I needed to take Eldey away from the rest of the group before mentioning the *other thing* that had been bothering me.

"Lusadé is close by. I know I didn't get into many details for the sake of the group, but other than a few minor wolf bites, Lusadé is no more than forty miles from here, and that was a day and a half ago."

"I was afraid of that too," Eldey sighed.

"One thing has been bothering me," I said.

"What is that?" Eldey asked.

"How does Lusadé know so many specific details about some of our conversations? Has he been able to hear everything I've said throughout our entire journey?" I asked.

"I'm not completely sure, but it might have something to do with my previous connection to Lusadé during his trip back to the Original Garden," the great auk sighed.

"Well, that would make sense, since he only seems to know things that I told you or your group," I replied.

"I knew that Lusadé would be a very real danger during this mission. He thrives on manipulation and deception, so I expected him to try to sway the others, as he did with Moana. A direct attack is not his style, but we have seen that he is growing bolder. I do not know what he is truly capable of, but I promise to do whatever needs to be done, should the time arise."

When the rest of the animals were out of sight, I went looking for Fausto. I found him with Strong by his side. I reached my neck up into a nearby bush and snapped off a twig. I walked over to him and drew, *hows?* in the sand. He looked at me quizzically, but then he sounded it out quietly to himself. Fausto realized I was asking him about the light*house* he had been building.

"I thought you'd never ask, my friend," he said, an enormous smile on his face, "Let me show you. I had to conceal it a bit, so I hid it toward the center of the island. I also wanted to make sure the lighthouse was mobile, so I could bring it down to the beach. I know some of you, like the Steller's sea cow, can't exactly climb up this arid volcano. Thankfully people aren't allowed on the island without a special permit. From what I saw on the National Park Service sign in back at the CDRS, no one is scheduled to be here for another three weeks. That means we're all alone to do whatever we need to do until then," Fausto beamed.

Fausto always saw the best in me. I'm not sure why, but looking deep into his eyes reminded me of looking into the cold, angry eyes of the serpent as he crushed Astuto. I had to shake that thought out of my mind and keep focused on the task at hand.

Fausto started to run, almost skipping, up the rocky hill waving to us, "Be patient. I'll be back shortly."

Even by tortoise standards, Fausto took a long time. He didn't arrive until after the sun had set. He looked deflated, but kept his upbeat outlook on the situation.

"Sorry for the delay. One of the wheels popped on the sharp volcanic rocks. I will come back here early in the morning and put everything together in the daylight down in the cove where it will be easier for all of your friends to get to. From what you've told me

George, we still have time. We can do this," he encouraged.

Fausto put his leash back on Strong because he couldn't let his dog *run amuck* on the island unsupervised. Fausto and Strong, the man and his dog, disappeared back down to the shore. We heard the boat engine start up, and they were gone. It was only one more night, but we were together. Everything would be better in the morning.

Fausto arrived before daybreak and began setting up the lighthouse. As he prepared to assemble the lighthouse, it was as if a newfound hope lit up my very core, like a lighthouse illuminating a stormy night.

Fausto diligently worked to assemble the lighthouse that would somehow 'reset' the relationship between animals and the people. But as the structure went up, I realized that Fausto's lighthouse was a far cry from a work of art. It didn't even seem safe to go near it. The lighthouse was about thirty feet high, painted a light green color. There was a door wide enough for all of us to cram inside, but the whole frame leaned slightly uphill. The top of the structure was composed of four windows and it seemed to be lit by a large flashlight of some kind which Fausto had 'borrowed' from the CDRS.

I guess in the grander scheme of things the beauty of the lighthouse didn't matter. Maybe Noah's Ark had been hideous too. Regardless, Fausto had taken it upon himself to trust a talking tortoise. He bent rules and regulations about Pinta Island to do this. He built this lighthouse in only a few weeks with no clear direction. His faith was beautiful even if its results were not. I was glad my facial expressions didn't show clearly back here, so it was easy to hide any disappointment I was feeling.

Faith was such an elusive thing at times. I had gone extinct and returned. I had made it back to the CDRS from Pinta Island. I had directed these six extinct animals from all over the earth back to me. I had spoken *to* a person and given him directions. My faith should have been stronger because I had seen the impossible, but there in that moment my doubts fought for control.

I took a deep breath, and with my writing twig wrote, *thanx for helping us* in the sand.

"The honor has been mine, dear friends," he replied.

Fausto continued working and putting finishing touches on the lighthouse. When he was finished, Fausto walked over to me, knelt down, and placed his hand on my shell. He was beaming with excitement.

"Well. There it is. It may not be the most beautiful thing, but it is finished," Fausto said, "What's next, George?"

I looked around at each face assembled before me; the wren, the auk, the pigeon, the heath hen, the sea cow, the wolf, and the man. That was the moment we needed a brilliant motivational speech. That was the moment we needed clear direction. That was the moment I wished someone else would lead, but this was my moment. I fumbled for clarity about what to say like I did the first night we met in the Garden. They all leaned forward with expectant and hopeful looks in their eyes.

"Well, I didn't think we'd actually make it," I said.

Their hopeful look turned to slight confusion and they looked around at each other. Fausto could only hear me hiss, in a nice way, to the group.

"What I mean is, we had to overcome the impossible to make it here to this moment. No one thought we could do this, because no one had ever tried it before. You have all shown remarkable courage and perseverance in your individual journeys. But we *have* done it! We *have* succeeded, and we *have* overcome the serpent. We are about to reset a new future between us and the people, a time of peace and hope because of each and everyone of you," I stated.

I looked at each member as I spoke, letting the truth of what I was saying sink in for them and for me. I then looked at Fausto.

"It sounded like you were giving a very great speech. I wish I spoke tortoise. I especially liked *the hisss, hiss, hissss* part. Please continue," he encouraged.

"It is only day 37. We even completed our mission with 3 three days to spare. Are you ready to do this thing? Are you ready to complete our mission?" I shouted.

Each animal raised their paws, their flippers, or their wings and shouted triumphantly. Fausto added his cheer as well.

"So in the story of the Ark, the animals got inside and waited, so let's try that," I directed.

Stella squeezed her head and upper torso into the lighthouse door. The rest of us filled in where we could.

"So did it work? Is everything better? Did we succeed? How do we even know if it worked? How?" Martha rambled.

I walked over to Fausto, hoping I could speak with him once again. I craned my neck up to him. Fausto slowly bent down to listen. I opened my mouth to speak, and I saw all the creatures lean forward to see what would happen.

I spoke, "Hisssss."

Fausto smirked and replied softly, " Well, hissss to you too."

As I feared, once we were huddled inside nothing had changed at all. I was at least hoping that I would regain the ability to talk to Fausto, but even that small wish did not come true.

I didn't understand. A jumble of questions invaded my mind. *Hadn't I done everything that was asked of me? Hadn't I miraculously steered six animals to Pinta Island from the ends of the earth to join me here? Hadn't I convinced a person to help us by talking to him? What did I do wrong? What was I missing?*

I willed myself to consider every aspect of 'rhyme and reason' that I knew, but I couldn't come up with anything. A wave of panic struck me as I realized my fate might soon be like that of Pat and Nessie, fleeing for my very existence. I knew a tortoise trapped on a small island had no hope of fleeing. My doubts began to roll in. The hope had been burning bright before we stepped inside Fausto's lighthouse, but now I could see the light at the end of the tunnel fading quickly.

As I had learned to do on this mission, I forced my fears to the side and willed myself to carry on. I put one leg up to reassure the group who had begun to grumble.

"We still have 3 days to figure things out. We just have to figure out what's missing. It'll be okay," I said calmly, "Eldey, can I speak with you for a moment outside of the lighthouse?"

Eldey slid down Stella's massive back, through the doorway, and jumped off next to me.

"That was rather delightful," he said, "Now how can I help George?"

"I just don't understand? What did we do wrong? I know I'm missing something, but I can't put my finger on it," I confessed.

"Maybe that's because you don't have any 'fingers'," he laughed.

"Did you just air quote me?" I laughed.

"Yes I did, but I have a point too. Just like you do not have any fingers, we don't have a piece of the puzzle about what needs to take place here. The answer must be in the 'rhyme and reason'," Eldey continued.

"Okay, let's go back to what you know about the Ark. Let's see if we can figure out what we are missing," I said.

"As I told you earlier, the people and creatures in the Ark waited 7 days for something to happen. If that was true, maybe things won't happen until day 44," Eldey reminded me.

"Ok, we can try that if we need to. We might not be able to communicate with each other, but we will all be here together with Fausto. Is there anything else that we are missing," I said.

Then I remembered one more potentially crucial detail from what Eldey had told me about his time in the Ark. I looked at Eldey who was also deep in thought.

"His family. Noah and *his family* had gone into the Ark after the animals. Noah wasn't alone when things changed. He had his mate and family," I blurted out.

"Ok. I think I see where you are going with this. Continue," Eldey replied.

I continued, "Each animal species only had a *single representative* in the Garden, but the man had been there *with* his mate when the first curse was implemented and things changed. Maybe the key wasn't us, as much as it was the people."

"I'm still following. So what do you think we should do George?"

Eldey said, allowing me to choose our next move.

"Eldey, you had once mentioned that it was always about them, and not about us. What if the final key is Fausto's mate and family?" I asked.

"You may be on to something George. It is worth a shot," Eldey said.

I walked over to Fausto and drew a rough outline of him, whose name I spelled correctly using his uniform name tag. Then I sketched a female person like the one I had seen marking the bathrooms that the tourists used so often at the CDRS. Fausto's expression lit up, and he seemed to be making the same connection that I was.

He smiled broadly and nodded, "I'll bring them to see you tomorrow."

With that, Fausto kissed each animal on the forehead, and put Strong back on his leash. Fausto was smiling and almost skipped the whole way down to the boat as if at any moment things would change and a rainbow would appear over Pinta Island. The only thing that appeared were some ominous clouds.

The next two days, most of us had hunkered down inside the lighthouse while Pinta Island was barraged by a freak storm. Stephen and Martha had hidden inside the end of my shell to avoid being blown out to sea. Boomer also stayed close to me too. Eldey and Stella rode out the storm choosing to swim just off the shore, to avoid being pounded against the dark rocky coast.

I had been in contact with Strong who was now Fausto's faithful companion. Strong seemed to be reliving the thrills of his days as a ship's dog.

"Fausto is with his family now, but this storm is too severe to come to you now," Strong explained.

"I know the storm is rough, and I don't want Fausto jeopardizing the lives of his family to get here. We will do our best to be patient until you arrive," I replied.

"Fausto has vowed to get there by day 40 no matter what. He still is not certain when this storm will subside, but he's hopeful," Strong reported.

"Yes. Fausto is always hopeful," I said before ending our conversation.

I was surprised that Fausto, a person, would willingly risk his life for the sake of a few extinct animals on a mission that he didn't understand. Thankfully late on the 39th night, while we were sleeping, the storm did pass. Pinta Island was returned to its hot normalcy. I had forgotten what it was like to be outside during a storm. For so many years I simply retreated into my enclosure during nights like that, and Fausto would come to check on me the next morning.

We were all up early the next morning and decided to fix the place up before Fausto arrived. The lighthouse was intact, but the door was askew and some of the lumber had been blown out of place during the storm. Martha carried some of the shingles back up to the roof and tried her best to seal any holes with chunks of mud. Stella swam back to shore carrying one of the shutters which had blown off during the night. I hated to say it, but Fausto's lighthouse looked worse than it had when we first saw it. Eldey found the flashlight that Fausto had mounted on the top of the lighthouse down by the shore. Miraculously it still worked.

When Fausto arrived I knew we were in trouble. Fausto wasn't on the small boat he had been using to travel back and forth to Pinta Island. He was on a much, much larger boat bearing the symbol for the Ecuadorian government. It was true that the Galapagos Islands belonged to the country of Ecuador, but why were *they* here? I wondered if Fausto had been arrested or if Lusadé had somehow thwarted us, by again deceiving the people.

I watched as Fausto jumped off the ship. Strong was jumping enthusiastically and tugging at his leash. Fausto motioned to the many people gathered aboard the Ecuadorian boat to give him a moment.

Every creature including Stella had no choice but to retreat into Fausto's dilapidated lighthouse to avoid being spotted. I wondered if we had been betrayed, putting my very existence at stake. To make matters worse, the feeling of dread returned. Something didn't seem right. I reared up to search for the serpent, but I couldn't see

anything out of the ordinary.

I walked toward Fausto as he raced toward me. As he approached me, he instructed me to embrace Strong. Strong and I leaned our necks into one another, and this thrilled the people onboard the ship who cheered loudly.

"George, I was trying my best to figure this whole thing out. The last time I was here, I felt like I had somehow let you down. Maybe I didn't do something correctly or maybe I had misunderstood what you needed me to do. I haven't slept since I was here last. I know that this might be the last time I see you. I want to make sure that I don't let you slip away, like I did last time, without telling you how much you have always meant to me. By some miracle, I have been given a second chance to truly express myself to you. I know you have been lonely for a long time, but I hope you know how truly loved you are by me, by the people of the Galapagos, by Ecuador, and by the world," he said, tearing up.

I wanted to say something in response, but all I was able to muster was a small hiss. I guessed that this would be my end; a tearful goodbye again to the one person who cared about me most and a disappointing ending to a failed mission.

Fausto continued, "You see George, people *do* care about *you*. They always have. Unfortunately, we didn't do enough to save you the first time and after your... after your passing. Although you didn't see it, we grieved for you as a nation. The Ecuadorian president and World Wildlife Fund just declared June 24th an international holiday; Extinction Awareness Day. With the celebration of the discovery of the Tasmanian tiger in Australia, and the odd arrival of a giant moa to the Tasmanian Zoo people are taking notice once again. Your story has even brought the president of Ecuador out to see you. He saw the story of the tortoise rediscovered and the bond you have with Strong televised last night. The president contacted me at the CDRS and said he wanted to see this rediscovered national treasure in person."

I couldn't believe what I was hearing. The president of Ecuador was here to see *me* and had dedicated a day to mark my extinction date. This was amazing, but I didn't understand how it would help us to finish our mission to reset things with the people. I realized that people did care. Not just Fausto, but the president of Ecuador. A wave of guilt flooded my thoughts. I had resented the people for so long, but now I saw how flawed my thinking had been. I thought back to Fausto's tear that had splashed on my nose our last night together before my 'extinction'. His compassion for me that night gave me the desire to join the mission. His love for me at that moment revitalized my hope. My hope which had dimmed to the point of near darkness lit up like the sun, and my faith was restored.

I listened as Fausto continued explaining, "George, that ship is full of news reporters and scientists. They think they're here to film the sweet relationship between you and Strong, but I have a feeling there will be more to film than that. The entire world will see what takes place here today, so let's get started. I have brought my family as you requested. Whatever happens here today George, know that I am truly a blessed man for having known you," Fausto said softly.

Fausto motioned for his family to join him. I remembered them from their frequent visits to see me at the CDRS, but now I relished in their patting and smiling. Fausto reintroduced his wife to me, talking loud enough for those huddled down in the lighthouse to hear. Fausto explained to his family why he had been missing so many nights over the past many weeks. I cringed with regret when I heard his youngest child say our rundown lighthouse was bigger than their house back in Santa Cruz.

I saw Fausto run back toward the ship and motion for the president and camera crews to come and set up outside the lighthouse. I felt nervous, but I could also sense the mixed bag of emotions emanating from within the lighthouse. That ominous feeling was still present, but I dismissed it because the people were here now. Even if Lusadé was lurking nearby, I was comforted by the fact that he wouldn't do anything in front of the people.

Once all of the cameras were in place, Fausto introduced the camera crew to me. The president asked if he could take his picture with me. I extended my neck up as tall as possible and smiled, well at least on the inside. Then Fausto announced that he had a few *other surprises* for those gathered.

At the mention of other surprises, I heard a few of the scientists gathered ask Fausto why he had built a lighthouse on a restricted island. He only paused for a moment before skirting the question.

"Let me do all of my introductions first, *then* I will answer any questions that you still have," Fausto said, redirecting their attention. "You see, as excited as I am to have a Pinta Island tortoise for you, I'm even more excited to introduce you to a few of his friends."

I saw the people look at each other shocked and intrigued. There were a few people who murmured that Fausto must be losing his mind, but he carried on without missing a beat.

"I know there have been several sightings of animals lately that we felt we would never see again. This is not a miracle per se or an act of science. You see from what I understand these animals have chosen to return to us for a reason I can't fully explain. How else can you explain a thylacine showing up on board a cargo ship in New Zealand, or a giant flightless moa wandering into the Tasmania Zoo 1,500 miles away from its ancient homeland?"

I saw a lot of strange looks from those gathered, but the president simply listened carefully to what Fausto had to say. He beckoned Fausto to continue his rather outlandish theory despite the disapproval of many scientists.

"You see, this 'mangy mutt' as deemed by the papers, George's newfound companion, is actually a Falkland Island wolf, which disappeared over 130 years ago," Fausto said, handing the president a paper entitled *Official Lab Report*. "This isn't just a theory that I made up. It makes sense if you're willing to believe."

The president read the lab report carefully, but said nothing. He passed the paper to several scientists in the crowd, silencing their skepticism. Then all eyes turned to the lopsided lighthouse across the hill, next to the far cove. I could see the large flashlight's slight glow from within the window of the lighthouse and hoped that would not detract from what Fausto was saying.

"You said you wanted to introduce us to the Pinta Island tortoise's *friends*, plural. Does that mean there are even more of these returned species," a reporter asked from within the crowd.

"The technical term is 'Lazarus species'. Strong, why don't you go summon the others? And please tell Stella to swim around to this side of the peninsula," Fausto said pointing across the way.

Everyone stood shell-shocked, no pun intended, by what was taking place. If nothing else, I figured we'd make believers out of those gathered. Even if we couldn't reset everything, we could hopefully help bring about some sort of lasting change between us and the people. Giving me my own international holiday was already a step in the right direction.

I have never seen a group of people more attentive or silent. Except for a few small questions, the people hung on every word as Fausto introduced each member of the mission. Martha flew circles around the crowd gathered, and the camera crew was enthralled by her. Everyone thought the Stephens Island wren was the most adorable little thing they'd ever seen.

Boomer stepped out, but many had never heard of the American heath hen. Not to be overlooked ever again, Boomer began strutting his stuff and dancing with all of his might. There was much applause when he walked over to me and we both did a slow-motion version of the last segment of his dance *in unison*.

Stella and Eldey were the last to make their grand reappearance before those gathered. Eldey rode the Steller's sea cow like a surfboard up the shoreline. Those gathered stood again awed by what they were seeing. Stella pulled up next to the rocky beach. The President walked over and placed his hand on Stella's snout. She let out a saltwater breath from her two large nostrils. The salt spray covered the President's face. He simply laughed like a child opening the best Christmas present ever.

The last creature to be introduced to the crowd was Eldey. "This is a..." Fausto began.

"This is a great auk of the northern Atlantic," the president interjected. "Since I was just a child I studied many of those creatures

I never got a chance to see and would never know, like this... this marvelous bird." A tear of apparent joy rolled down his cheek, and he carefully embraced Eldey who snuggled into the president's shoulder.

Many people gathered also began shedding tears of joy at what they were seeing. We were all soaking it in, not knowing if what we were experiencing at that moment would cause a lasting change or not. We still had the mission to accomplish and had to at least try to get Fausto and his family in that lighthouse with us before the sun set on day 40.

The president laughed another hardy laugh and wiped a joyful tear out of his eye, "I half expected to see a dodo bird riding in on a quagga next."

The president sure knew his extinct animals. Fausto's demeanor changed at the mention of the dodo. The president seemed to sense he had struck upon a bad subject, but before he could ask, Fausto simply said, "Our friend the dodo, was sadly lost en route to Pinta Island."

"Fausto, can you explain how this has all come to be? I mean you said it's not an act of science, so how is this even possible?" the president prodded.

"Mr. President, I can't explain it other than what George here has communicated to me over the past many days," Fausto said, shaking his head. "I know it's an act of faith to believe this, but I will show you what I *do know*."

Fausto proceeded to show them the map full of sketches and calculations, and the president nodded. We all noticed that the day was quickly fading amidst all of the celebrations and explanations. I was as growing impatient with the proceedings, just like Astuto had with the ice breakers in the Garden that first night. The sun would be setting soon, and I had no idea what would happen after today, day 40 ended. I walked over to Fausto's leg and gently pulled on his pant leg.

Fausto looked down at me and nodded. He then explained to those gathered, "As I understand things, my family and I must join these seven animals in that lighthouse. I honestly don't know exactly what will happen, but it seems like a test of faith for the animals and us. That's why I wanted to invite you Mr. President and the media to record whatever is to take place here today."

Stella began swimming back around to the lighthouse while the other animals began flying, waddling, and walking along the Oceanside toward our destiny in that small lighthouse. Eldey knew I had to walk back to the lighthouse, so he chose to go with me over the rugged terrain.

"I can't believe we did it Eldey. I mean the people seem to be ready to help us already, and it had nothing to do with the lighthouse at all," I said excitedly.

"It does seem like things are changing. I told you we just needed to have faith. But you know this mission cannot fix *everything* between the people and us. I just hope that it can bridge many of the differences we have had in the past. I know things can never be perfect again outside of the Garden, but..." Eldey's body was jerked backward in an instant.

I couldn't believe what I was seeing. To the horror of all those watching, man and beast; Lusadé, the giant snake began coiling up around Eldey. It was happening all over again, and I was powerless to stop it. I raced toward the serpent in a rage. I bit into Lusadé's tail so hard that I lopped the tip off. At this, Lusadé loosened his grip. I snapped my beak a second time, deep into the taut flesh of his lower back. My second bite caused him to release Eldey who staggered away gasping for breath.

The people seemed too stunned to do anything to help. They didn't understand what stood in the balance at that moment. The animals, on the other hand, knew exactly what was at stake, but they were petrified in fear. Not one of them moved to my aid, not even Strong. Eldey continued to cough and sputter. Lusadé turned his attention away from the great auk and toward me.

"George, I told you that we both had to do what we thought was right. I have followed through on my end of the deal. I did what Gene Huston 204 was in the best interest of all creatures past, present, and future," he seethed.

"But why did you have to kill Astuto? He did nothing to harm you," I retorted.

"That old dodo! George, we both know where he is right now. He's no worse off today than he was 40 days ago when you started this pointless mission. He's in the Garden, safe and sound; a place where you and I can never return George. We are trapped here and can *never* make it back there," Lusadé hissed.

I didn't know if that was in fact true. From what Eldey had told me, completing this mission should reset things and put me back into the Garden. *Focus George, you're missing something again. What would be the reason for all of this? There's got to be a rhyme and reason here.*

Eldey coughed, his one wing hanging limply, "Do not lie to him Lusadé. You did go back once. I have no idea what happened to you when you went back to the Original Garden, but it changed you. You were not always like this, not back before you lost Silvia on the ramp of the Ark."

Upon hearing his mate's name, Lusadé's demeanor changed. "You know this isn't what I wanted, Eldey. I never asked for this. You know that I tried to save her. If that boy had just watched where he was stepping, things could have been so different. I tried to save us all, but I failed."

"You did not fail, my friend. You were deceived in the Beginning. Lusadé, I know the true you. We were friends once, and I know that I can help you if you let me," Eldey pleaded, staggering to maintain his balance. "You were tricked, deceived to do the wrong thing in the beginning, even before the people did. You said a stranger told you the *truth*, but you cannot see that that stranger used Silvia's death to manipulate you. That stranger tricked you into deceiving the people to eat the fruit from the forbidden tree. What did he tell you that made you do it? Why would you deceive the people and willingly set things in motion when you knew the ultimate outcome?"

"Silvia. Once I ate of the tree, I saw that if things didn't fall apart, and the people weren't tricked, I could never be with Silvia again. I would have all of paradise without my true love. I would have been the only creature not *complete* in the Garden. I would have had an eternal hole in my heart and a sense of loss that no one else would ever have. You almost made me do the one thing that would have taken Silvia away from me forever. I would have lived alone in the Garden, while *every other creature* including the people celebrated. It wasn't good for the man to be alone, but it wasn't good for *us* to be alone either, Eldey. You had a family once. You know what it's like to love a family, Eldey. I won't ever go back to the Garden. There's nothing there but misery....total, eternal misery!" Lusadé shouted, snapping his bleeding tail toward the great auk knocking him backward across the hill.

Eldey's head hit a rock, and he lay motionless. I could still sense his presence, so I knew there might still be hope if I could stop the serpent. I saw Lusadé sigh deeply at the sight of his fallen friend of old, before whipping his head back toward me. His beady eyes drilled straight through me once again, draining me of any ability to move. I knew that my shell prevented him from simply constricting me, but I was still terrified of what else he might do.

"Lusadé, I know what it's like to be alone, totally alone," I shouted at the mighty serpent.

He simply laughed, "You foolish tortoise. Don't you see it? You have no idea what *true loneliness* is. You've been alone for what; forty years? You are ridiculous, George. You have the hearts of millions. These people love you. The president of Ecuador loves you! The people have named a holiday after you. You are as far from alone as any creature ever was."

I had never thought about how being deemed 'Lonesome George' gave me notoriety greater than any other animal, even more so than those cute and cuddly pandas. Benjamin wasn't the only one who had the people shed tears of joy to see her.

Lusadé hissed, "The people *hate* me, and have since the beginning. Everywhere I turn, they blame me for *their mistakes*. They blame me for the fall of mankind. People have always been self-seeking and have always refused to admit any wrongdoing. I didn't make them do it. They did it of their own free will. It was *their fault*, but they will always look for someone or something else to blame. I am their scapegoat."

"They don't know the whole story, Lusadé. The people don't know that you yourself were deceived. Maybe if you explain it to them...," I said, trying to talk him down.

"You think that they want to hear from me? You see Tortoise; I have been alone since the Ark because of them. That foolish boy took the only thing I ever cared about from me. He took my mate, my hopes, my future. I willingly chose to trick the woman and the man in the beginning because they deserved it. I was cursed because of what I did at the Beginning and that curse eventually led to Silvia's death, *but* it let me have a life with her, even for a brief time. Don't you see there's no way out of this George until the people are out of the way? I'm glad I ate of the tree before I made the biggest mistake of my life, erasing Silvia from existence. I *hate* them George, and they do have a right to hate me," he responded angrily.

"Well then, I guess we must choose our paths and agree to disagree. I'm deeply saddened by your loss. I really am. It's true I've never had a mate of my own, but I can't let your anger toward the people hurt my friends anymore," I said, snatching his tail in my mouth.

I began dragging the massive snake away from the lighthouse and away from the people. Everyone still stood away from us, shocked, not knowing what to do. I wouldn't let Lusadé hurt anyone else. I needed to save the ones I loved, and I only saw one way to do it. Making a straight line toward the distant ocean, I dragged the writhing serpent away from everyone.

"George, what do you think you're doing?" the snake asked, "It's almost sunset, and you have failed to finish your mission. You can't hold me here *and* join your friends in the lighthouse. You need *seven* animals to have a chance of success. I know Eldey told you that six is a very dangerous number. Without you, your mission fails and you, like me, will be a Garden outcast with no way to return."

I didn't respond to him. The way I saw it, if I ignored him, he couldn't get to me and change my mind. I continued my slow and steady plodding toward the rocky cliff at the far end of the peninsula where I used to watch the sunset with my family in my final days with them. I could feel tears; real tears, welling up in my eyes as I faced my eternity, the end of my existence.

"George," Lusadé said more calmly, "George you know that you can't do what you're thinking about doing. If you take me over that cliff with you, it's the end for both of us. You will not have changed anything between your friends and the people. Please, George, there's got to be a better solution. Can't we talk about this?"

I considered this, and my plodding slowed. My brain seemed to question everything I was doing. *Maybe you could find other options together with the serpent? Lusadé had been to places and seen things that you have not. You could learn from him, possibly go back to the Original Garden and truly reset things without risking a greater curse.*

My mind countered this thought. *No! This is another one of his clever tricks. If you stop to talk with him, the sun will set, and you will fail the entire mission. That's exactly what Lusadé wants. Maybe the serpent has to be out of the way for there to be any hope of change between the creatures and people. Remember, you need to trust that this plan will work and do what you know is right.*

I regained control of my thoughts. Sensing my determination to end this, Lusadé made a final plea, "George, think about what you're doing. I admire you for being a tortoise of your word and for protecting the ones you love. As noble as that is, let's just assume we go over that cliff together. How do you know that you will take me to oblivion with you? We both know that *you* can't swim at all, but *I* can. What you're attempting will probably fail, and then what will you have accomplished? Nothing! Is it really worth it? Are *they* really worth it?"

I watched as the sun started its final descent. I blocked out Lusadé's words and focused on finishing what I had to do. I knew I needed to end this before it was too late. My final thought before taking the plunge was, *Mom, I wish you were here to see one last Pinta Island sunset with me. Goodbye world.*

I held onto Lusadé's tail with everything I had. I took one final glance at the people gathered on one side and my friends on the other. My claws hung over the rocky cliff. A small stone rolled over the edge bouncing off several boulders before splashing into the water far below. The waves lapped against the rocky coast below me. I closed my eyes and hurled myself with all of my might over the edge of the cliff, feeling the massive serpent still flailing behind me.

I expected to feel a cold splash of water but was greeted with a harsh jerk backward. I was shocked to find that the snake had grasped hold of a small shrub on the edge of the precipice. I was dangling from the end of the serpent high above the Pacific Ocean twisting back and forth in the breeze.

I didn't know how long I could hold on, but I was determined to take the snake with me. I didn't want his words about my death being for nothing to be true. I tightened my beak into his tail to let him know I wasn't going anywhere. The sun was even farther down on the horizon, and I knew I couldn't let Lusadé hold on much longer. I tried to swing my weight back and forth to make him lose his grip.

Suddenly above us, a huge hairy figure peered over the cliff. I knew that this couldn't be a person rushing to my rescue. There was only one possible, farfetched explanation. Somehow Pat had made her way to Pinta Island. I didn't know what that meant. I had no idea whose side Pat was on. Unlike Nessie who had been so resistant to understanding the truth of the situation, Pat had seemed to believe me about Eldey's remorse for her exile. She also seemed to understand that our mission might be her way back to the Garden. I had no idea what lies the serpent had used to fill her with doubt.

She shouted over the cliff to us, "Lusadé and George, we can settle this once and for all. There is another way which you have both missed. Being *three* boomerang species, I have discovered another 'loophole' while fleeing from the people," Pat shouted.

She seemed to raise her hands slightly and move her fingertips downward ever so slightly. This made me pause and reflect on what she just said. *Had she really discovered a new loophole that no one else has considered? Maybe three boomerang species had a new-found power? It did fit into the whole rhyme and reason mantra that I had learned during this mission.* But there seemed to be something more, so I continued to try to listen while swinging above my eternal death below.

"You have both been so blinded by your distrust in each other that you missed the complete picture," Pat seemed to be speaking very intentionally, and I tried to interpret what she was trying to communicate. "We need to look at this rationally, putting our own individual agendas aside. Lusadé, I know that the loss of Silvia still haunts you, but stopping George isn't the way. You have explained many things to me and have helped me since my failed mission. For that, I am truly grateful. You have taught me that I can't trust everything Eldey says and that everyone is capable of manipulating details to get what they want. I have seen how true that is. *You* have given me someone to believe in, now *you* need to trust *me.* I am doing what's 'best' for everyone," she said again, twitching her fingers.

I didn't know what she was trying to communicate. My mind was at a breaking point. *Had I been seeing things? Had she really tried to move her fingers in an air quoting motion to focus me? If so, why? What did it mean?*

Then it occurred to me. Pat was trying to prepare me for my end. *She* was the loophole we hadn't considered. *She* could be the seventh animal needed to complete the mission even if I could not.

Her wild hair blew in the soft breeze, illuminated in the glow of the red orange sunset. I looked at Pat's face which beamed with hope and optimism, but her blue eyes seemed to flicker with sadness.

"Lusadé, you need to let me help you. I can help us all find peace. Let go of the tree on *three*, and I'll help you," Pat called.

Even though I couldn't see his face, Lusadé must have believed that Pat was there to help him. I knew that Lusadé probably told

Pat the same twisted lies as he told me about the added curse, the misery, and how we could never return to the Garden as boomerang species.

"One, two,... three," Pat counted.

I felt the snake's muscles relax, and he let go of the shrub. Pat's massive hand grabbed Lusadé's neck. Her power was unbelievable. She held Lusadé in midair with me dangling from his tail with ease. Pat looked into the serpent's eyes and then down to me before saying, "I wish there was another way. I am truly, truly sorry to you both. May you both find the peace you have been searching for."

With that, Pat swung her long, hairy arm out and hurled Lusadé and me away from the cliff's edge. I braced myself for what was to come. We both plummeted through the air before smacking into the cold Pacific Ocean. The frigid water hit me with a jolt, but I knew I had to hold onto Lusadé's tail until the end.

We both sank down, down into the depths. The crimson light of the setting sun rippled through the increasingly dark waters as we continued into the abyss. It was as if all of creation was waving goodbye to us. Lusadé continued to fight me, flailing to free himself, but he seemed to realize that our fate was sealed. I felt the snake's body stop fighting and go limp just before the end came. I could only hope that all I had done had been worth it, but I would never know. I felt the darkness overtake me and then it was finished.

EPILOGUE

"George," I heard a familiar whisper. "George, you need to wake up now."

I slowly forced my eyes open, but I couldn't see anything except an overwhelming light. I gave my eyes a few moments to adjust to the glow, but I still felt disoriented.

"George, you did it! You really did it! We didn't think you were going to be able to do it, but you did. With a little unexpected help that is," Martha sang.

"Could someone back up a step or two and translate what Martha is trying to say?" I said as politely as possible, trying to avoid offending Martha. "Are we back at the lighthouse or at the CDRS or is this some new exhibit that we were all taken to after I was rescued from another failed attempt at swimming?"

I felt a familiar weight on top of my shell and slowly stretched up my neck, twisting it around 180 degrees to look directly into Eldey's warm inviting eyes. I felt an overwhelming sense of comfort and relief, knowing that soon everything would make sense, or so I hoped.

"Well, I do not remember many of the details of what happened after I spoke to Lusadé. I remember pleading with him to think about what he was trying to do, and then I remembered waking up as everyone rushed to the cliff to find you," Eldey admitted.

The lull in the conversation seemed to be killing Martha. She exploded in another, more helpful tangent of what had happened.

Martha recalled, "We all watched as you and Eldey strolled toward us down by the lighthouse. The people watched too from up on the hill. No one, including the people, had time to react to Lusadé's hostile attack. We saw the great serpent grab Eldey, engulfing him in tightening coils. Then you, you bit his tail off, at least a teeny tiny piece of it. We bet that tasted disgusting, but we don't know for sure since we've never tasted snake before."

"I honestly don't remember," I said, scratching my head.

"You were awesomely, amazing George! We watched you drag the snake who was flailing back and forth and back and forth to the cliff. We could hear him screaming and pleading with you to reconsider what you were planning. Honestly, we didn't know what you were thinking, but we knew you had a plan," Martha explained.

"We didn't expect you to jump over the cliff like that," Boomer interjected.

"It was more of a slide than a jump because tortoises can't really jump. Whatever you call it, it was unexpected," Martha added.

"I tried to swim around the peninsula quickly to help you, but I wasn't fast enough," Stella said regretfully.

"It was at that point that Pat showed up," Eldey explained. "It was a little hazy, but she seemed to have been waiting somewhere nearby to see what would happen between us and the people before she acted."

"Pat?" I said trying to recall my last moment before plummeting into the Pacific. "I do vaguely recall her showing up to throw Lusadé and I over the cliff, but I still don't understand how Bigfoot found her way to Pinta Island?"

"Maybe it would be best if she explains it to you. I am still not quite sure how she did it myself," Eldey admitted.

Slowly, the animals parted, making way for Pat to step forward. She was massive and almost as tall as Moana. Pat had long grayish-brown hair covering most of her body except for her mannish face and hands. She cleared her throat before explaining the finer details to me.

Apparently, my initial animal all-call had made her aware that something strange was taking place. It also allowed her to listen in on parts of my conversations with multiple members of each triad. She was able to contact me in the same way I could call her. It seemed to be a connection between 'boomerang species' like us. Due to our previous conversations, Pat knew where we were headed and when we would get to Pinta Island.

"I knew I had to find my way to Pinta Island. For so long I have been hiding from the people, moving only at night, so sneaking to you wasn't that unusual for me. I made my way south through the Rocky Mountains and then 'borrowed' a small fishing boat to get to Pinta Island," Pat explained.

She had been studying the people for years, still hoping that she'd be able to muster up the courage to 'talk to them' herself. Pat admitted that fear had kept her from even trying because she knew if things went wrong, she would lose her existence.

"I waited on Pinta Island, watching Fausto construct his light-house each day. Many times I wondered if I could simply talk to him myself since you seemed to trust him with your life. But each time I thought about communicating with him, I panicked. I figured it was safer to wait for you and the three triads to arrive," Pat explained.

"What made you decide to help us? I know from talking with Nessie that you both feared facing eternal extinction," I said.

"I saw that there was only one hope of returning to the Garden, and that was to help you. I thought it was better to risk it and possibly get back to the Garden where I belonged than spend eternity fleeing from the people," Pat admitted.

"But what about Nessie? Did she return with us? Is she here too?" I asked, looking through the growing crowd of creatures.

"I had spoken with Nessie after your conversation with her. She knew she could not stop you, so she decided to be as far from Pinta Island as possible to prepare for the impending curse. She was more content fleeing and trying to survive than in risking her existence," Pat clarified.

"I see, so Nessie still remains back there as the only boomerang species left on earth? I'm sorry I couldn't convince her. What happened?" I asked.

I needed to know what had happened after she had thrown Lusadé and me over the cliff into our icy grave. I wondered if Stella had found me, or if Fausto and the people were able to rescue me as they had before.

"You died George," a voice said from behind Stella. Astuto walked around the massive sea cow and bowed.

"But... you are dead... you..." I stammered, trying to make sense of what was happening. I felt as lost as I did my first night in the Garden.

"What an 'astute' observation George," the dodo mocked, emphasizing the air quoting with his puffy white wings. "We are all back in the Garden. You and I both died making sure the mission could succeed. The rest, at least those in the lighthouse, were sent back here after they succeeded."

"Okay, I guess that makes sense, but how am I here? I thought that if I died back there before the mission ended, I would lose my existence," I asked, happy they had been wrong but confused about what had happened.

"It has always been about 'rhyme and reason' George," Eldey said, jumping off of my shell and placing a wing on my shoulder. "You willingly sacrificed yourself to save others. You had faith that even by eliminating Lusadé, the mission could still succeed. You took a metaphorical and actual *leap of faith*, and you were rewarded for it. Fausto and Stella did try in vain to revive you, but to no avail. We all feared the worst, and many tears were shed by creatures and people alike at least until we found you back here in the Garden."

"Eldey managed to get to his feet in time to rally us to finish our mission. Amidst the grieving, Stephen pointed out that there were still seven creatures that had made it, with the arrival of Pat. We all wanted to at least try to complete the mission; to honor you, as the final glimmer of sunset began to fade," Strong added.

"I tried to explain to Fausto and those gathered that we planned to go back and possibly return in our own species' triads later on using pictographs. My pictures were not as clear as yours George. Fausto was confused by what we were trying to communicate to him," Martha explained.

"But then I remembered that Pat had learned sign language for her original return trip," Eldey recalled, "although a collection of extinct animals on Pinta Island was amazing in the people's eyes, accepting the appearance of a mythical Sasquatch in the Galapagos was a little harder for the people to grasp. Thankfully, one of the scientists in the crowd of people realized that Pat was trying to communicate with them using sign language. This seemed to calm their fears. With Pat's help, we didn't need to *speak* to communicate with them."

"So the lighthouse idea worked then?" I asked, surprised.

Eldey simply laughed light heartedly and said, "I do not understand what happened or how it happened, but when the animals followed the shining flashlight into that little green lighthouse, followed by Fausto and his family, there was a strange flash of light and all the creatures were returned to the Garden.

"I see," was my amazing reply.

So the plan had worked somehow. The other animals including Pat and myself had been able to reenter the Garden safe and sound, but I wondered if things between the animals and people had been set right. Other than my international holiday, I wondered if we had really made a difference back there.

"I can see you have a lot of questions," Eldey said sympathetically.

"Do we have time to explain everything to him again?" Astuto asked, trying to speed things up a bit.

"May I ask one more question, Astuto. I promise to withhold the others for as long as possible. I think we will all have more than enough time to talk about everything for a long, long time to come now that we're *all* extinct," I said.

Astuto sighed, "What is your last question? Let me guess. It's something earth-shattering like; why doesn't a legless lizard have legs or why does a blue-tongued skink have a blue tongue?"

I simply laughed at the old dodo's attempt at humor and asked,

"What happens now that I'm one of you?"

"Well George, we have a choice, as we always do here in the Garden. We can stay here in the Garden enjoying its delights and perfection, or we can head back there and spend more time with the people. From what Benjamin and Moana have said, things have changed for the better since our mission ended," Eldey explained, trying to wrap things up for the cranky dodo who was beginning to pace.

"Benjamin and Moana?" I asked.

"I knew the tortoise couldn't ask only one more question," Astuto huffed.

"Well, being the last of their kind back there, with their extinction several years off, I summoned them back to the Garden last night, to see how things were going back there. They said that they were planning to come back to the Garden soon, to go back with a *family triad* to start over. Moana and Benjamin both agreed the time was right to return with the people and asked us who would want to join them," Eldey explained, looking at me to gauge my reaction.

I paused only a moment thinking how great it would be to see Fausto again and see how things truly had changed now between us and the people. After all, I was a worldwide celebrity and wanted to be there for the first-ever celebration of my own personal holiday. Realizing this self-absorbed thought was probably bothering Astuto who could again read my thoughts if he so chose, I simply smiled before responding, "I'm in!"

AUTHOR'S NOTE

I have always had a love of two things since I was young; extinct animals and the stories found within the Bible. My love of extinct animals began in 6th grade when I did a research paper on the ivory-billed woodpecker, which may or may not be extinct. It instilled a passion in me to understand why and how so many different animals went extinct in our recorded past. Their individual stories of extinction are amazing, and I wanted to share them with others.

Some animals went extinct due to poor planning on the part of people. Others like the heath hen, the passenger pigeon, and the thylacine people tried in vain to save from extinction. It was too little, too late. These extinction stories have helped us make better choices concerning animals that are struggling to survive today.

Even when I visit zoos today, I am most amazed by the animals which are critically endangered, the ones which my children and grandchildren may never get to see. I would wonder what they would say if they could speak. Do they hold a grudge about their current situation? Do they like their life at the zoo? What would they say to us, *if* they could speak? That is why the story in the Bible about Balaam's donkey has always fascinated me so much. It's part of the 'rhyme and reason' element which Eldey, the great auk, speaks of so often in the story. If a talking donkey was recorded in the past, maybe it could happen again.

I didn't know about *Lonesome George* until a few years ago when a fourth-grade student I was teaching started crying in the computer lab. I had no idea why, since my students were supposed to be selecting an animal to research. Most students had selected a panda or cheetah, the usual, but not this particular student. When I asked her why she was crying, she said that the Pinta Island tortoise was going to be extinct. There was no hope in saving the real Lonesome George from extinction. This student was crying because she felt devastated by the death of that tortoise and his entire species.

It was that day in the computer lab that I realized how much certain animals mean to certain people. I felt a greater desire to teach future generations about George, and other lesser-known endangered species, as well as some of the fascinating stories of extinction in recent times.

Even as I was writing this book and gathering information for it, my daughter asked about some of the animals. I explained to her that some animals like dinosaurs went extinct millions of years ago, while some animals went extinct because of people. She asked me what being extinct meant. I explained it meant there are no more of a certain kind of animal, like the dodo, so we can never see a real one in the wild or in a zoo. She started screaming that she wanted to see a dodo. Her youthful passion solidified for me the importance of sharing these animals' stories with future generations.

I knew I wanted 'Lonesome George' to lead my ragtag bunch of extinct animals on their mission to save the world. Then it was my turn to be saddened by George because a few months into writing this book, while looking up George's weight, I discovered that the real Lonesome George had died much sooner than scientists at the Charles Darwin Research Station had expected. This affected my book idea, but it did give me the ability to have him identify his own extinction date, June 24, 2012.

I have tried my best to keep the facts about each animal as true as possible. I have taken some liberties with some 'gray areas' in extinct animal debates, such as whether the quagga is simply a plains zebra or whether the heath hen is really a subspecies of the lesser prairie chicken. I have also tried to build my characters around the 'rhyme and reason' rules found within the Bible; building on those 'gray areas' as well. So if Jonah could be trapped in the belly of a whale, why couldn't a dodo? If a donkey could talk to a man, why not a tortoise? I hope George's mission inspires thought-provoking conversations about both the biblical and the extinctional stories represented throughout this fictional adventure.

CPSIA information can be obtained
at www.ICGtesting.com
Printed in the USA
BVHW032003181021
619253BV00006B/312